Praise for *Boys Like You*

"More tha ... ve story, *Boys Like You* is a redemptive remedy for despair...I love it wh... a book can b... ..."
—K. A. Barson, author of *45 Poun... ...r Less)*

"A story of family, first love, and forgiveness. I couldn't stop reading. I loved it!"
—Miranda Kenneally, author of *Catching Jordan*

"Juliana Stone's YA debut is romantic, heart-wrenching, and unputdownable. I want more!"
—Michelle Rowen, national bestselling author

"Fast paced with characters you care about, *Boys Like You* by Juliana Stone is a delicious, emotional read."
—Monica Murphy, *USA Today* and *New York Times* bestselling author of *Second Chance Boyfriend*

"The tension between remorse and a desire for closure success-fully propels the narrative...the intensity of the couple's sexual relationship and the dramatic experiences they have faced will attract teens."
—*Booklist*

"The as-happy-as-it-could-be-under-the-circumstances ending will definitely satisfy, and Stone writes it with confidence and style."

—*Kirkus Reviews*

"The story handles challenging subjects like sex, drunk driving, and faith after tragedy in a sensitive and age-appropriate way without veering into melodrama…just what readers need."

—*School Library Journal*

Also by Juliana Stone

Boys Like You

SOME KIND OF NORMAL

JULIANA STONE

sourcebooks
fire

Published by Sourcebooks Fire, an imprint of Sourcebooks, Inc.
P.O. Box 4410, Naperville, Illinois 60567-4410
(630) 961-3900
Fax: (630) 961-2168
www.sourcebooks.com

Library of Congress Cataloging-in-Publication Data
Stone, Juliana.
  Some kind of normal / Juliana Stone.
    pages cm
  Summary: Told from their separate viewpoints, popular Trevor, who suffered traumatic
brain injury in a drunk driving accident, and his assigned tutor Everly, a pastor's beautiful
daughter who is hiding a devastating family secret, not only begin to redefine themselves,
they find common ground and even love.
  (13 : alk. paper) [1. Tutors and tutoring--Fiction. 2. Brain--Wounds and injuries--
Fiction. 3. Family problems--Fiction. 4. Secrets--Fiction. 5. Love--Fiction.] I. Title.
PZ7.S877875Som 2015
[Fic]--dc23
                                        2014042622

Printed and bound in the United States of America.
                    WOZ 10 9 8 7 6 5 4 3 2 1

For my mom and dad. I love you both. That is all.

Before
Trevor

I used to be the guy who had it all.

I had the girlfriend most guys drooled over—easy on the eyes, curves in all the right places, and always up for a good time. I played guitar in the hottest band around and made first string on the football team. My best friend was like a brother to me, and my family was relatively free of drama. Sure my dad worked a little too much and my mom bitched about it, and yeah, my little sister could be annoying as hell, but we were good.

I was invincible. I had goals and dreams, and I was damn close to getting them.

Until I wasn't.

Until a night went so wrong that I ended up in a coma, and by the time I came out of it, months had passed. By then I was already running to catch up to everyone else, and running to catch up wasn't something I was used to. I was the guy at the head of the line. I was the lucky one. *Until I wasn't.* And like everything else in this new life of mine, it totally sucked.

Thinking about it makes me sick to my stomach. I hate it. There are nights when I can't sleep. Nights when all I want to do is close my eyes and see nothing. Hear nothing. Smell nothing. I don't want to remember how I used to be, and I sure as hell don't want to remember that night.

Except that I can.

I can remember every single detail.

It was hot. The kind of hot that makes you sweat like crazy and leaves your lungs feeling heavy. The moon was out, and it never went away, kind of like perpetual twilight.

My girlfriend wore a tight black halter top and a white skirt that barely covered her ass. I gave her hell for it, but I liked how the other guys checked her out. I liked knowing that she was mine. And I really liked the fact that we'd get busy in some dark, quiet spot among the trees.

Of course, that didn't happen because I drank too much. I got wasted, like stupid wasted, and I puked. Even my girl, Bailey, was disgusted. So yeah, the "getting busy" thing never happened.

Then I got in a car with someone I knew was almost as wasted as me. And that is without a doubt the stupidest thing I've ever done. I remember thinking Nathan shouldn't drive, but he laughed me off and said he was fine.

I remember thinking that we should call my dad. He was always good for a pickup if one of us screwed up. And man, we were screwing up. But at the time it seemed like too much work to make it all happen, so I did nothing.

If I'd done that? Called my dad instead of getting in the car with Nathan at the wheel? Things would be so damn different. I'd still be the old me. Not some loser with shit for brains and a TBI (traumatic brain injury). Now there's a great handle.

But I don't like thinking about *what if* because it depresses the hell out of me. *What if* doesn't matter anymore because I have to deal with *right now*.

And for me, *right now* is crunch time. I gotta believe that *right now* just might change my life. And the scariest truth of all?

Right now is all I got.

Before
Everly

Twelve months, two weeks, and three days is exactly three hundred and eighty-two days. I'm fairly certain it doesn't mean squat to anyone else, but to me, it's everything. To me, it's how I measure my life, because nothing that happened before then matters. Not now and maybe not ever.

I used to be that girl. You know the one. I had it all.

Until I didn't.

Three hundred and eighty-two days ago, my whole world imploded, and ever since then, I've been trying to figure out how to get it back to what it was. How to unsee and unhear everything that happened.

You see, those things, the things that could break me, I hold them close, buried so deep that sometimes I don't even think they're real.

But they are. They're as real as the blades of grass beneath my toes. Or the big fat cucumbers in the back garden. They live in between those three hundred and eighty-two days, like the sawdust that fills the cracks of the floorboards in my father's church. And it's the sawdust that chokes.

Every morning I wonder, is this the day that I can forgive *him* for what he did? Is this the day that I can forgive *her* for not knowing? I mean, how can she not know? That thought alone haunts me every single day, which leads to other questions. Is it my place to tell her? Is it my place to make him?

Is this the day I can break free from the silence that weighs me down?

Every morning as I sit across the table from my father and watch him eat his toasted bagel with chunky peanut butter, spread so thin I don't get the point of even putting it on his toast, I wait. I wait for something inside me to shift.

I wait for him to talk about it. To explain the lie that is his life.

I wait for something to change.

I wait for it, and I die a little when it doesn't happen because I want it so badly.

I watch my mom breeze into the kitchen and kiss him on the cheek, her hands lingering on his face because she loves to touch him. I watch her frown because the Nutella on my toast isn't a healthy choice, so she grabs her homemade strawberry jam and puts it in front of me.

I let her touch my shoulder, lean over, and kiss me before running her hands through my little brother's hair.

I watch her smile, and I wait for her eyes to light up the way they used to. Because for as long as I can remember, my mom's smile was the most beautiful thing in the world.

But her smile never quite reaches her eyes, and her penchant for humming hymns from church borders on crazy. She knows things have changed, but for the life of her, she can't figure out what those things are.

So I pop my toast in my mouth and force the dry crust down. I know that I'll have to put on a fake smile and head out into the world and pretend that my life is just as perfect as it was before. No one can know the secrets that hide behind our front door. The secrets that are slowly tearing my family apart.

To everyone in Twin Oaks, we're the Jenkinses—the perfect and loving Pastor Eric Jenkins; his beautiful wife Terry, who spends all her time volunteering for the less fortunate in the community; and their kids. Isaac, the free-spirited little guy who loves baseball, fishing, and above all else, his father.

And then there's me, Everly, the All-American girl, with a heart of gold and truckload of morals to go along with it.

That's how I was brought up. That's what he taught me.

Ironic isn't it?

So here I am, day three hundred and eighty-three. I'll push my feelings aside and pretend that everything is freaking A-OK. I'm a good daughter who's learned from the best, even though the best is flawed. Even though the best is beyond redemption.

Apparently, in my world, the best means being a hypocritical jerk. A liar. *A cheat.*

I hate pretending. But most of all, I hate him for what he's done to my family. Him. My father.

I love my father.

I hate my father.

How screwed up is that?

Chapter One
Trevor

The only thing worse than being stuck in Twin Oaks for the summer without my best buddy, Nathan, is being stuck in Twin Oaks for the summer and having to spend most of it with Everly Jenkins. She's the person my guidance counselor assigned as my tutor. Don't get me wrong, the girl is cute as hell, but I have zero in common with her. And from what I remember, her nose is stuck so far up in the air I'm pretty sure it's in a different time zone.

Jesus. Everly Jenkins.

She goes to church every Sunday, and considering her father is the pastor, I get it. I've been to church exactly once in the last five years and have no plans on attending anytime soon. Not because I don't believe in a higher power or anything like that. I just don't think that I need to prove it every damn Sunday.

Her reputation is that she's straight as an arrow. Again, no judging. I just like a bit more of an edge to the people I hang with. Besides, during freshman year, Nathan and I "borrowed" my cousin's truck for the weekend and got caught. To our classmates the stunt elevated us to a weird sort of celebrity status, but that year in English class, Everly had done a speech on the perils of delinquency. Damn. *Perils* of *delinquency*. At the time I'd thought I was nowhere near her radar, but I'd been wrong. That day she was talking to me. I knew it. Everyone knew it. And of course, I'd acted like it didn't matter. I mean, who the heck cares about delinquency when you're fifteen? But the truth of it was I didn't like being under her microscope. Didn't like the thought of her judging me.

And yet here I was again. About to be analyzed and probably found wanting.

I pulled Dad's old rusted Mustang to the curb and cut the engine. It ran on for a bit, chugging and jerking as if it still had somewhere to go, and I made a mental note to tell him the carburetor was screwed.

I snorted. *Mental note.* What a joke.

It was the second Monday of June, and the disaster that had been my senior year was almost behind me. I had one more hurdle to jump, and then I could finally call an end to the most craptastic year ever. All I had to do was pass my government test and I could finally end this all and move on. I hoped that, with Everly's help, I'd get it done.

I tapped the steering wheel, eyes on Everly's house, and tried to remember the last time I'd actually had a conversation with her but came up with nothing.

That didn't mean it didn't happen. Sometimes my memory was a little hazy, and as I stared across the lawn, I gave up trying. What was the point? It's not as if I was going to chat her up about the new Gibson Les Paul I'd seen online or the bush party everyone was talking about, the one in the woods behind the old drive-in.

I sighed and focused. Come on, Trev. Get your shit together.

Her house was white, and like everything else about Everly Jenkins, it was picture perfect. There was the picket fence. The expertly trimmed hedge and the greenest grass I'd seen all summer. A miracle in itself considering our spring had been the driest in years. Heck, even the hanging baskets on her porch looked good; I wouldn't be surprised if they were fake.

Everly Jenkins's place looked nothing like mine. Not that I lived in a dump or anything, but the grass had always been the least of my dad's worries, and my mom didn't exactly have a green thumb.

I smiled for the first time today. God, my mom. She'd even managed to kill a plastic planter because she'd put it too close to the oven. It had been a fake poinsettia, and we'd woken up Christmas morning to find the red leaves melted to the pot. My dad still kidded her about that one.

I groaned and closed my eyes, pushing back the long hair that fell over my brow. It was early yet. Not even noon, and already I was tired. That familiar throb was there, just behind my eyes, and I prayed like hell a headache wasn't on its way.

They wiped me out, and it was exhausting trying to pretend that I was fine when all I wanted to do was close my eyes and block everything out.

I heard a door slam shut and spied Everly on the front porch.

Busted.

I threw open the car door and winced. My right knee had been banged up but good in the accident, and when I sat for too long, it got stiff and sore. Grabbing my laptop, I walked around the car and pushed open the gate.

But Everly was already headed my way, ponytail swinging behind her, a laptop case slung across her shoulders. She wore a white T-shirt that fit her the way a T-shirt was meant to fit a girl. Tight in all the right places. (Hey, I'm a guy, so these are the things I notice. Sue me.)

I stopped walking for a few reasons.

One. I'd forgotten how damn beautiful she was with all that dark hair and blue eyes the color of a new pair of jeans.

Two. I had no idea why she was walking toward me as if we were supposed to be going somewhere. *Were* we supposed to be going somewhere? Was that something I'd missed?

And three. Damn. The girl had great legs, so the fact that her cutoff denim shorts showed them off wasn't something I could ignore. And well, the T-shirt.

I took a moment and looked her over. Like I said, I'm a guy first.

I watched the blush creep up into her cheeks. Saw how she

lifted her chin as if to say "F you." Pretty much killed whatever she had going on.

We'd never really clicked, she and I. Not since grade six when I'd kissed her in a closet at Jackson Breckman's house and told the entire class about it. I'd been pretty pumped. Heck, she was the girl all the boys liked, but she was also the girl who was hands off. Pastor's daughter and all.

Everly had been *mortified*. That was the word I think she'd used. She'd told me that she would never talk to me again. That she *knew* I was the kind of boy who would spread dirty gossip and that the *only* reason she'd kissed me in the first place was because she'd been dared to.

Oh, the tragedies of being a twelve-year-old. So other than the delinquency lecture, we'd pretty much had zero contact.

"Hey," I said.

She smoothed her hands down the front of her shorts and shifted her weight. "Hey, yourself."

A pause.

"You're late," she said, eyes narrowing a bit.

Huh. She wasn't going to make this easy.

"Well, shit, Everly. I didn't know we were punching a time clock or anything."

"Ever," she replied.

Confused, I opened my mouth and had to wait a moment for my brain to catch up. It did that from time to time, and I was always afraid the wrong words would come out. It made for awkward conversations sometimes, which sucked when trying to scrounge together some kind of attitude. Some hint of the guy I used to be.

"What?" Good one. When in doubt, only use one word.

"Ever," she said again, this time a little softer. "I prefer Ever now."

"Oh," was all I managed to say.

For a few moments that was all we had. The sun. The sprinkler going crazy on either side of us (reason for the nice green grass). And silence.

"So I guess we're not studying here," I said, eyeing the house.

"No," she replied quickly, turning around as some young kid ran down the steps and shrieked when he hit the water. She shook her head and yelled. "Isaac! You better make sure you don't track mud into the house or Mom won't be happy. I'm—" She glanced back at me. "We're heading to the library."

She didn't wait for her brother to answer.

Everly Jenkins blew past me and headed straight for the car. She yanked on the door, we both winced at the sound the dried-out hinges made, and then she disappeared inside.

Her brother was drenched and still watching us, so I gave the kid a wave—he looked like he was around ten years old or so—and headed back to the Mustang.

The library it was.

I slid into the driver seat and tossed my laptop into the back. I was about to turn the key and rev the engine when Everly—or rather, Ever—pushed a piece of gum in her mouth and inserted a pair of earbuds. I wasn't used to girls ignoring me.

That right there was my move. The best way to avoid conversation was always earbuds.

I started the car, my eyes still on her, when suddenly she whipped her head up. Her cheeks were still pink.

"What?" she asked, eyes narrowed. Her attitude was all wrong. She was prickly as hell and nothing like the girl I remembered.

I shrugged and said nothing as I pulled out into the road. She seemed different somehow. Couldn't put my finger on it, but it seemed to me like I wasn't the only one who'd changed over the last year or so.

We cruised a couple of blocks, and then I hung a right onto Main Street. The library was downtown just past the town square. I'd just turned left onto Chestnut Street when I caught sight of Bailey Evans and a dude I didn't recognize. The guy had his arm slung across her shoulders, and she was looking at him, offering her mouth up for a kiss.

Bailey is my ex-girlfriend, just one part of a shattered past that I'd failed to hold on to. I wasn't in love with her or anything— we'd never been about that—but I missed her. Or maybe I missed the idea of her. Of having someone to hold on to.

Or maybe I just missed getting some action. It had been a while.

Everly turned to follow my gaze, but she didn't say a word, and a few moments later I pulled into the library parking lot.

I cut the engine and cleared my throat as it ran on for a bit and then sputtered to a stop.

She nodded toward the hood as she took out her earbuds.

"That doesn't sound too good."

"Don't worry. It's not going to explode or anything."

For a second her eyes lightened, and I swear there was a hint of a smile hiding in their depths. "No, but I bet your mileage is crap. You might want to get that carburetor fixed."

"That is probably the sexiest thing a girl has ever said to me." I was teasing. It's what I did. But as soon as the words left my mouth I winced, because man, could I sound more stupid?

Her eyes widened slightly. "Well, then I feel sorry for you, Trevor Lewis."

"Oh," I said. "And why is that?"

"If that's the sexiest thing you've ever heard, then obviously your reputation is overrated."

Huh.

She stepped out of the car, and it took me a couple of seconds to catch up.

Well, that was unexpected.

Chapter Two
Everly

Trevor Lewis bit his bottom lip when he read.

We'd just gone over the basic structure of our government (if I was going to tutor him, we were starting from the bottom up), and I was surprised at how much he already knew. I wasn't expecting that. But then, I'm not exactly sure what it was that I'd expected.

Everyone knew about the accident. That his best friend Nathan had gotten behind the wheel of Trevor's car, either high or drunk (I'd never been clear on which, and for all I know, it could have been both). He'd crashed the car, and Trevor ended up in a coma for months. I guess I just thought he'd be somehow less than what he'd been before. So far, he seemed pretty much the same to me.

I settled into a chair across from him and tried to concentrate on the book I'd brought along, but I found myself peeking over the top of it and looking at his mouth. At the way he worried his bottom lip with his teeth.

It was kind of adorable, something my little brother did, and totally not in keeping with Trevor's bad-boy persona.

His eyebrows were furrowed as he concentrated, and he kept tugging on a piece of hair that hung in his eyes. His plain black T-shirt showed off impressive biceps, and though I couldn't see them, I knew that his faded jeans, so worn out they looked as if they were about to fall apart, hung low on the hips. It was hot but he wore heavy black boots, and I noticed a sheen of sweat on his forehead.

He sure didn't look like someone who'd nearly died in a car accident a year ago. In fact, with the beam of sun coming in through the bank of windows highlighting the dark blue streaks in his hair, he looked more alive than anyone I knew.

But then again, hadn't he always?

Trevor Lewis. The bad boy with the smile of an angel. The kind of boy who got away with most everything because he was a charmer. Had that down to an art form by grade six. In eighth grade he convinced our teacher, Miss Harmon, to let us have our year-end dance out at Baker's Landing. You know, 'cause that was so much cooler than the gym. Everyone was excited at the idea, and Trevor went with it.

He thought that maybe his band should play.

Oh, and maybe his band should, you know, get paid to play. And he managed to get Miss Harmon on board with that.

When they changed the location, my parents wouldn't allow me to go unless they chaperoned. As if. Who wants to go to their eighth grade dance with their parents watching? Not me. I missed the dance in protest, and of course it was all anyone talked about that summer.

I totally blamed Trevor and decided there and then that he was on my very own personal blacklist. It was easy to do. The guy was confident, cocky even, and usually in the middle of whatever was going on.

And he always had a girl…or two. I thought of his ex and the guy we'd seen her with earlier, and I wondered about that. I'd heard that she'd dumped him a couple of months after he'd come out of his coma because he wasn't the same guy as he was before the accident.

If it was true, then she was as shallow as I'd always thought.

I snuck a peek at him again. He looked good as new to me.

Not that I'd seen him much over the last year. Because of the accident, he'd missed the entire first semester of school, and when he'd returned, well, we didn't exactly eat at the same lunch table. He hung with Nathan Everets, his buddy Link, and more girls than I'd ever care to wade through.

My eyes fell back to Trevor's mouth, and I thought of a dark closet, the smell of Pine-Sol, and his infectious grin. Trevor Lewis was trouble, and if I let him, he could make trouble for a girl like me. The guy was way out of my league.

So why was I thinking that his mouth was so interesting?

Squirming, I dropped my eyes to my book, but the words were a total blur, so after a few moments, I gave up and glanced at my cell. Only an hour to go until I was supposed to meet my best friend Hailey at the pool. She was a lifeguard, and after her shift we were going to hit Big Burger and then maybe a movie.

I know. Exciting times in Twin Oaks, but when you're stuck out in the middle of nowhere, you pretty much take what you can get.

Trevor's finger tapped along the table, and for the first time I noticed that he had tattoos across his knuckles. They looked like a bunch of nothing to me, but I suppose the weird markings meant something to him.

"Courage."

Startled, my eyes shot up, and then, bam, my heart took off so fast and hard that for a moment I forgot how to breathe. I felt like I'd just been caught sneaking a cookie from the proverbial jar.

"Excuse me?" I whispered, totally thrown off balance by the way he was looking at me. As if he was trying to figure something out.

Trevor stretched out his fingers and laid his hand on the table. He pointed to the markings. "It's Sanskrit. The one on my other hand means strength."

"Oh." Like I knew what Sanskrit was.

"It's Indian or Hindu or something like that." Trevor shrugged. "Nathan's into that shit, and after I came out of the coma, I had a lot of stuff to deal with." He studied the markings for a few moments. "Most of it sucked." He smiled, not a full one but a small glimpse of something pretty nice. I found myself smiling in return.

"We went to New York at Christmas. It was the first time I'd gone anywhere since I'd been out of the hospital, and man, that city blew me away." He frowned, his eyes intense. "Have you been to New York City?"

I shook my head. God, I hadn't been out of the state.

"It's an amazing place, and I'm jealous as hell that Nathan's there for the summer. I met his girlfriend, Monroe, and the night before Nate and I had to fly back to Louisiana, all three of us got tattoos. We all got the same ones."

A pause.

"Courage and strength."

I cleared my throat, because suddenly there was a frog as big as a donut stuck down there. "It's really cool."

Trevor nodded. "Yeah. I like ink, you know? I like anything that inspires me. Words. Music. Tattoos." His eyes met mine again, and even though it was as hot as a furnace in the library, I shivered. "You got any?" he asked.

"Any what?"

"Tattoos?"

"Me?" I had to laugh at that. Wow. Before last year that would have been grounds for major punishment. Heck, up until my senior year, I hadn't been allowed to wear lip gloss. Now I wasn't so sure that my mom would even notice, and since I avoided my dad whenever I could…

"No," I said, shaking my head. "My skin is untouched."

His eyes widened a bit, and I felt heat creep up my neck. Great. Now I was blushing again.

"Untouched," he said with that lopsided smile that made my stomach dip. "I like that."

"You do?"

"Yep. A clean slate. There's something almost poetic about that, you know? Tragic too. How many people get a do-over?"

Trevor reached for my hand, and though my first instinct was to snatch it back, his long fingers enveloped mine before I had the chance. He turned my hand over so that my palm faced up and then traced the little blue lines that ran down my wrist.

I can't lie. It felt weird and good, and my heart took off once more, so fast that I was surprised he couldn't hear it.

"This is…kind of…like ink," he said, his words a little slow as if he was thinking hard. "But it's alive."

He glanced up again, and all I could do was nod before my eyes dropped to his hand. Mine was still there, small and pale next to his large palm and tanned skin. I saw the thin blue veins that ran down my wrist, the ones that carried blood from my heart, electrifying my cells and feeding my body.

His thumb rested just beneath my pulse, and I swallowed thickly. Crap, he was going to feel how fast it was, and that would be embarrassing.

"Your fingers are rough." I blushed harder and thought that there was no way I could sound any more like an idiot. Not even if I was trying.

"Yeah," he answered. "It's from playing guitar. I practice a lot so my calluses are nice and strong."

"I used to play piano."

Wow. Good comeback. I guess it was better than a clarinet or trombone, but really. Dork much?

"I mean, I still do in church and stuff."

"I know. I saw you play once."

Surprised, I shook my head. "Where?"

"Church."

"But you don't come to church."

"How do you know?"

I was silent for a moment and more than a little confused. "Because I've never seen you there."

He grinned. "So you miss me then." His smile got bigger. "You know, when I'm not there."

"Trevor. I'd have to see you there in the first place to miss you when you're not. And I like I said, I've never seen you in my church."

"But the only reason you know I'm not there is because you must be looking for me in the first place, right?"

Okay. I couldn't really argue with that logic, even though it made no sense whatsoever. I figured he was trying to mess with me and relaxed.

"I used to practice every day after school."

"Used to?" he interrupted.

Again he surprised me. He was sharp.

"I don't hang out at the church all that much, and I'm not really home too often either."

That was an understatement.

"Why?"

"Because my dad's there."

Okay. I did not just say that to a guy who was practically a stranger.

"Anyway," I said in a rush, hoping he wouldn't notice my slipup. "I didn't really enjoy piano until I heard some old Elton John songs."

"Really," he said with a smile. "He's stellar. Retro, but stellar."

"Yeah."

"So what's your favorite?"

He was still holding my hand. It was still hot. And I felt vaguely light-headed.

"Favorite?"

He flashed that smile again. The one that had charmed Miss Harmon back in eighth grade. "Your favorite Elton John song."

"Oh." That was an easy one. "Blue Jean."

He frowned for a moment. "You mean David Bowie?"

"No. Elton John."

"Got it, 'Tiny Dancer.'"

"Yes," I nodded. "That's it, from—"

"*Almost Famous*," he finished for me.

Had he always looked this intense?

"What?" he asked. He smiled again and I thought that on a scale of one to ten, his smile was a total eleven. "You're into the classics. That's cool. Didn't picture that."

"Really. What exactly did you picture?" Shoot. Did I really want to hear this?

"I don't know. PBS and that Jane Austen?"

Okay. First off, I was impressed that he knew who Jane Austen was, and secondly...*he knew who Jane Austen was!*

I dropped my eyes, because I was pretty sure that my cheeks were as red as the roses planted just outside the library. Trevor Lewis wasn't anything like what I thought he'd be. He wasn't stupid and he wasn't arrogant. He wasn't slow or weird.

He seemed pretty normal to me.

You know, for a guy with tattoos and blue hair.

Mrs. Henney, the librarian, chose that moment to clear her throat, and it startled me. I snatched my hand from his.

Trevor Lewis made me nervous. I wasn't exactly sure why, and I didn't want to spend a whole lot of time thinking about it. Besides, I had way too much on my mind. I needed to put this into perspective. Trevor was my excuse to be out of the house all summer. A guy I was tutoring. A distraction maybe, but nothing more than that.

"I have to go." I stood up, nearly knocking over my chair while Trevor reached for his book and laptop.

"I'll drive you home."

"No."

He raised his eyebrows. "Did I do something?"

Taking a deep breath, I shoved my free hand into the front pocket of my jean shorts. "I'm meeting Hailey at the pool."

"Cool." He closed his laptop. "Let me give you a lift."

"No really," I replied. "I want to walk."

"Not gonna happen." He was standing now. He nodded toward the door. "Let me drive you to the pool. I don't mind."

Not gonna happen.

The words echoed in my head, but it wasn't Trevor's voice I heard, it was my father's. And they'd been knocking around my brain for three hundred and eighty-three days now. They were three words I was trying to forget. Three words he'd spoken to someone. A someone who wasn't my mom. A someone I was trying to forget.

Something broke inside me. Something hot and heavy and mean. Something that pressed into my chest and made my eyes smart with unshed tears. Great. If I cried in front of Trevor Lewis, I just might die.

"I said that I wanted to walk, Trevor. Do you need me to speak slower? What part of that don't you understand?" As soon as the words left my mouth, I wanted to snatch them back.

For a moment there was nothing but the sound of Mrs. Henney as she shushed us.

Trevor ran his hand over his chin and studied me for a few moments, that slow grin still in place though it had pretty much left his eyes. "Don't worry, Everly. Sorry. *Ever.* I'm having a good day today." Sarcasm bit into his words. "I understand all of it." He looked away and muttered. "Every single word."

His eyes swung back, and I saw anger in their depths, which only made me feel worse than I already did.

"Just so you know, I'm not a moron. I might have been in a coma and all." His eyes narrowed and he winced as if in pain. "Maybe my words come out a little slow sometimes, but you don't have to talk to me as if I'm some kind of loser. I didn't expect that from you."

"You don't know me," I shot back.

"No, I guess I don't. That's one thing we can agree on."

The feelings inside me—the hot, heavy, angry ones—had nothing to do with Trevor and everything to do with my dad. They were always there. Waiting for a chance to explode. They were etched into flesh and bone, and they colored everything in my life.

I thought of my mom and her sad eyes that poked out from underneath her perfect bangs when she thought no one could see. I thought of the denial that she clung to every single day, denial that she pretty much ate for breakfast, lunch, and dinner. And I thought of my father. Of how this morning as he spread peanut butter over his stupid bagel, he'd said that he'd be dropping Isaac off at a friend's before heading into the city for errands.

Errands. You'd think he'd at least come up with a new excuse, because that one was getting old.

I didn't ask him when he'd be back because I didn't care, and he didn't volunteer that information, so I figured that he was up to no good.

There it was. The sad story of Everly Jenkins. That was all that I had time for, and it was exhausting.

"I'm sorry. I didn't mean to offend you. Really, I didn't. That was a stupid thing for me to say. I'll see you tomorrow." The words were wooden and the apology pretty darn sad, but it was all I had.

Chapter Three
Trevor

"You look tired, honey. Are you sure you're up to going out?"

I glanced at my dad for help, but his nose was buried in a biker magazine and he didn't bat an eye. Kind of convenient, the magazine, but in a house run by the woman standing in front of me, with both hands on her hips and that penetrating gaze that could see through anything, not really a surprise.

My dad is a big guy. Not only is he tall with broad shoulders, he's built like a brick house. He's got bulging biceps, an affinity for tattoos, and a shaved head to boot. The tattoo thing we have in common, and though I can look him in the eye because we're pretty much the same height now, I'm more on the lean side. On the football field I was the go-to wide receiver because I was built for speed, while my dad would have been the center or fullback.

He's an intimidating dude, and when he wants to, he can look pretty damn scary.

Except he's so far from scary it's laughable. Don't get me wrong. My dad's temper has a slow fuse, and when it's lit, he has no problem using his size to intimidate anyone who wrongs him. And he's more than willing to back that attitude up with his fists. No one pushes him around. I mean, no one.

Well, except for my mom.

She has him by the balls, and he's totally fine with it. He told me once that a good woman was hard to come by and even harder to keep. He said that when I found the right girl, I'd do whatever I needed to do to make her happy. Case in point? A few years back, Dad took up line dancing because my mom wouldn't stop talking about it. *Line dancing.* Can you imagine? Talk about a bull in a china shop.

At the time I thought it was lame, and Nate and I used to razz him about it. *A lot.* I mean, he was about as far away from those line dancing guys as you could get. But my dad would just shake his head and grin. He told Nate and me that even though he had two left feet, it was worth it because it made my mom happy. He said that one day we'd learn what it meant to put someone else first.

One day we would learn how a smile could knock us on our ass.

All of that was fine—hell, it was his life and all—but I couldn't help but think that when Mom got all up in my shit, he should at least stick up for me. Wasn't there some kind of guy code?

"Trevor? Did you hear me? I think you're a little pale. Maybe you should just stay in. Your first day studying must have been intense. You might have overdone it."

Here we go.

"I'm fine."

The words came out a little sharp, and I heard my dad rattle his magazine—his warning for respect. Whatever. I needed to get out. I'd been pissed ever since Everly blew me off at the library, and these days, my temper doesn't have a slow fuse. It can turn on a dime, and right now, I felt something brewing.

I needed to get out.

If only I could find my damn cell phone. It was here, among all the crap tossed onto the kitchen counter. There was at least a week's worth of newspapers piled up (who actually read the paper anymore?) along with an impressive amount of junk mail.

"Are you looking for this?" Mom asked gently, rooting out my phone from beneath an issue of *Better Homes & Gardens*. Huh. Since when did my parents give a shit about landscaping?

"Thanks," I said, taking my cell from her. "Link's gonna be here in a few."

"Where are you guys going?"

Mom and I glanced up as my sister Taylor walked into the kitchen. Two years younger than me, she was almost sixteen, and her attitude these days fluctuated between hostile and bitchy and, well, not much else.

"Out," I replied in answer to Taylor's question.

"Can I come?"

"No."

"You suck."

"Yeah. I know."

Mom crossed her arms over her chest and frowned. "You're not going anywhere, Taylor. Or did you forget you're grounded?"

My sister scowled. "Seriously? I wasn't that late."

Mom moved toward Taylor, and I took a step toward the back door, glad that Taylor had drawn Mom's attention.

"Your curfew is eleven and you tried to sneak into the house an hour and a half late."

"But it's summer! None of my other friends have to be home until, like, one or whatever."

"Yes, well, I don't care about your other friends. I care about you. And in this house we have rules."

Taylor's scowl deepened as she glared at me. "Like he ever came home before midnight."

She was right about that. I don't think I'd ever been given a curfew. A lot of things had changed after my accident, and maybe it wasn't fair, but Taylor was getting a lot of flack, and I didn't blame her for being upset by it.

"We're not talking about Trevor right now," Mom continued. "We're talking about you, and while we're at it, I'd like to know who brought you home an hour and a half late."

I watched the exchange with interest, mostly because it was refreshing not to be the one under Mom's microscope. I got why she was so in my face, I really did, but man, she was suffocating sometimes.

"A friend," Taylor said, her eyes sliding away.

"I'd like to hear the answer to that."

Those words came from my dad, and his nose was no longer buried inside his magazine. He pushed up out of the old rust-colored La-Z-Boy, his eyes on Taylor.

"Just a guy from school."

"A name would be good," Dad said, and I could tell he wasn't impressed with his daughter.

"Caleb Martin."

Huh. He was bad news.

Taylor's eyes widened slightly, and I knew she was begging me to keep quiet. For a moment I had one of those weird blips, almost like my brain slows down and then speeds up again. It's a freaky sensation, and I hated it.

"Trevor, are you all right?"

I nodded, not trusting myself to answer, and shoved my cell into my front pocket at the same time a knock sounded, and then one of my oldest buddies and the drummer in my band, Link, walked through the door.

"Hey, Mrs. Lewis." He smiled at my mother and nodded to my dad before his eyes slid over to Taylor.

"Nice hair," he said with a grin.

"You suck," she said, glaring at him.

Link threw his hands into the air. "What did I do?"

"Nothing," Taylor shouted. "Forget it." She pushed past my dad and headed back upstairs.

Link rocked on his feet and shoved his hands into the

front pockets of his jeans. "Man, your sister. What's up with her?"

"Who knows?" I replied.

Link raised his eyebrows in question. "You ready?"

"Yeah," I said with a rush. "Let's go."

My mom stepped in front of me, her hands sliding up either side of my face. Her fingers were cool, their touch gentle. "Where are you going?"

"Gonna hit the movies," Link answered.

My mom's eyes softened, and for a moment I saw the fear that still lived inside her, and I felt like a shit. It was fear that I had put there, and I'd be the happiest guy on the planet if that look would just go away. But I had a feeling it was not happening anytime soon. Maybe it never would.

"We'll be okay, Mom. We're just heading over to the next parish. Their drive-in is running up."

"It's what?" she asked.

"Running up." Man, get me out of here.

A heartbeat passed. Maybe two.

My mom cleared her throat, her eyes falling away.

I glanced over to Link and shrugged.

"Okay," she said stepping away. "Be safe," she whispered.

"I got him," Link said with a grin. "No worries."

"You better, Lincoln. Don't forget. We know where you live."

That was my dad, and I nodded to him before following Link out to his truck. A beat-up and rusted Ford, it sounded like shit, and I was pretty sure the exhaust wouldn't pass any kind of emission test, but to Link, it was the best ride ever. He'd saved all his money two years ago, and as soon as he'd gotten his license, he'd bought the thing from Old Man Ben's used car lot.

And Old Man Ben had owned the thing since it was new.

I slid inside and leaned back, just now thinking of what I'd said. Running up? I'd meant to say the drive-in was still up and running. That was the problem with my brain these days. Sometimes I skipped words or got the order mixed up and didn't know it until later, if I figured it out at all.

Link threw the truck in reverse, and after a few seconds, we were heading out of town.

"So how did it go?"

"How did what go?" I replied. But I knew what he was getting at. He'd been ribbing me about Everly ever since he found out she'd be the one tutoring me for my government test.

"Don't make me hurt you," he said with a chuckle.

Link was a good guy, with an easy smile and an *I'm up for anything* kind of vibe going on. His mom was black and his dad was white. And Link? Well, he'd ended up somewhere in the middle. His dreads were an ode to his mom (though she made him keep them trimmed to just below his shoulders), but the blue eyes, they were all from his dad.

He was probably the funniest guy I knew, and he would do anything on a dare. Like once he'd run naked across the football field during cheerleading practice. It had earned him fifty bucks and a week's worth of detention. But that was Link. Up for anything.

"It was all right."

"All right?" He snorted. "Everly Jenkins is one of the hottest chicks in Twin Oaks. Damn, that girl has a nice ass. And her attitude? Off the charts. AT-TI-TUDE."

Okay. Link was one of my best buddies, but I was starting to get annoyed. I really didn't want to talk about Everly.

"She's got attitude for sure," I muttered.

"I know, right?" Link sped down the road. "I took civics with her last semester, and after that Jason guy moved out of state—"

"Jason guy?"

"Yeah, you know the dude she dated for, like, two years."

Huh. How did I not know that?

"Anyway," Link continued. "Brett Smith tried his hardest to get in her pants. Like, the guy pulled out all the stops. He must have asked her out five or six times. The dude seriously doesn't know what the word *no* means. One day he grabbed her ass, felt her up real good. I was about to step in because, you know, I don't like that kind of shit, but she slammed her foot down on top of his." Link snorted and glanced at me. "And she was wearing these high-heeled things. It had to hurt like hell. And then she nailed him with a hard right."

"What do you mean *nailed*?"

"I mean she slammed her fist into his face."

"She punched Brett Smith?"

"Damn straight she did. Dude's nose was bleeding all over the place, and he cursed her up and down." Link's grin was huge. "She didn't care. She sat in her seat and took all her shit out, her books and stuff, put them on her desk as if nothing had happened, and then she told Brett that the next time she'd aim for his junk. Told him that she had a pair of steel-toed boots at home and she'd be wearing them to school until the end of the semester." Link slapped the steering wheel. "Asshole totally deserved to get his balls kicked in, though it never happened because he didn't go near her again."

"Huh." It was all I had.

"Yeah," Link replied. "That chick is fierce."

About ten minutes later, we pulled into line at the drive-in, and once inside, we cruised for a spot near the back. It's where all the action's at. The downside is that the walk to the concession booth is long, but the upside is…it's where all the action's at.

Monday night at the Starlight Drive-In was double-feature night. Sadly for Link and I and all the other guys who'd shown up to hang out in the back, the movies were both chick flicks. Which meant that most guys would end up getting lucky or arguing with their girl. That's the thing about chick flicks—they either make a girl question her relationship or they get her in the mood for some heavy making out. It was a fifty-fifty shot, but since I was solo, I guess it didn't really matter all that much.

A bunch of guys we knew from school were already parked,

and a couple of them were tossing a football around, cheered on by a group of girls, most of whom were already halfway to loaded.

I nodded to a cute blond sitting on the tailgate of a truck. Her name was Jess, and we'd partied together in the past. She patted the empty spot beside her and I grinned. Things were looking up.

After we parked, Link and I hiked to the concession booth. We were both taking it easy tonight, Link because he was driving so no booze for him, and I knew that if I came home with beer on my breath, my mom would kill me. That's if she could get past my dad. And like I said, Dad is built like a brick house. No way was I messing with that.

I volunteered to pay for our food and had just ordered two large popcorns and a couple of cokes when I heard a soft voice behind me.

Everly.

I don't know how I knew it was her. I just did.

I grabbed the tray off the guy in the red-and-white-striped apron and turned around. Everly and a girl from school, Hailey I think her name was, were chatting with Link.

I walked toward them and stopped a couple of inches away, not smiling when I saw her, not reacting at all. The girl thought I was a moron. She'd been pretty clear about that.

She was still wearing the same clothes she'd had on at the library. White T-shirt that fit just right and those short shorts that showed off a whole lotta tanned leg. Her girlfriend was dressed for a night out in jeans and a jacket.

"I hope you brought a gallon of bug spray."

Everly looked at her girlfriend and then back to me. "Excuse me?"

I nodded to her legs. "You're gonna get bit up for sure, and we'll be able to play connect the dots on your legs."

"That's all right," Link said, putting his arm around the other girl. "I've got my fishing crap in the back of the truck, and I know I've got lots of spray. So, you girls going to hang with us or what?"

"No," Everly said.

"Yes," her friend said.

Everly's eyes darted to mine, and I saw something there but I wasn't sure what it was. "I mean," she said slowly, "we can or not…it's up to you."

Was that her way of apologizing for being such a bitch at the library? Did I care? I studied her for a few seconds, because I could see this going one of two ways. Either we were gonna be friends or not. Friends made for a much better summer.

The other option wasn't one I wanted to think about. At least not yet.

"Follow me," I said with a shrug. "We're parked at the back."

I guess I was going to find out.

Chapter Four

Everly

By the time I reached the bottom of my popcorn bag, my cell had pinged at least five times, and my stomach was churning so badly, I thought I might be sick. Not surprising, I'd wolfed down the bag as if I was starving when I wasn't hungry at all. Mostly because I wanted to look like I was at least into the movie. Which I wasn't. At all.

I'd lost my appetite somewhere between the concession booth and here. Trevor hadn't bothered introducing me to his friends, though I suppose after the way I'd treated him earlier, that shouldn't be surprising.

What was surprising was the speed with which Hailey ditched me. That stung. Oh, she'd played the "I'll sit with you if you want me to" card, but I didn't want to look like a jerk. I'd told her to go ahead and hang with Link. I got it. He was super hot. But still…

So here I sat, on the hood of Link's truck, pretending to watch a movie, with nothing but an empty bag of popcorn to keep me company. Hailey and Link were in the back of the truck, and last time I glanced back, she was stuck to him like glue.

Traitor.

I get that I wasn't great company these days, but still, what was up with that? I snuck a peek once more and sighed, swinging my eyes to the screen but not before catching sight of Trevor.

He was leaning against the truck beside us with a group of kids from school, none of whom I knew all that well, and other than a few curious looks from a couple of the guys, they kept their distance. Some blond girl kept poking Trevor in the ribs and giggling like an idiot. She looked ridiculous.

She looked happy.

And I was just plain old pathetic.

I set the empty bag of popcorn down and fished out my cell phone. All of the texts had come from my dad.

Just back now. Where are you?

Nice of him to come home.

Mom must be at prayer group?

Where else would she be? It's not like he was home, keeping her company.

Call me or text me right now.

Wow. Will do, Captain.

The last ping had been for a missed call. Again my dad.

With a sigh, I texted him back because I knew that he'd keep bugging me until I acknowledged him.

At the movies with Hales.

A few moments went by, and then a text came back.

Next time let me know what your plans are. We're going to have a chat about this. Come home right after the movie.

Whatever. I stared at the text for a few more moments and then shoved my cell back down into my front pocket. Night had fallen and I shivered, putting my hands under my thighs, trying for some kind of warmth.

The drive-in was full, and yet most of the kids here weren't inside their vehicles. They were hanging out in groups like the one beside me, drinking, laughing, hooking up. I spotted several cars and trucks with fogged-up windows and skipped my eyes over them, only to land on a couple a few rows up who were pressed into each other.

It was dark and hard to tell where the girl ended and the boy began. He had her pushed up against the car, his hand buried in her hair, and he was kissing her. He was kissing her like there was no one around. Like they were the only two people in the universe. He was touching her and pushing up against her and I couldn't look away.

Not even when his one hand slid down her hip and rested against her lower belly. It was intimate and it spoke volumes. I guess I was a pervert because I kept watching. Their kiss deepened, and as she tugged on his shoulders, trying to get even closer, I held my breath.

I thought of Jason, a guy I'd dated for a long time. Never had

I felt that way about him. So desperate to get close to him. So desperate to connect. To matter.

Something inside me tightened. It swelled and pressed into my chest so hard that it was painful. I was one of probably five hundred kids out here under the stars, and for some reason, I'd never felt so alone.

I tore my gaze away from the couple and tried to focus on the movie, but it was hard because suddenly there were tears pricking the corners of my eyes. God, here we go. Hot, painful tears. Angrily, I wiped them away and jumped off the truck.

I didn't have a plan. I just wanted to get away. I rounded the truck, and Trevor glanced up, a smile on his face—a smile meant for the blond girl—and for a second I froze, letting the beauty of his smile wash over me.

But it wasn't mine, so I turned sharply, heading the other way.

Hailey called my name, but I raised my hand as if to say *I'm good* and kept walking. What a joke. I was a joke. My life was a joke.

What the hell was wrong with me?

Trees surrounded the back end of the drive-in, and once I passed the first few rows, I started to run. I didn't stop until my chest burned, and by then, I was deep inside the forest.

It was quiet, and man the quiet was heavy. It was the kind of quiet that felt as if it was alive. It was the kind of quiet you could hide in.

My breath misted in front of me, and I wrapped my arms around my chest, shivering as my eyes adjusted to the gloom.

My ponytail had come loose, and hair stuck to the clammy skin at my neck.

If my life was a movie, this would be where the stupid heroine (me), out alone in the dark woods, gets attacked by some deranged madman. I kind of laughed at the thought. If my life was a movie, it would totally suck.

I leaned back against a tree, wishing the tightness, that hard coil of pain and confusion inside me, would just melt away. Maybe if I counted. Maybe if I thought of puppies and rainbows, I'd be fine. Maybe then I wouldn't feel like I was standing on the edge of something that I knew would wreck me.

So I did. I closed my eyes and counted to twenty, and then I started over. I wasn't sure how many times I did it or how much time had passed, but a snap echoed in the dark, and suddenly I knew I wasn't alone anymore.

"Hey."

I knew that voice.

Slowly, my eyes opened. Trevor stood a few feet away, hands shoved into the front pockets of his jeans. His dark hair fell forward across his brow and touched the tops of his shoulders. I saw something sparkle at his ear. A piercing?

"Are you all right?" he asked.

I shrugged and said nothing, afraid to answer because I wasn't sure that I could. That damn lump was still stuck in my throat, and even though I blinked several times, the tears were still there, just waiting for an excuse to embarrass me.

"The movie sucked," he said quietly. I guess he wasn't going away anytime soon.

I cleared my throat but still said nothing, trying to hold in a shudder but failing miserably. It was damp, and I was cold and more miserable than I'd been in a long time.

Trevor reached for the edge of his long-sleeved Henley, and my eyes widened when he began to pull it up over his head. He wore a T-shirt underneath, but even so, I saw a lot of skin as he raised his arms over his head.

Mouth dry, I didn't know what to say.

"Here," Trevor said as he moved toward me. "You're cold."

He stopped just in front of me, so close that I could feel his body heat, and I shivered again. He held out his hand and I hesitated, staring at his shirt, because anywhere other than into his eyes was preferable.

I didn't want him to see what was inside me. I wasn't ready for that.

"Everly?"

I reached forward and held my breath when our fingers connected. I swear something passed between us, but I was so emotional that I had no idea what it was. But it was there. And it was electric. Like a shock.

I angled his Henley over my head and slowly threaded my arms through. My chest rose and fell, faster than I'd like, and I kept my eyes lowered as I pulled out my hair. I played with the tangled ends, afraid to look up.

A heartbeat passed. And then another.

"Better?" he asked, his voice low.

I nodded. His shirt was still warm and it smelled like him. Fresh and clean and just...Trevor.

Several long moments passed. Several long moments where the quiet faded away and the crickets made themselves known. In the distance I heard the vague echoes of those at the drive-in, but here in this small patch of sanctuary, I heard Trevor's breathing and my own fast-beating heart.

I knew he was watching me, but I kept my eyes averted, still too afraid to let him see what was inside them. Too afraid that his intense, penetrating gaze would rip apart my defense shield. And that little bit of defense was all that was keeping me from falling apart right now.

"Do you want to talk about it?"

My bottom lip trembled. Shit. *Get hold of yourself, Everly.*

I shook my head and exhaled slowly.

Trevor took a step so that he was beside me, and he leaned back against my tree, hands folded above his head. He glanced up through the branches at the stars that twinkled over us.

I followed his gaze and relaxed into the bark once more, this time with the added barrier of Trevor's shirt. The silence enveloped us, and we both let it. It was just easier somehow, and after a while, that big lump in my throat dissolved and the tightness in my chest faded to nothing.

"There's going to be a blue moon this month."

Wow. I'm silent all evening and that's my opening line?

"Blue moon?" Trevor pushed off from the tree and stood facing me. I tilted my head slightly so that I could see him better. I knew he was tall, and maybe it was the dark or maybe I was just feeling small and vulnerable, but right now, he looked larger than life. "What's a blue moon?" he asked.

"Every so often, there are two full moons in one month. The second one, that's the one they call a blue moon."

"That's kind of cool."

He inched a bit closer, and I found it harder to keep my breaths nice and even.

"I'm sorry about today. I didn't mean to suggest that you had some kind of brain damage or anything."

Oh. My. God. Brain damage? Could I have been any more insensitive?

"I'm sorry. I didn't mean to say brain damage." Oh God. I said it again. "I meant…" Just stop. Right now.

"It's okay, Everly. I know what you mean." Trevor shifted his weight, but his eyes never left mine. "Is everything okay with you?"

Surprised, I didn't answer right away. I tried so hard every single day to be normal and, at the very least, some sort of version of the old me. Guess I was failing at that too. "Why would you say that?"

He shrugged. "I don't know. You look sad or something."

"Is it that obvious?"

He moved again. Another inch and now there was only a whisper between us.

"Yeah," he said slowly. "It kinda is."

"I'm fine. Just tired."

"You're lying."

"Why do you care?"

"I don't know." A slow smile crept over his face. "Maybe because I'm a moron?"

I opened my mouth to reply but had nothing, and the two of us stood there for a long time, so close I only had to lean forward and I could bury my face in his chest. And that's pretty much all I was thinking about right now. What he would feel like. Warm. Hard. Alive.

"I can't figure you out," he said so softly that at first I wasn't sure he'd even spoken.

"Why would you want to?" I blurted.

"I don't know," he murmured. "Maybe because you're nothing like I remember, and for once, I'm pretty sure that thought has more to do with reality and less to do with"—he tapped his forehead—"the brain malfunctioning."

"You are." I blew out a breath.

"I'm what?"

"You seem the same."

There was that lopsided smile again. "I don't know if that's a good thing or not, but trust me, Everly, I'm not that guy anymore."

Slowly he reached for me, and I inhaled sharply when his hand tucked a long strand of hair behind my ear.

"Well, I'm just a girl," I finally managed to say. "No big mystery here."

"Wow."

"What?"

"You have a very different view of yourself from the one that I see." His tone was light, teasing even, and I relaxed a bit.

"Really."

"From the whole universe, if you want to know the truth."

"The whole universe?" I tried to hide my grin but it was hard. "That's pretty big and far-reaching."

"Yep." Trevor moved to the side. "Good thing I've got the whole summer to work on it."

"On what?"

"On figuring you out."

The thought of Trevor Lewis figuring me out was not only terrifying, it made no sense. I chewed on my bottom lip, curious. "I was such a bitch at the library. Most guys would just blow me off."

"Most guys like a challenge."

"I disagree. Most guys like the easy win. The slam dunk. The whole nine yards."

"I'm not most guys, Everly." He wasn't teasing anymore. "A year and a half ago, I would have blown you off. I would have told you exactly where to go." He shoved his hands back into the pockets of his jeans, and I noticed goose bumps on his arms.

"Truth?" He shrugged. "Maybe you're right. Maybe most guys would just say screw it. Or maybe I need to pass the government test so badly, I'm willing to spend the summer with a girl who's cold as hell one moment and the next she's talking about ink and Elton John. We're going to be spending the summer together, so we should at least try to get along. Don't you think?"

Panic. I felt it nipping at my toes, clawing its way up my legs until it landed hard in my stomach. So I dug in. "I'm sure your pretty little blond friend won't like that."

"Who? Jess?"

"Is that her name?" I knew exactly who she was.

"Jess is just a girl I know," Trevor said. "But you're…" His voice trailed into nothing, and my stomach tumbled again. This time harder.

"I'm?"

That slow grin was back, and if my stomach tumbled before, it was now spiraling out of control. Whoosh. Not an entirely pleasant feeling, and in fact, I didn't like it at all.

"You're more complicated than that."

I laughed nervously. "I'm not complicated at all."

He grinned. "Well, lucky for me, I've got the entire summer to figure out if you are, in fact, a bitch or just a complicated girl who was having a bad day."

I didn't know what to say to that, so I said nothing. I exhaled and glanced back up at the moon as if it was the most interesting thing in the world.

Oh no. Nope. That was so not going to happen. I did not need someone like Trevor Lewis on a mission to figure me out. Mostly because there was too much that had to stay hidden.

Chapter Five

Trevor

It was Thursday afternoon. Everly and I (I couldn't call her Ever, just couldn't) had finished discussing due process of law and procedural due process of law, oh, and let's not forget about substantive due process of law. We were slowly making our way down an impressive list of things that she'd organized, and even though my brain was pretty much fried, I kind of liked this stuff. I just hoped that it stayed where it was supposed to stay. Deep inside my brain for when I'd need it later.

The nagging headache I'd woken up with was still hanging around, but whatever. I'd learned to deal with a lot more than a stupid headache in the last year, and it was totally worth the pain, just so I could be here and watch Everly.

Something about this girl intrigued me. Was it her smile? The way her eyes got really dark when she was concentrating and that little frown appeared between her brows? Was it the way she chewed on the end of her pencil (like now) when she was thinking?

Was it the fact that she'd punched Brett Smith in the throat and threatened to kick him in the gonads?

Or was it the fact that there was a piece of her hidden away? I'd felt it Monday night, and I felt it now. It was in everything that she wasn't saying, and everything she wasn't saying filled the silence up with little mysterious pieces of her. It was those little pieces that I wanted to explore. It was those little pieces that made her different from any girl I'd ever met before.

We'd been studying all week and had fallen into a routine. I showed up at her place just before noon, and we'd head to the library to study. If she wasn't meeting Hailey at the pool afterward, I'd drop her home around five.

We hadn't talked about anything other than government. I hadn't brought up the drive-in, and she'd not said a word either. Not even when she returned my Henley, smelling all fresh and full of Sunlight detergent.

But something was up today. She was distracted, and I'd caught glimpses of that sad look in her eyes.

My cell pinged and I reached for it, grimacing when I saw that it was Jess. For, like, the tenth time. She wanted to hang out later, but I…

I glanced over my laptop at Everly. She was gnawing on the end of a pencil again, tapping her fingers along the top of the table.

"Something up?" I asked.

Her head whipped up, and she studied me for a few moments and then shook her head. "No."

"You sure?"

A nod.

"Yep."

Huh. She wasn't making this easy for me. I don't want to sound like an arrogant dick or anything, but yeah, this is totally going to make me sound like an arrogant dick. I'm not used to having to work to make a girl like me. It's just always been easy. Mom says that when I put my mind to it, I can charm the pants off anyone. Said I'd been doing it since the day I was born and Dad had to practically wrestle me from a couple of enamored nurses. Something about my rosebud mouth.

Apparently Everly Jenkins hadn't gotten that particular memo.

"What are you doing tonight?" I asked, watching her closely.

Everly's eyes were dark again. She cleared her throat, which was a delaying tactic, one I'd learned she used a lot when she was trying to figure out what to say. Or more importantly, what not to say.

"I have youth group."

"Youth group."

Her eyebrows shot up.

"Yes. Youth group. As in a bunch of teenagers, who would be the youth, who have nothing better to do on a Thursday night but get together, which would be the group, in the church basement."

"Sounds exciting."

"It is.

"What do you guys do?" I was picturing choirs and hallelujah and much praising of the Lord.

"We talk and stuff."

"About what?"

"The weather."

Wow. She really was in a mood.

"That makes exciting seem lame," I teased.

"It's not a joke, Trevor. It used to be a lot of fun."

"Used to," I repeated slowly. "So what changed?"

There went the pencil again. Tap. Tap. Tap. Tap. She shrugged. "I guess I did." The tapping stopped. "Why are you asking me all these questions?"

I leaned back in my chair, happy that we were engaged on some level other than due process of law.

"Why are you in such a bad mood?"

She tossed the pencil. "I'm not."

"You're full of crap."

She leaned forward, elbows on the table, and for a second, my gaze dropped. How could it not? She was wearing this pale yellow blouse, and the top buttons had come undone. I could be a nice guy and tell her about it, but right now, I was about as far from being a nice guy as snow was from Louisiana.

Everly Jenkins had cleavage and—I grinned—was wearing a matching yellow bra.

"What are *you* doing tonight?" she asked, oblivious to the fact that the more she leaned toward me, the more of that creamy, smooth skin was exposed. I noticed little daisies decorating the bra straps.

"I don't know. That depends."

This here. This was flirting at its best. The kind of flirting that a guy enjoyed, mostly because it was kind of like foreplay. There was something between Everly and me, and man, I wanted to explore it. Considering I hadn't been all that interested in any girl since my accident and breakup with Bailey, that was saying something. For the longest time I'd been afraid of rejection. I mean, what kind of girl wants to date a guy whose marbles aren't always intact?

"On what?" she asked, a little out of breath now.

"On you."

I could tell she was surprised. "Me?"

"Yeah. You."

Mrs. Henney shushed us, so I leaned closer and lowered my voice. "Let's do something tonight."

"Why?"

"Why not?"

Everly glanced over to Mrs. Henney, who was looking at us like we'd committed some sort of a crime or something. When Everly's gaze swung back to me, I felt like I'd been hit with something. It made me stop for a bit and think. Was this just a physical reaction to a pretty girl? Or something more?

"I've already told you I have youth group."

I had to blink, because suddenly Everly was out of focus.

Her big blue eyes wavered a bit, and my stomach rolled. Okay. I could deal with this. Sometimes my vision goes a little wonky. It doesn't happen that often, but the headache that had followed me around all day should have been warning enough.

I was an ace at acting as if everything was good. I took a moment. Shit. My stomach didn't feel so hot. I took another moment.

"So I'll come," I finally managed to say.

"To church."

I waited as the wave of nausea finally rolled away and then breathed out nice and slow, toying with my laptop case as a distraction.

"Yeah, to church. I'll come."

"You won't like it."

Okay, I was starting to get annoyed. That, coupled with the fact that all of a sudden, my head felt as if it was being ripped apart from the inside out, made my voice a little sharp, but shit, what was her problem anyway?

"How do you know what I like?"

Heat surged through me, and I had a weird moment when I felt as if I was standing outside my body. My mouth was dry, and I reached for the water bottle on the table beside my laptop.

Except my hand didn't do what I wanted it to. I stared at the water bottle, trying to figure out why I couldn't get to it. I'm not real sure how long I did that, but suddenly I felt Everly's hand on my arm.

She was talking to me but it sounded like she was talking

from far away, like when you're in the city and just getting off the subway at night. If you shout, the walls make it seem as if your words can fly anywhere.

I tried to tell her that I felt like shit. I tried to grab the water bottle. I tried to tell her that I'd go to her stupid youth group meeting because for most of our study session, all I'd thought about was getting her alone. Which was kind of defeated by the whole youth group thing, but a guy would take what he could get.

But none of those words came out. My mouth was still dry, and my vision was really starting to freak me the hell out.

She leaned in real close, and I could smell that light summery scent that was all Everly. But no matter how hard I tried, I couldn't understand what she was saying, and I banged my knee against the table. Once. Twice. And as my anger increased, a third time.

God, I was hot.

I was hot and pissed and scared.

What the hell was happening to me? My skin felt too small for my body, and my brain felt like it was going to explode. Saliva was pooling in my mouth which (A) was gross, and (B) freaked me out more than the vision thing.

Mrs. Henney was in my face now, the bottle of water I wanted in her wrinkled hands. She offered it to me. I saw the bottle floating in the air like an astronaut, just drifting in front of my eyes. Why couldn't I grab it?

Then I was fading. Going away somewhere dark, and the

last thing I remember thinking was that Everly was going to see something I was pretty sure would be the most uncool thing ever. And that maybe I was dying.

And that totally sucked.

Chapter Six
Everly

It was Saturday morning, and I had the kitchen to myself. Mom was off to yoga class, her neon yellow pants still burned into my retinas. Seriously, no female over the age of ten should wear that color. I don't care if your butt is tight, it's just kind of wrong. But my mom was all about sunshine and happy, or at least the appearance of sunshine and happy, so yellow was her color of choice lately.

She'd done a drive-by, kissed the air near my cheek before grabbing her water bottle, and was gone. Dad was in his office, working on his sermon for tomorrow (thank God, because it was too early to play pretend), and Isaac was still in bed.

I'd been up for a while and had been sitting in the same spot at the table, staring into a cup of cold coffee, wondering what Trevor was doing. Was he still in bed? Was he okay? Was he still as freaked out by what had happened as I was?

My stomach rumbled just then, and I thought that maybe I should make myself something to eat. Something adventurous like a poached egg or French toast. On second thought, both of those choices seemed like too much work. Bagel and chocolate spread it was.

I was just about to get off my butt when my dad walked into the kitchen. He helped himself to the last bit of coffee in the pot and leaned against the counter. He was his regular Saturday self. Hair slightly askew, unshaven, and sleep still in his eyes.

He was beautiful, my dad, but we all know that beauty can hide dark and sinful things, because the reality was that my beautiful father was a snake. He just hadn't shed his skin yet.

"So how's Trevor?"

Funny. His voice still held that extra bit of warmth that wrapped every single word he uttered in a blanket of nice. Safe. Trustworthy. It was his secret weapon.

Too bad it was a total lie.

I shoved my cup away. Guess today wasn't the day he was going to come clean, which meant that today wasn't the day I could stop playing pretend. I'd thought about confronting him. I thought about it every single day. And every single day I thought *no, today isn't the day I want his lie to be real*, because once his lie becomes my reality, I'd have to face a whole lot of other stuff I wasn't ready for. It was a coward's way out, but right now, being a coward was getting me through life.

So I took an extra moment to get my game face on (go, Everly, go) before I answered him with the most epic answer ever.

"I don't know."

And I didn't. The truth was I hadn't been able to stop thinking about Trevor since Thursday. The whole thing had been awful to watch, and thank goodness Mrs. Henney had been there. She'd shoved her sweater under Trevor's head and just held him. I'd never felt so helpless in my life, so I couldn't imagine what Trevor had been feeling. The ambulance had whisked him off to the hospital, leaving me to deal with all the kids who'd been there. Their questions had been stupid and I left without answering any of them.

"Did he, like, bite his tongue off?"

"Is he going to die?"

"I hope whatever he has isn't contagious, like a disease or something."

"It was a seizure, wasn't it?"

Earth to Everly. Startled, I nodded.

"Hmm. I'll keep him in my prayers."

"You do that." The words fell out of me before I could stop them, and I tensed, fingers gripped to my coffee mug.

I heard his feet scuff the floor, and inside my head I said every single bad word that I was never allowed to say, and I repeated a few of them. The really bad ones. He pulled out the chair across from me and set his cup on the table.

"What's going on with you, Everly?" Again with the warmth. Even now when I knew that he was angry with me. The warmth. It was nauseating.

I glanced up and shrugged. "Nothing."

My dad, who was in his early forties, was a cross between Jared Leto (I guess the Jesus factor was a bonus, considering he worked one of his day jobs from a pulpit) and the guy who played Superman. His hair was still as dark as mine, though when he forgot to shave, there were a few silver hairs on his chin. His eyes were blue, but not the dark blue that mine were. His were so light that when I was little, I thought he'd somehow trapped the sun inside them.

"Are we going to talk about what's been going on with you?" he asked. "You haven't been yourself, and Everly, I've got to tell you, I'm concerned."

For one perfect moment I let the warmth of his voice wrap me in that blanket of "it's going to be okay." For that one perfect moment it washed over me, and for that one perfect moment I felt some kind of hope.

But as much as a lot of folks in this town think that I live inside some weird, perfect world, I'd love to tell each and every one of them that there aren't any perfect moments that are real. Not really.

So this one passed, and as I stared into my father's eyes, the familiar pangs of hurt rushed up from my heart and crushed my larynx.

Again, I shrugged because I had nothing else. My throat was so tight I couldn't speak, so I grabbed my coffee cup and downed the rest of it, nearly choking on the cold, overly sweet remnants that hung at the bottom. Smart move. Wiping the back of my hand across my mouth, I glared at him, in this moment blaming him for every single crappy thing that I could think of.

"Everly," he said slowly, so slowly that those three syllables could have been four.

"Why don't we talk about you?" I managed to squeeze out.

Silence.

My dad cleared his throat. "Is there something you want to say to me?"

Man. There were hundreds of words inside me, dying to be heard. Thousands probably, and now that he was finally giving me the chance to say them, which ones would I pick? Which ones were the sharpest? The most brutal? Which ones would pierce through flesh *and* bone?

"I…"

The only problem was that I was going to fall apart before I'd be able to get any of them out. It's just the way I was built. I, Everly Jenkins, am a crier, and an ugly crier to boot. I cried when I was happy. I cried when I was upset or angry. And I for sure cried whenever I was confronted with something like wanting to tell my dad that I knew about his secret.

Breathe. Just breathe.

"Everly, whatever this is, we need to talk about it. I'm here for you, sweets, you know that. I can help you. Does it have something to do with Trevor? Was he taking drugs? Is that why he had a seizure?"

Wow. I think I had to pull my jaw off the table.

"Just because he has long hair and tattoos, you think he does drugs?"

"That's not what I said."

"It's what you implied."

He frowned. "Everly."

"Why do you go to New Orleans so much?" The words came out in a rush. They weren't sharp and they sure as heck wouldn't pierce through flesh and bone. But they were a start.

This was his chance to explain. His chance to be honest. His chance to tell me that everything was going to be fine and that he still loved all of us. His chance to maybe admit he was human after all and not this perfect, upstanding pastor who was nothing more than a big fat lie.

"Is that what this is about?" he asked.

He got up and set his coffee cup on the counter before reaching into the cupboard for his extra-chunky peanut butter. "I counsel a troubled youth group, Everly. You know that." He grabbed a bagel out of the bread box, sliced it, and then tossed it into the toaster just like he'd done every single morning since *that* morning.

The tears, oh the tears, they were right there, like hot little bullets just waiting to spring from my eyes. But I forced them back, my body tense like a boxer's before a fight. When my father turned to face me, his eyes didn't hold the sun anymore.

You're lying.

I wondered if he could read my thoughts. I wondered if he

knew that ever since *that* morning, I'd thought the same thing over and over again. *You're lying. You're a liar. You're a lying piece of crap.*

"Right. The troubled youth group." I pushed back from the table. "Can I have the car? Like, you don't need to go to *New Orleans* or anything today, do you? Can the troubled youth of *New Orleans* live without you today?"

The sarcasm, it was heavy, and I knew my father didn't know how to handle this side of me. I'd always been his angel. His good little girl. The one who believed all the bullshit and the lies. The one who still believed that her dad was a man above all others. A guy who lived by the words that he preached.

"Everly."

"Good," I said abruptly. "I'm going to visit Trevor."

I pushed past him, scooped the keys out of the little porcelain dog near the fridge, and ignored the silence that followed in my wake as I ran up the stairs, not stopping until I was in my room.

The face that greeted me in the mirror was angry. It was full of blotchy patches of skin and eyes that were too shiny. I yanked a brush through my hair and slipped into the first thing I grabbed out of my closet, a blue summer dress that was faded and old, but whatever. I was never going to be a fashionista like Hailey, so why should I care?

After slipping into a pair of flip-flops, I grabbed my purse and ran out the front door before he could stop me.

Twenty minutes later, I stood on the porch of Trevor's house, nodding like an idiot as his mother told me that Trevor didn't want to see anyone right now.

Mortified, I glanced down at my toes. What was I doing here anyway? Trevor and I weren't exactly friends. I'm not sure what we were, but I knew that I should not have expected him to want to see me.

"Oh, okay, Mrs. Lewis. I'm so sorry to bother you"—I glanced at my watch and winced—"so early on a Saturday morning. I guess I wasn't thinking."

"Please," she said softly. "Call me Brenda." She stood back a bit, her brows furrowed. "Have you had breakfast? I'm just in the middle of making waffles and strawberries."

"Oh, no." I cleared my throat. "Thank you so much, but I've got…ah…" Nothing whatsoever to do because right now, my life is sucking huge donkey balls.

"It's no trouble, really." Her eyes were soft, the lines around her mouth deep. "I'd love to talk about how Trevor's doing with his studies. That's if you have the time?"

Time? That was a good one. I had all the time in the world, because Hailey was gone for the weekend on her family's annual camping trip, and there was no way I was going home. Not now.

"It's no trouble, Everly, really."

I gave a half shrug, mostly because I had nowhere else to go and, well, the smell of cinnamon was making my mouth water. "I could stay for a bit."

"Good," Brenda Lewis said, her smile wide as she stood back and motioned for me to come inside.

She had a nice smile. A slow crooked smile. Kind of like Trevor's.

Chapter Seven
Trevor

I'll be the first to admit that when I came out of the coma and realized what had happened, what my future might be, I was a total dick. Yep, I was that guy. Total dick with a capital *D*.

The thing was, everyone kind of expected it, and man, did I deliver. I threw some serious tantrums, the kind my family hadn't seen since I was at least two years old. I broke a lot of shit and used words to hurt (when I could get them out, because in the beginning, that was stupid hard to do).

But over the last six months, I've learned to deal with it, or at least I thought I had. You see, I was almost there. Almost halfway to normal. Until Thursday night. Man, I hadn't seen that coming. Thursday night, I completely lost my shit.

Seizure.

The word alone gives me the goddamn creeps. Seriously. I hear the word and picture a guy all twisted up with snot running out of his nose and spit falling from the corner of his mouth. I picture a rabid dog with a foaming snarl or a screwed-up mental patient.

I close my eyes and see a freak on the floor.

And now that was me. I was the freak on the floor.

Back when I was still in the hospital, the doctor had told us that it wasn't uncommon for someone who'd suffered a TBI to have a seizure. Usually they occur in the days and weeks just after whatever incident caused said TBI. He'd told us that they could still occur months or years afterward, but it wasn't *as* common.

Which kind of sucks, because in that year, you start to think that maybe (at least on the outside) you can get back to normal. If you learn to hide all the defects, the ones on the inside that no one can see, then maybe you can live your life as if nothing had happened. I could go back to being Trevor Lewis, the guy who had it all.

That's what I was aiming for, and yeah, it was damn hard work. The headaches alone were exhausting, and the nights when I couldn't sleep didn't help. But my memory blips weren't as bad as they used to be, my guitar chops were slowly coming back, and once I passed the stupid government test, I would graduate and leave for New York City.

So I was a dreamer. Sue me. I had a plan, and for the last year, it was that plan that had gotten me through. New York City, my buddy Nate, and our music.

But now?

I splashed cold water on my face and glared at the mirror above the sink. Now the fact that I was me but I *wasn't* me was real hard to ignore. I still looked the same. All the evidence of the accident and coma were buried. The scar from when they'd cut open my skull because my brain had swelled was hidden beneath my hair, a jagged line that no one would see unless I shaved my head. Since I liked my hair on the long side, that wasn't happening any time soon.

I worked out like a son of a bitch, and other than my knee, my body was good. Physically I was probably in the best shape I've ever been in. I had all my teeth. They were straight. White. My eyes looked the same. Nose had escaped the accident unscathed.

Every single thing about me looked the same, and yet it wasn't.

Seizure. If ever one word can define you, that was it for me.

I wouldn't be the same again. Ever.

My fists clenched, and for a moment, I let the rage swell. It pushed up from my chest and fired through my cells. I can't lie. In a sick way, it felt good.

My perfectly normal face stared back at me, and I wanted to smash the mirror and obliterate the image, because it was a total effing lie.

Shit.

Chest heaving, I dragged my eyes away, because if I did punch the mirror, my dad would have my ass. I don't know how long I leaned over the sink in the bathroom staring at the faded porcelain and the crack that ran along the edge, but it was long enough for my eyes to blur. Long enough for the hard, cold fear inside me to grow and expand until I had a tough time breathing and my skin was covered in sweat.

I had to get out of there.

Stopping at my room long enough to grab a T-shirt, I didn't bother changing out of my sweat pants and headed for the front door. I was almost home free, but I stopped when I heard her voice. Everly. What. The. Hell.

I'd told Mom to send her away. I mean, why was she here anyway? Did she want another look at the freak?

That pin inside my head—the one attached to a crap ton of anger just waiting to explode—well, that pin pulled and I swung around, heading for the kitchen before I could (A) think about it and realize maybe this wasn't such a good idea, or (B) stop myself once I did realize that I was probably going to make a complete ass out of myself.

Everly was at the kitchen table and turned when I walked into the room.

"Why are you here?" The words tore out of me, and inside, my heart beat as fast and furious as a Metallica drum track. Double kick and hitting hard. I wanted to break something. Anything.

My gaze swung widely until I caught sight of my mom, her soft brown eyes shadowed with a whole bunch of stuff that I was responsible for.

"Trevor," she said quietly. "Take a moment, okay? Just breathe."

"Don't talk to me like I'm a goddamn baby," I shouted.

Shit. This wasn't going well.

The last time I "pulled the pin," as my dad liked to call it, I'd put my fist through the drywall in the garage. When it came over me, the rage was hard to control, and this morning my feelings were all over the place. So yeah, I knew I should have run out the front door, but here I was and there was no turning back.

"Breathe," Mom said again, moving toward me.

I stared down into her eyes when she put her hands on me. Saw the hurt in them when I flinched. It was hard to explain, but I felt twitchy, like my skin was pulled too tight. And I had to be honest. I was scared shitless that I would hurt her.

"I gotta get out of here."

"Trevor, please. Just sit down with us. I made your favorite. Waffles and strawberries."

She didn't get it. No one did. Hell, I didn't even get why I acted the way I did sometimes. It was like there was an ocean of stuff inside me, rolling in like constant waves buffeting the shore, just waiting for a chance to break. And when they did? When they crashed onto the beach and annihilated the sand, there would be nothing left. The weird thing is that sometimes it was the nothing that I wanted, because feeling nothing was somehow better than this.

"Where are the car keys?" I asked, shoving past my mom.

Taylor appeared from nowhere and scooped them off the counter. "What the hell, Trevor? Are you insane? You can't drive. Not after…" Her eyes shot to Mom's. God, she couldn't even look at me.

"Not after what, Taylor? Just say it." I practically growled the words.

Silence. Yeah. Not surprised. Everyone was so concerned about treating me like a baby that they didn't for once consider I hated it. I was gonna be eighteen in a few months, not eight.

"I had a goddamn seizure, Taylor. And maybe I'll have another one. And another one after that. Maybe I'll have the biggest freaking seizure on record, and then we can all call it what it is. Epilepsy. Yeah, that's me. That's my future, so why don't you just goddamn well say it?"

Taylor's eyes got real small, the way they did when she was pissed off. Good. I could deal with pissed off. Pissed off went hand in hand with the way I was feeling right about now.

"You're such an asshole."

"Epileptic asshole," I shot back.

"You expect me to feel sorry for you?" she shouted.

Taylor was small. She was small and blond with a pretty dated Goth thing going on, but when she wanted to, she could be fierce. I'd seen her stand up to a chick twice her size at school and win the face-off.

"Well, I don't feel sorry for you, Trevor. I don't feel sorry for you one bit, and I'm sick of everyone in this family treating you as if you're some fragile doll that's going to crack if we do or say the wrong thing."

My mom stepped between us. "Taylor and Trevor, please."

"No," Taylor spat. "He doesn't get to shit on us just because he feels sorry for himself, and you don't get to expect me to treat him like he's going to fall apart if I say seizure or epi-effing-lepsy." She held the keys up in the air, taunting me, and then shoved them in her pocket. "So you had a seizure? So what? Is the world supposed to stop spinning? Am I not allowed to enjoy my goddamn waffles and strawberries?"

"Taylor!" My mom's voice reached that pitch, that critical point where I knew she was going to either explode or break down. "Language."

"See?" Taylor said shrilly. "You yell at me for swearing but Trevor gets a pass? Maybe I should get into a car with some drunk loser and maybe I should end up in a ditch somewhere with a major TBI so that I can swear and stay out late and do whatever the hell I want."

The waves inside me? Yeah, they were crashing hard, and I knew bad shit was going to happen unless I got the hell out of there.

I yanked around and headed for the front door, ignoring my mother's pleas and my sister's shrill screams. Her meltdown was going to be epic. I suppose it was a good thing that my dad had already left for his repair shop, because I was pretty damn sure heads would have rolled.

I ran out the front door and didn't stop running for twenty minutes, and by that time, I found myself at Baker's Landing, which was a nice piece of property owned by my buddy Nate's grandparents. Chest heaving, I slid down near the edge of the large pond and then fell back, arms crossed over my face to block out the sun. My knee was throbbing, I was thirsty as hell, and, well, just plain old pissed off.

I don't know how long I lay there, but I do know that when I realized I wasn't alone anymore, I was still in a bad mood.

A shadow crossed my face, and I sat up slowly, glancing to the side.

"Hey."

It was Everly.

I didn't answer, but I did move over a bit when she plopped down beside me. For a long time, the two of us stared out at the water, watching the swans who'd called this place home for years glide across the pristine surface.

"It's pretty out here," she said. "I have a place I like to go to, to just chill and think. The old mill, but it's not nearly as nice as this."

"How did you know where I was?" I asked, ignoring her attempt at conversation. She picked at the grass, which made me notice her dress. Which made me notice all that smooth skin, because the dress was definitely on the short side. And here I thought church girls always dressed like old ladies.

"Your mom told me you might be here. She said that when you got upset, you liked to come to this place."

"Yeah, well, my mom should just keep her mouth shut," I retorted angrily.

"Really?" Everly asked. "She's your mom. She's supposed to be up in your business."

"Whatever," I muttered. "I'm sick of it. All of it. The doctors who keep telling me things are looking up and then bam, a seizure. I'm sick of how scared my parents are every time I leave the house. How my dad likes to pretend that things are the way they were before when they're not. Nothing is ever going to be the same again. I'll never be the same again."

I had to stop talking, because I could barely catch my breath. The anger inside me was leveling off, but it left me jumpy.

Silence filled the space between us, and then she spoke softly. "Are you okay?"

"You're joking, right?" I asked, a nasty tone to my voice.

Everly shook her head. "No." Her voice lowered. "No, I'm not."

"Everly, I'm so far from all right that I wouldn't recognize it if it came up to me and said hello." I paused, frowning. "I was almost there. I thought there was a chance, you know?" I sighed. "But now I'm the guy who had a seizure in the library."

I glanced up and found her dark blue eyes settled on me. I wanted to look away, because this girl was freaking me out a little. It felt as if she could see inside me, and with all the crap going on in my world, there was a lot of stuff I didn't want anyone to know.

I yanked on some more grass and tossed a handful into the air, feeling more of the anger leave me as the blades fell back to the ground. "I like to go to the football field and watch the cheerleaders practice too."

"Excuse me?" she asked.

"When I don't come here. Sometimes I'd rather watch a bunch of girls jumping around than a pack of swans swimming across the lake."

A hint of a smile twisted the corner of her mouth, and for the first time today, I felt a little bit of lightness.

"She did say that as well, but I was pretty sure you were here."

"Oh yeah? Why is that?"

"Because school's out and there is no cheerleading practice."

Right. I didn't answer but focused on the swans.

"About Thursday," she said softly.

"I don't want to talk about it."

A pause.

"Okay. But we're still going to study, right? I'll see you on Monday?"

I shrugged. At the moment I didn't want to do anything but stare across the water and wallow in being a lame and sorry ass. A few more moments of silence passed, and I began to think about what had just happened. And with those thoughts came a bit of shame.

"I guess you're probably not used to the kind of scene you just saw at my house." I watched her closely, trying to gauge her reaction. She tucked a long piece of hair behind her ear and chewed on her lower lip for a few seconds. I'd noticed it before, but man, the girl had a nice mouth.

"You'd be surprised," she whispered.

"Really?" I somehow doubted that. The Jenkinses were the poster family for Pleasantville, USA.

"Really," she repeated, turning fully so that she was facing me. She was inches away, and that sweet summer smell was all over me. I had to give Everly props for making me totally forget the reason I was out here in the first place, because right now, in this moment, all I could think about was how soft her mouth looked.

And how amazing she smelled.

She licked that incredible mouth, and I thought that maybe she was nervous.

"I'm no different from anyone else. My family is no different. In fact, you'd probably be shocked if you knew the truth." Her voice caught, but she cleared her throat. "We're all hiding something, Trevor. None of us are perfect."

There was something in her voice, some small bit of hurt that bled through her words, and I couldn't take my eyes off her.

"What are you hiding?" I asked before I could help myself.

She gave a small shrug. "Meet me at the library on Monday and maybe I'll tell you."

We stared at each other for a long time. How long? I'm not sure, but it was long enough for the swans to get curious and make their way over to our side of the pond. Long enough for small beads of sweat to glisten across her forehead.

And long enough for me to realize that I wanted to kiss her. Like, really kiss her. Skin and tongues and heat. The old me would have made a move, confident of the outcome. But this new me wasn't so sure about anything anymore, so I did nothing.

"Do you want a ride back?" she asked eventually.

"Nah," I replied. "I think I'm going to hang here for a bit. Pretty sure Mom and Taylor are going to go at it for a while."

A pause.

"Do you feel like company?"

I couldn't help but smile, and I liked how her cheeks got red when I did. "Only if that company is you."

She blushed harder, and her eyes moved away as she whispered, "Okay."

I relaxed back onto the bank, and Everly did the same, her body so close to mine that I felt the heat coming off her skin. I closed my eyes, inhaled her fresh clean smell, and for the first time since I'd woken up, I felt some kind of peace.

Chapter Eight
Everly

One of my earliest memories is sitting on my mother's knee, there in the first row at church, watching sunlight stream in from outside to halo my dad's head as he gave his sermon. The beams were like little pieces of heaven, and I was convinced they came straight from God to bathe my father in his goodness.

Because in my young mind, my father *was* good and strong. He was the guy who hugged me as much and as often as I wanted. Kissed me on the nose and called me his sweets. He was the man who tucked me into bed and read *The Velveteen Rabbit* over and over and over again because I asked him to.

My dad was that guy. The man all my friends loved, the man who was bigger and stronger and smarter than anyone else I knew. His voice was love and his eyes were promise.

He was so handsome that a smile or a touch on the shoulder made most women giggle like little schoolgirls. My mom used to tease him about it. She called it the Pastor Factor. And she said that it wasn't just his charisma and charm that filled our church each and every Sunday. It was his ready smile and the way he could make anyone feel special just by looking at them.

She had a point, but I always thought it was my father's voice that drew people in. Like he had some magical quality that hypnotized and cajoled until you couldn't help but agree and say *amen* and sing his praises.

He was good. He was better than good. I'd give him that. And up until a year ago, he had me fooled. The sad thing is that sometimes I wish I was still fooled, because there's something safe about floating through life on a cloud of ignorance. It is, as they say, bliss after all.

Sometimes it felt as if my sanity was hanging on the edge of a tiny little crack, and every day that crack got a little bit bigger. And every day I wondered, *is this the day that I'll shatter? Is this the day that I lose it and ruin the perfect lie that is my life?*

Turns out Sunday wasn't the day for cracking and spilling. Nope. It had been no different from any other that I could remember. I'd gotten up early, gone for a run, had breakfast with Mom and Isaac, and after a quick shower, got dressed for church. I wore a pale pink skirt and a sleeveless white blouse, my hair pinned back and only a hint of gloss on my lips. Understated and proper, just like the girl I was supposed to be.

Dad always left early—said he needed time alone to go over his sermon—and we joined him half an hour before service began. I played the piano and sang a few hymns. He did his thing, and the people, well, they gave him their love and money and that was that.

But as I sat there beside my mother in the first row and watched and listened as my father talked about forgiveness and acceptance, I felt different. It wasn't just that I felt betrayed and angry—I'd been feeling those things for months and months. No, it was something more devastating to me. I didn't see sunbeams anymore—they'd disappeared along with my mom's bright and easy smile. They'd been replaced by a darkness that seeped deeper into my family every single day, and there was nothing I could do about it.

Forgiveness.

Acceptance.

What. Ever.

I wanted my sunbeams back, and I totally didn't see that happening anytime soon because I knew there were some things that were unforgiveable. Some things that the truth could never fix. And that realization was probably the saddest moment of my life. Considering I was seventeen, what did that say about my future?

So I was still pondering all of that stuff Monday afternoon as I sat in the library waiting for Trevor. Mrs. Henney came by and asked if Trevor was okay. I smiled and said he was fine, aware that the two girls one table over were listening closely. What else could I say? It's not as if I knew anything, and besides, it felt weird discussing Trevor behind his back.

Mrs. Henney hung around a few more moments, as if waiting for me to offer something more, and when it was obvious that I had nothing, she cleared her throat and moved on.

Hailey was on her way home from her camping trip, and she'd texted me at least twenty times in the last half an hour. They were nauseating and super fluffy texts filled with happy faces and the name Link. I was happy that she was so into this guy, but I had to be honest, I was a little jealous as well. How could I not be? The texts. They were unending.

Hales: do you think love at first sight is real

Me: no

Hales: I think it's totally real

Me: I think lust at first sight is what you're talking about

Hales: you're wrong

Me: then why ask

Hales: because you're my friend and you're supposed to agree with everything I say

Me: that I am and no I don't

Hales: wow, you're grumpy

Me: yep

Hales: so do you think Link is hot or what?

Ugh. Insta love is annoying.

It wasn't until I read Hailey's last text that I realized I'd been waiting in the library for nearly twenty minutes. I sent Trevor a text—he was super late—and waited another five before scooping up my bag. I was irritated.

I thought of that slow crooked smile and the way he'd looked at me. I was irritated, and—there was no other word for it—I was disappointed. For some stupid reason I thought we'd connected Saturday. We lay beside each other at Baker's Landing for a long time, not touching, but somehow it felt as if I was wrapped up in Trevor Lewis. And that had felt…nice. No. Nice is too easy of a word to describe what it felt like, but for now, I guess it would have to do since I had nothing else.

Tossing my bag across my shoulder, I marched out of the library, wincing when I walked into the sunshine. I checked my phone one last time and muttered to myself as I took off down the sidewalk.

He could have at least called to let me know he wasn't going to make it. That's what you did so as not to inconvenience someone. And that's what I was feeling. Very inconvenienced.

I'd taken maybe ten steps when something tingled along the back of my neck. Some invisible radar that made me hyper-aware. Slowly I yanked the buds from my ears and glanced across the street toward the park.

A guy leaned against one of the big old oak trees, hands shoved into the front pockets of his jeans, a bag at his feet. His head was down so he didn't see me, because his hair covered most of his face while his one foot tapped the ground furiously.

Trevor.

I must have said his name out loud, because he raised his head. Or maybe I hadn't said anything at all and it was coincidence.

But as I stared across the street at him, I couldn't deny the little bit of happiness I felt. Chest tight, I waved again and then lifted the hair off the back of my neck.

I felt like I was back in sixth grade, staring across the closet at this boy who was larger than life. A boy whose gravity pull was so strong, it was enough to suck me in.

He lifted his chin as if to say *hey* and gave a small wave.

I could have done one of two things at this point. I could have given him the sort of salute he deserved. You know, the big old bird salute. Or I could let his gravity work its magic and pull me in.

Two guesses as to which one won.

"Everly," he said, a hint of gruff in his voice.

I'd crossed the street and stood a few inches away, wary of his pull and not entirely sure I'd made the right choice.

"You're really late," I retorted.

For a moment his eyes dropped, and I felt like a shit.

"Sorry, I just…" His voice trailed off as he stared across the street at the library. "I've been out here for almost half an hour. My dad dropped me off on his way back from lunch, but I just…"

A few awkward moments passed as I watched him, and it was then I knew.

"Mrs. Henney can be a little overwhelming. I get it."

His eyes shot back to mine, and for the first time since we

started this whole thing, I felt as if I was seeing the real Trevor Lewis. Sure, he looked like he had his shit together, but he was scared and kind of messed up, and I was pretty sure he didn't want to talk about what had happened with Mrs. Henney. We both know as soon as she saw him, she'd be all over that.

"Do you want to study at my house?"

I did not say that. What the hell?

His eyes softened, and the way he tilted his head to look down at me had my heart leaping all over the place like a fistful of jumping beans.

"Are you sure?"

No. My dad was home, and being around him was about the last place I wanted to be. Pretending that all was shiny and happy in my world wasn't exactly easy, at least not lately. But pretending in front of a crowd? That would be plain awful.

A slow crooked smile was making its way across Trevor's face, and there went those jumping beans again.

Trevor Lewis might be damaged, but he was also dangerous, and I knew him well enough to know that his smile wasn't exclusive. The power of that smile was legendary. I had to remember that even though a direct result of the power of said smile was a stomach full of butterflies, we were only study buddies. Nothing more.

Today, he was relieved that he didn't have to face his demons. There would be no Mrs. Henney. No one staring or asking inappropriate questions.

I totally got that, and I knew his beautiful smile wasn't one hundred percent for me.

As we slowly headed down the street to my home, I couldn't help but wonder what it would feel like to be the girl on the receiving end of that smile and to know it was all for her.

Chapter Nine

Trevor

Everly's family was a lot different than I expected. For one, her mom doesn't look anything like the woman I remembered from when I was younger. Not surprising. When I was twelve, I wasn't checking out my classmates' mothers because I was more interested in frogging and football than girls.

But I wasn't twelve anymore, and right now it was a fact that Terry Jenkins was hot. I'm not talking "she looks good for an older lady" kind of hot. I'm talking she looked like she could have starred in one of those CW shows that my sister watches. As a mom, of course, but an insanely hot mom.

I totally saw where Everly got her looks.

Her dad seemed like a really nice guy and not overly churchy at all, which was a relief, because the last thing I needed was to be grilled about my family's absence. He was dressed in jeans and a T-shirt, and we chatted about football while he grilled up some burgers. Mrs. Jenkins had come in when I was packing up my laptop and invited me to stay for dinner. I said yes, because truthfully, I wasn't ready to go home yet—being around Everly made me feel good—and these days, I'd take some good when I could get it.

When I was with Everly, I didn't think about the word *seizure* or picture contorted freaks in my head. We studied the constitution, debated certain merits, and though I'm sure I skipped words or said some things wrong or backward, she didn't point it out or make me feel like a loser.

I'd been doing that a lot more since Thursday, but the doctor told me that it could happen when I was under stress, and if having a seizure isn't something to stress about, I don't know what is.

Speaking of stress, I was getting the feeling that I wasn't the only one who was dealing with it. Something was off with Everly. She'd gotten real quiet when her mother came home, and a couple of times I'd caught this weird look in her eyes when she was looking at her father, like she was halfway to sad. And halfway to anywhere other than happy wasn't a great place to be. I should know. I'd been halfway to somewhere else for the last year.

"Burgers are ready," Mrs. Jenkins said as Everly's dad walked in from outside.

Mrs. Jenkins insisted that I sit beside Everly, and after we said grace, her little brother Isaac kept the conversation rolling with 101 questions about music and football and Mustangs. The kid had noticed my dad's car that first day I'd picked up Everly, and like most boys under ten, he had a one-track mind. Now it was cars, but when he got to my age? Yeah. We won't go there.

Isaac asked me at least three times if I would take him for a spin, and each time, I'd told him that the car was in the shop. Technically, it was true. Dad was fixing the carburetor, and I didn't feel the need to share the fact that I had to go six months without another seizure before I'd be able to drive again.

"The salad is great," I said, nodding to Everly's mother.

She smiled this great big smile, and I sat up a little straighter.

"You're so sweet," she said, reaching for the wine bottle. "Isn't he sweet, Eric?" She poured herself another glass, took a sip, and then settled back in her chair, eyes on me before sliding to Everly and then back to me.

"The caramelized walnuts and goat cheese are what make this salad a standout." She giggled and I thought that maybe she'd been into the wine while Pastor Jenkins had been outside grilling up the burgers. "It's always been one of Eric's favorites." She took another big sip of wine, "You still like it, don't you, Eric?"

A pause. I glanced around the table.

"My salad?" Mrs. Jenkins asked, emphasizing the words as if they meant something other than what they really did. That was the thing about adults. Why don't they just say what they mean?

An uncomfortable silence fell over the room as Pastor Jenkins frowned and took a few moments to answer. "Of course I do, Terry. You're a wonderful cook."

"Yes," she said softly, and for one second, I thought she

looked as sad as my mom used to look, back when I first woke up. It was fifty percent unsure and fifty percent afraid. "Yes," she said again. "I should make it more often."

We ate in silence, though when I say we ate, I mean that Isaac and I dug in with gusto. Everyone else just kind of picked at their food, and I don't think Everly ate more than two bites of her burger.

Pastor Jenkins cleared his throat and looked my way. "So, Trevor. I understand Everly is helping you out with your government exam."

I nodded. "Yes, sir. I...ah...I need it to graduate."

"What are your plans after you get your diploma? Everly here has been accepted to Brown."

Huh. She hadn't mentioned that to me. I shot her a quick look, but she was staring at her plate as if it was the most interesting thing in the world.

"I plan on heading to New York, sir."

He shook his head. "Please, call me Eric. What's waiting for you in New York?"

"Music," I replied. "There's a liberal arts college I want to go to, but that's not for sure just yet." Which meant I had no idea if I could do college.

His eyes softened a bit. "You've had quite a year. Your parents must be proud of how you're handling things. Working hard, moving on. Chasing your dreams."

I'm not sure if *proud* was the exact word I'd use to describe what my parents felt about my situation. *Relieved* would be a better choice. Grateful even better.

"They had it way worse than me." The words came out before I could stop them, and Pastor Jenkins gave a knowing smile.

"There is nothing more stressful for a parent than feeling helpless because your child is suffering."

I couldn't be sure, but I thought that Everly snorted when he said that. A quick glance to the side told me she was still more interested in picking at her burger than eating it. Maybe I was hearing things.

"Trevor." That was Mrs. Jenkins again. "Am I mistaken in thinking that you enjoy singing as well as playing the guitar?"

"I…"

My brain rolled back to this morning when I'd grabbed my Les Paul and tried to run a few scales. They sounded like crap. I'd been too distracted and eventually had given up, playing a few chords over and over again until Taylor screamed at me to shut the hell up. She was still mad and blamed me for the fact that Mom had grounded her an extra two days because of her epic meltdown.

Maybe she didn't deserve it, but then, she'd apparently dropped the f-bomb more than once. My parents are fairly tolerant when it comes to certain things, but the f-word wasn't one of them. The f-word was not allowed. Ever.

"I'm slowly getting my chops back," I eventually replied.

She was filling up her wineglass again, and I caught the way

Everly's bottom lip stretched thin as she stared across the table at her mother.

"Eric used to play the guitar for us, but it's been a long time. Honey, why don't you get out your acoustic and play us a song after dinner? That would be so nice. Don't you think that would be nice?"

"I haven't played in ages, Terry."

"No," she answered, rolling out the one word. "No, there are a lot of things you haven't done lately."

Okay. Now she was saying what she meant, and I was wishing she'd kind of kept that one to herself.

"Jesus," Everly muttered.

"What was that?" her father asked, though his eyes never left her mother.

"Nothing," Everly replied. "Nothing," she said a little louder before turning to me. "Are you done eating?"

There was still food on my plate, so technically I wasn't, but the look in her eyes said that I was.

"Yeah."

She pushed her chair back. "I'll take you home."

I had no idea what was going on with her family, but there was a weird vibe I hadn't noticed before. Mrs. Jenkins was reaching for the nearly empty bottle of wine, eyes on her husband, and I could almost hear the f-word falling from her lips. It was like she was daring him to say something.

From my experience, limited as it was, alcohol and weird vibes meant trouble. It was time to go.

I thanked Mr. and Mrs. Jenkins for dinner, and though they protested strongly and said dessert was going to be delicious, I think they were probably relieved when I left. Or at least the pastor was. Everly's mother was already searching for another bottle of "God's juice," I think she called it.

I scooped up my stuff and followed Everly out to the car, and we took off toward home.

Except we didn't go to my place. She kept driving, and I kept quiet. It just kind of felt right to sit there and not say anything. Eventually she pulled into Baker's Landing and cut the engine.

"Do you want to…" Her eyes were shiny, her voice a little wobbly. I nodded.

"Yeah. We can sit by the water if you want."

I followed her to the edge of the pond and sat my butt down beside her. I wasn't sure what was going on, but something had happened back at her place, and I could tell that she was upset.

"Hey, are you all right?" I asked, nudging her with my knee.

She took a few seconds, shook her head, and whispered, "No."

Shit. I wasn't real good at this kind of thing. Most of the girls I'd dated—and not that Everly and I were dating, so this was just a general snapshot of what I knew—but when those girls got all emotional, it was usually because (A) I hadn't paid enough attention to them, or (B) they thought I liked someone else (hell, I can't help it if a guy and a guitar is all it takes for some random girl to send you inappropriate text messages), or (C) I'd just broken up with them.

For each of those scenarios, I was good. I knew what to do, how to act and how to react. But this here? What was going on with Everly? This was new territory, and I wasn't sure of the right protocol. I guess it's because I'd never really been *friends* with a girl. Sure, I'd done the friends-with-benefits type of hookup, but this was so not that. This was something more. Something undefined, at least for me.

Did I put my arm around her? Did I just shut the hell up and listen?

I thought about it for a few moments and opted for the shutting up and listening, because those shiny eyes of hers were now filled with tears and I didn't want to do something wrong and make them spill.

"Remember what I said on Saturday?" Her voice was so soft and low, I had to bend close so that I could hear her. "About the hiding?"

"Yeah, I remember."

"There's stuff going on…stuff that I know…stuff that I think my mom kind of knows but isn't really sure about, you know? And I don't know what to do. About the knowing part. If that makes sense."

Okay. That was both vague and telling at the same time. She turned toward me and looked so incredibly sad that I couldn't help myself. I reached for her, because I wanted to and because this girl who normally had it together looked more lost and afraid than anyone I knew.

My arms went around her shoulder, and she half collapsed, half crawled onto my lap, her face buried in my neck.

She was warm and soft and hurting. And suddenly I wanted to be the guy she confided in. The guy she turned to. It was hard to explain, but there was this rush of something that settled in my chest. It was tight and emotional and real. I knew it was real because it kind of hurt.

"Do you want to talk about it?" I asked carefully.

She shook her head and settled in some more, the entire weight of her body sunk into mine. It was a weird time to think it, but the thought crossed my mind that we sort of fit together perfectly.

"No," she replied. "Can we just stay here for a while?"

Stay here for a while? Everything about this felt good, and I'd stay the whole damn night just to be her guy, the one she needed.

"Whatever you need."

"You must think I'm the most pathetic girl on the planet." She moved and glanced up at me.

I reached for a single, solitary tear that had slid from her eye and lay against her cheek. Carefully I wiped it away and shook my head.

"Nope, that's not even close. I think that like you said, you've got some stuff going on. Stuff that you're having a hard time dealing with, and I get that. I've been there. I guess we all get there sometime. It's just some of us get there first and some of us stay there a long time. You need someone right now."

Her bottom lip trembled and her eyes slid away. I grabbed her chin so that she could see me. Really see me.

"And I'm glad it's me."

For a few moments neither one of us said anything else, and then she kind of shuddered and melted against me.

"Thank you," she whispered.

I'm not sure how long we sat there, but it was long enough for me to realize that I wanted to know this girl in a way I'd never felt before. This wasn't about partying and hooking up. It wasn't about sex either (though I'm not going to lie, I'd be all over that if she was willing).

It was about meeting someone who kind of knocked you on your ass. A girl who wasn't anything like I imagined. A girl who was hiding stuff, and just like me, she was hoping no one would notice.

So maybe we could hide together, or maybe we could fix each other. Personally I was pretty damn sure that my situation wasn't fixable. In fact, with a seizure, it had gotten worse. But maybe Everly's situation was different, and as I held her and listened to her crying quietly in my arms, I thought that maybe I was the guy. You know, the one who could fix her.

Or at the very least, I thought that maybe I was the guy she'd let try.

Chapter Ten
Everly

We didn't study Tuesday because Trevor had an appointment with a specialist at the hospital. He didn't elaborate on what the specialist needed to see him about, and since it was none of my business, I didn't ask. Besides, I was mortified every time I thought of how my mother had acted at dinner.

She'd been drunk. My mom, Terry Jenkins, who only drank the occasional glass of wine, had gotten drunk and acted weird in front of Trevor. And if that hadn't been bad enough, I'd fallen into his arms like an emotionally unstable crazy person who'd cried her eyes out and then hiccupped most of the way to his house.

But it had felt good. Not the embarrassed part or emotionally unstable part or crying part either. The holding part had felt amazing. His arms around me had felt better than good, and I'd spent a lot of time thinking about it. Comparing him to my ex-boyfriend, Jason. So much so that when I met Hailey down at the pool, she'd known something was up pretty much right away.

I waited for her shift to end, and then we walked over to buy some ice cream. As I pondered my choices, she turned to me, eyebrows askew.

"Why are you so distracted?"

"I'm not."

"Yes, you are."

Annoyed, I made a face. "Why would you say that?"

She ignored my question and ordered us both a chocolate cone with chunks of peanut butter.

"Is it Trevor?"

"No."

"Are you sure?"

"Of course I'm sure."

"Then why are you blushing?"

"I'm not…" I started, but I totally was. In fact, the longer she stared at me with that half smile on her face, the hotter my cheeks felt.

"Did he kiss you?" she asked, handing me my ice cream cone.

"What? No, we're just study buddies."

"Uh-huh."

I licked the top of my cone. "He's pretty intense."

She got this "duh" expression on her face. "Of course he is. Trevor Lewis is an artist. A guitar player. Those dudes are all intense. Link's the same."

"Really?" I replied. "So you and Link are dating?"

"Dating?" She looked horrified. "No one dates, Everly. Geez, what is this middle school? We hang out." Her grin widened. "A lot."

"So you're hooking up."

"No, it's more than that."

"Then what is it?"

She giggled. "I don't know, but I'm having fun finding out. He's so artistic, you know? Like he paints and has even done some sculpting. He's got this thing at his house, it's this big…" She laughed, holding her arms wide. "I don't know what it is exactly but…hello! Sculpting? What guy does that? And oh my God, does he know how to kiss."

Great. I had to listen to a detailed account of Link's fantastical tongue and this technique he used with his… I'm not sure what she was talking about, because my mind was wandering into uncharted territory.

The Trevor Lewis kind of uncharted territory.

"So do you like him?" Hailey asked.

"Who?"

"Trevor, you idiot."

By this time we were nearly done our cones. "He's intense."

"You already pointed that out and I agreed, remember?"

I knew Hailey well enough to know she wasn't going to let this go.

"I don't think it matters if I like him or not."

Hailey grabbed my arm. "Why?"

"He's leaving when the summer is over, Hales. He's heading off to New York City to hook up with Nathan Everets. He's got his life planned, you know?"

"And you don't? You're going to college in the fall and so am I. So what? That doesn't mean we can't have fun this last summer. In fact, it means we're supposed to be having the best summer of our lives. This is it, Everly. Our last blast of fun before the next phase. And who's to say that a relationship can't survive college?"

"Relationship?" I snorted. "So that's what you have going with Link? You guys just started hanging out last week and…"

"And what?"

Did I have to spell it out? "He's Link. I don't think he's ever had a serious girlfriend."

"People change, Everly."

I thought of my parents. When had things changed for my father?

She hugged me. "Besides, we're not sixteen-year-old kids anymore."

"No." I shook my head and tried not to laugh. "We're a whole year older."

"I'm serious," she said with a giggle. "Our lives are about to change forever, and right now is the time for us to experience anything and everything. If we don't grab what we want now, it might pass by and we'll never know."

"Never know what?"

She shrugged. "Well, for starters, you'll never know if Trevor Lewis is the best thing that could have happened to you right now, in this moment."

"Wow. You've been reading too many John Green novels."

"And you're being way too pessimistic for a teenager."

"We're teenagers, Hales. We're supposed to be pessimistic."

We reached my place, and I noticed that my mom's car was in the driveway, which was strange since normally she didn't get home from volunteering at the old folks' home until at least five o'clock.

"What's up with your mom?" Hailey asked as we paused at the end of my driveway.

Okay. That wasn't how our conversations ever went.

"What do you mean?" Instantly, I was on high alert. I'd not said one word to a soul about what was going on at home. I knew the cracks were starting to show, but still, the only one who'd witnessed it had been…

"Did Trevor say something to Link?" I asked hesitantly.

"Trevor? No, why would he?"

"Well, what do you mean?" I asked, not answering her question.

"Nothing, really. I ran into her at the coffee shop this morning, and she just looked, well, honestly she looked like she'd been crying."

I didn't know what to say, so I shrugged and said nothing for a few moments. I hadn't come down for breakfast until Mom had left for work and Dad left for his part-time job at the local community college.

"PMS?" I offered up.

"God, she must be as bad as my mom is. Man, she's brutal

lately." She scrunched up her face. "I bet they're going through menopause. My grams told me she was like a witch when she went through it."

I eyed my mom's car again. Why was she home already?

"I'd ask you to come in, but I have a feeling her PMS is still hanging around."

"That's all right. Mom and I are heading to the city for a bit of shopping, remember?"

Oh. Right. I passed on that when she'd asked me the day before.

"Are you sure you don't want to come? We could swing by and scoop you up in half an hour."

"I'm really not in the mood for shopping. Go have fun with your mom."

"Yeah, while I have a PMS-free window," she said with a giggle. She paused. "Has Trevor said anything to you about the big party Friday night?"

I shook my head. "No."

"Oh." Hailey looked surprised. "I'm sure he will. Link and I are going and so are the rest of the guys from the band. I heard that Nathan might be home for the weekend, and Brent is back too."

Something hot twisted inside my chest. It felt like everything was changing way too fast. Like I was spinning in circles and everything that meant anything to me was disappearing.

"Don't worry about it," I said with a tight smile. "Trevor and I aren't...well, we're not anything. Like I said earlier, we're just study buddies."

Hailey gave me a big hug and whispered, "But you guys would be so good together. I bet he asks you."

"I'm not exactly Trevor Lewis material."

Hailey stood back and frowned. "What do you mean?"

"Hailey. He dated Hannah Modar, and we all know she's been having sex since the eighth grade, and then he moved on to Jade Dearling,"

Hales rolled her eyes and nodded when I mentioned Jade.

"And he just broke up with Bailey. I'm nothing like any of those girls."

"No, you're not. You're just you."

"Yeah. But why would Trevor be interested in someone like me when he can be with someone like Jess? Or any of those other girls? They're playing at an entirely different level than me."

"Who's Jess?"

"Who's Jess?" I repeated loudly. "She's the girl who was all over him at the drive-in."

"Oh," Hales replied, dragging out a one-syllable word until it sounded like four.

"Exactly."

"I still don't get why you think those girls are somehow above you. That's just ridiculous."

"Well, it doesn't feel that way," I muttered.

"Is it because they're having sex and you're still a virgin?"

"Um, yeah. That's a pretty big difference between me and them, don't you think?"

"What I think is that you're overreacting. Sex is a big deal, and it's supposed to mess with our heads, but you can't let it rule your life. Either you're doing it or not. You just have to be true to yourself. You'll know when the right time and the right guy comes along."

"But isn't that what most boys think about? Like 24/7?"

Hailey made a face. "Well, yeah, but that doesn't mean girls aren't thinking about it 24/7 either. That's kind of a sexist comment."

I shook my head. "Not me."

She squared her shoulders. "You're full of crap. You don't honestly expect me to believe that you've been hanging with the very hot and very available Trevor Lewis and not once has sex crossed your mind."

I opened my mouth but nothing came out.

"See? You can't lie to me, Everly Jenkins."

She was right about that.

"Sure, I've thought about sex, but…"

Her eyebrow popped up as if it was a little soldier standing at attention. "But?"

"He hasn't even tried to kiss me."

She elbowed me. "I bet you'll find out this weekend."

Hailey's expression was comical, and I couldn't help but giggle with her. "I guess we'll have to wait and see."

She gave me another quick hug. "You sure you don't want to come with us and buy something super trashy to wear to the bush party?"

"No, go and have fun with your mom."

"Okay," she said, taking a few steps backward. "I'll text you pics later so have your phone handy because I might need your opinion. Lord knows my mom has no fashion sense."

I watched Hailey until she rounded the corner and then pushed past the gate, only then spotting my brother sitting under the large oak tree, picking at the grass.

"Isaac, what are you…"

But my sentence remained unfinished because it was then that I heard the raised voices. Or rather, raised voice. My mother's. I couldn't make out the words exactly, but did it really matter? My parents never fought, or at least they'd never fought in a way that we noticed. But maybe the polite ignorance they'd been dancing around for the last year wasn't good enough. Maybe a loud in-your-face fight is exactly what they needed.

Or maybe this was finally the end.

I slowly slid into the grass beside Isaac and tried to ignore the butterflies diving around in my stomach. They were nervous butterflies. Anxious and unsure. And man, did they make me feel yucky.

"Has that been going on for a while, buddy?"

His skinny shoulders hunched a bit and then he nodded.

"We should probably hang out here for a while then," I said gently, feeling hot tears prick my eyes as Isaac slowly nodded. He didn't say a word. He inched closer to me and rested his head in my lap as he continued to pull at the grass and send it flying.

I glanced up at my house. My perfect, beautiful, and well-maintained house, with the neat driveway and clean, respectable vehicles parked there. Our grass was lush, the flowers vibrant, the paint fresh.

As I listened to my mom's voice get loud and then fall again, I couldn't help but wonder. Why couldn't they maintain our family the way they did their things? Why was the picture they presented to the world so much more important than the people behind the portrait?

And why was my dad living a lie?

Pretty heavy questions, and I wasn't naïve enough to think that I'd get answers anytime soon. In fact, I had a feeling things were going to get worse before they got better, so I should get used to it.

This was my so-called perfect life.

Chapter Eleven
Trevor

We decided to continue studying at the library, and though it was hard that first day, with Mrs. Henney and her 101 questions, I got through it. Not because my skin was thick like an alligator's or slick like Teflon, but because I knew Everly didn't want to be home.

So I sucked it up, and after the initial stares and whispers, things settled down. Wednesday and Thursday went by quickly, but today had been slow as hell. Something was definitely up with Everly. I tried to ask her about it, but she shut me down with one of her looks.

This Everly was closed off, and normally I'd be up for a challenge, but not today. Today I had a lot of stuff on my mind, and having the headache from hell didn't help. My eyes hurt, and after an hour, I told Everly that I was done. I could tell she was pissed—about what, I had no idea—but then again, so was I. After texting my dad for a ride, I scooped up my laptop and books. I asked her if she wanted a lift home, but she shook her head. Said she was going to hang at the library for a bit and that I'd see her next week.

At that point I set my books back down on the table and shoved my hands into my front pockets because they were fisted and angry.

"Did I do something to piss you off?" I asked, watching her closely. In the space of a few weeks, I'd learned that Everly was a crappy liar. I'd also learned that when she was upset or angry, her eyes looked glassy and much darker. Kind of like they looked right now.

"Nope," she answered crisply. "Just make sure you study the Fifth Amendment rights because I'll be grilling you about them Monday."

"You're angry."

"No, I'm not."

What was it with girls? Why can't they just say it like it is? Girls get pissy or whatever, and it's a big thing that carries on for days or weeks. Shit, when guys have a disagreement, they get in each other's faces, have it out, and go back to being buddies.

"Everly," I said carefully, not wanting to leave until I'd at least scored a smile out of her.

"What are you doing this weekend?" she asked abruptly.

Okay. That was out of left field. Surprised, I shrugged. "Nothing." A pause. "Why?" I asked slowly. "Do you want to hang out?"

"No." Wow. No hesitation there.

She stared at me for a long time, and I tried like hell to think of what I could have said or done to warrant this mood, but I came up with nothing. I decided to let it be. Lord knows my dad had certainly done that many times over, because like he said, girls are strange animals, and we'd be fools to try and figure them out.

"Okay," I said, scooping up my bag. "I'll talk to you tomorrow."

"We study on Monday."

"I know, but I'll talk to you tomorrow."

That had been hours ago, and it was still bugging me when our doorbell rang. Friday night in my house is date night for my parents, so they'd left around six, heading to the city for dinner and a movie. Taylor was still grounded, so her bitchy scowl was intact as she flipped through the TV channels like a madwoman.

And me? I'd been sitting at the kitchen table texting with Link and Nathan for the last hour. The two of them were trying to convince me to go to this big summer bush bash, but I didn't want to. Everyone would be there and I just…

Shit.

Summer parties in my corner of the world consisted of bonfires, drinking, and music. The drinking I could handle. I wasn't doing it these days, especially not now that I was taking new meds since Tuesday.

It was the music thing. I knew that Link would be there with a couple of acoustics, and I'd be expected to play. Shit, I could barely keep my concentration going long enough to run a few easy scales. How was I supposed to play and sing with everyone watching?

The doorbell went again.

"Holy fu—"

"Language, Taylor." I mimicked my mother perfectly and shot a look into the family room. I was teasing, but if looks could kill, I'd be dead.

"I hate you."

"I know."

"Well, can you get that? We both know it's not for me. It's not as if I'm allowed to go to, like, the hottest party of the summer."

I headed for the front door, but I knew who it was, and before I had a chance to answer it, it flew open and my best friend walked through as if he'd never gone away.

"Dude," Nathan grinned, hauling his girlfriend Monroe in behind him. "I'm not taking no for an answer. Link's already out there, and I'm not leaving without you."

I grabbed his shoulder the way guys do and then pushed him back before smiling at the small girl beside him.

"Hey, Monroe."

"Trevor." She reached up and kissed me on the cheek. "You look great," she whispered.

That wasn't surprising, considering the last time she'd seen me, I'd still been weak and kind of broken. Too skinny and too slow from all the time I'd been in a coma. It had been a tough haul, getting my muscle memory back.

Nathan was quiet for a few moments, and I saw Monroe squeeze his hand. Something flickered in the depths of his eyes, and I knew he was thinking back to another party. Back to another night when our world had exploded into shattering glass, twisted metal, and for me, scrambled brains.

"Trev, I've only got tonight, man. Tomorrow we're with my family and then Monday we're heading back to New York. You gotta come. It will be like old times. The whole gang back together."

"Hey!" Monroe punched him in the shoulder, a big smile on her face. "What about me?"

He laughed and kissed her. "New friends too."

They looked like they had the world by the balls, and watching them, I realized that for the first time ever, I was jealous of my buddy.

Jealousy didn't taste so good.

"New York looks good on you," I managed to say.

Nate grinned. "It's so much better than we even thought it could be. Dude, I busked in Times Square last week. Times Square! The vibe, the scene…it's what we thought it would be but way better." He slapped me on the shoulder. "When you finally get your ass out there, you'll see. We're going to rule, man."

I nodded, tried to smile even, but it was hard to ramp up my enthusiasm level when I had no idea if my head was going to explode.

"Are you okay?" Monroe asked softly, her hand on my arm.

I hadn't told Nate about my seizure and instructed Link not to say anything either. I was still dealing with what it meant, what it could mean, and I didn't want to deal with Nate's guilt too.

I knew he felt it.

I knew he felt it twist like a knife, but I was exhausted enough, and taking on the burden of his guilt would probably send me over the cliff I'd been straddling for days now.

"I'm good," I replied, fake smile pasted to my face.

"So are you coming or what?" Nate asked.

I glanced toward my sister. She was watching some stupid bachelorette show, the volume level was at eardrum-damage, and her everybody-hates-me scowl was getting old.

"What's up with Taylor?" Nate asked.

"Grounded."

"What did she do?"

"Nothing that Trevor hasn't done before," she shouted from the family room. Man, my sister had some ears on her.

Taylor pretty much made my decision. "Let me grab my cell."

The ride out to the bush party didn't take long. We lived in the middle of nowhere, yes, but bush parties always took place in the forest behind the old abandoned drive-in on the edge of town. The cops usually knew what was up and kept an eye out, but unless things got out of control, they left us alone. Wasn't like there was anything else to do.

By the time we got there, it was dark and the glow off the tops of the trees could be seen from the road. That meant some kind of bonfire.

"Lots of cars," I said as we pulled up beside a beat-up and rusted Chevy. I recognized it as belonging to Brent, our old bass player. A year older than us, he'd already graduated and surprised the hell out of everyone when he up and joined the army. I hadn't seen him in ages.

"He's on leave," Nate said as we piled out of his car. "And he's gonna be stoked that you came out."

I was happy to see the guys. It was the other stuff that I was concerned about. Already stressed, I worried that my words would come out wrong or even worse, there would be whispers behind my back about the seizure.

I had no idea who knew and who didn't other than Link. What if I had another one? That thought made me sick, and I tried to ignore how my stomach was all twisted, but it was damn hard.

"Come on. There's Brent." Nate nudged me.

I could leave right now. I know Nate would take me home if I asked him to, and he wouldn't ask questions either. But that sucked almost as much as being here and being afraid.

"You coming?" he asked.

I glanced toward the bonfire and immediately caught sight of Brent. He was waving his arms in the air like Superman, and I could see his grin from here. I couldn't chicken out, not now. I needed to man up and just deal.

I put my game face on and followed Nate toward the bonfire. The night was warm and pretty muggy, but it was the kind of night that I loved. The sky was bright, lit to the heavens with stars, and the air felt alive, full of possibilities.

It took a while, but eventually I relaxed a bit, mostly because Nate, Brent, and I were treated like gold. Everyone was in a good mood and the atmosphere was chill. One of the guys on the football team had speakers set up on the back of his truck, and an odd mixture of country and rock filled the air. This was my scene, and it had been too long.

Jackson Byers, a guy from school, had the balls to ask me about what had happened at the library. Said he'd heard that I'd been taken to the hospital in an ambulance. I told him it was an exaggeration. He didn't give up.

"But dude, an ambulance?"

"Do I look like there's something wrong with me?" I stared him down, flexing my fists as I did so.

"Nah. You look as badass as ever."

Someone offered me a beer, but I shook my head, and after it happened the second time, I grabbed a can so I could have something to hold and ward off any more offers.

I was getting into some vintage Green Day—"Jesus of Suburbia" is epic—when someone nudged my hip and two warm arms slid around me from behind. My first thought was Everly, which was crazy. The girl had pretty much blown me off today. Whoever it was giggled and stumbled into me, obviously loaded.

"I've mad at chu."

Ah. Jess.

She circled around so that she was in front of me, though her arms were still wrapped around my waist. "I've been texting you all week about this party."

Any other time, I would have been all over this. Jess was cute, nice, and obviously ready to party. But these days, Everly Jenkins was the only girl I was interested in, and even though I wasn't sure she was interested back, I wasn't going to take what Jess was offering.

I wasn't that guy anymore, which maybe should have surprised me. I'm damn sure it would have surprised half the guys I knew. I was single, so it's not like I was cheating on anyone. And let's be serious. Guys our age think about sex all the time, and to say otherwise is an outright lie.

But Jess wasn't Everly. End of story.

"Sorry, been busy."

She pouted, hands falling to my hips, which was awkward because now parts of us that shouldn't be touching were touching.

"Whoa," I said, trying to disengage, but the girl had talons for fingers and she was dug in but good.

"I'm glad you came," she said, talking real slow, drawing out each syllable in what I called alcohol speak.

I looked around. Where the hell was everyone? I spotted Nate by the fire, picking up an acoustic and strumming a few chords for his girl. Brent was close by, chatting up the Murdock twins, which wasn't surprising. Other than Caleb Martin, Brent was the biggest player this side of the Mason-Dixon line.

And Link…

My stomach did that weird tumble again, and I carefully picked Jess's claws from my hips as I stared across the clearing. Link sat on a log beside the fire with Hailey on his lap, and a few feet from them was Everly.

She was nodding to the guy beside her, and he was leaning down, so close that I didn't have to see his face to know exactly what he was thinking. And it wasn't how awesome she smelled, though I'm sure he'd noticed that. It wasn't how nice her hair looked either or how shiny her eyes were.

The guy was looking to score, and who could blame him?

His hand was at the small of her back, and from my vantage point, I saw a whole lot of skin on display. Soft skin. Soft skin that he shouldn't be touching. I wanted to smash my fist into his face. Total Neanderthal move on my part, but there you have it. At the moment it appeared that I was a knucklehead.

"Trevor, hello! I'm right here."

I pulled back from Jess and finally got her hands off me. "Look, Jess, I'm sorry. This…us…it's not gonna happen."

She followed my gaze and glanced over her shoulder. "Everly Jenkins? Really? I heard she's got her V pin stuck to her chest like glue."

But I was already walking toward the one girl who mattered. The one girl who'd given me nothing but attitude today. The one girl I wanted to touch and kiss and throw my arms around.

She was the only girl I wanted, and I frowned as the guy

beside her straightened and looked up, right at me before he offered his hand and Everly took it.

Caleb Martin. Damn.

They headed into the night.

"No effing way," I muttered, dodging a tackle from one of my old teammates.

"Where you going?" Nate asked, holding up his guitar. "Let's jam."

"Can't."

Caleb Martin didn't belong anywhere near Everly Jenkins, and I had no problem letting him know it. Some might argue that because I hadn't come to the party with Everly, I had no right to get up in her business. Maybe I didn't, but I was pretty sure about one thing.

I wasn't leaving without her. She just didn't know it yet.

Chapter Twelve

Everly

I tried to ignore the butterflies in my stomach, but that was pretty hard to do considering my heart was beating so fast I thought that I was going to pass out.

Caleb Martin was going on and on *and on* about his daddy's cottage and a lake and a boat and a Fourth of July party.

What. Ever. God, he liked to listen to himself talk. And Hailey wasn't any better. She was sitting in Link's lap, listening to whatever was on his mind as if he was Jesus giving a sermon. I had to admit that they looked cute together, but still…she should be paying attention to what was going on with me. At least a little bit.

Because what was going on with me was pretty pathetic. I didn't know how to act like I didn't care that Drive-In Girl was practically mauling Trevor, so I prayed that no one would notice.

Not that anyone other than Caleb was paying attention to me. I felt like I was in sixth grade all over again. Playing with the big boys and having no clue.

I exhaled. Good. Breathe. *You can do this.*

I nodded when Caleb asked me if I liked to water-ski. Um, no, but it seemed easier to just agree with whatever he was saying. He'd been pretty much glued to my side since we arrived nearly half an hour ago. Which was weird. It's not as if we ran in the same social circles, but then, I guess I presented a bit of a challenge. I knew what some of the guys in town thought of me, and I knew that they considered "nailing the pastor's daughter" as some sort of win.

Whatever. It used to bother me, but now it seemed so immature and silly, considering all the other stuff going on in my life.

The bonfire glowed red, and I stared into the flames because I didn't know where else to look. Why had I agreed to come to this party?

Oh. Right. Because Hailey convinced me that I needed to. You know, because it was going to be fun. A blast. A totally epic party, I think she'd said, adding that as a bonus, I could show Trevor Lewis what he was missing.

I'd told her I didn't care what Trevor Lewis thought.

She rolled her eyes and grabbed a skimpy top from her closet.

Her enthusiasm, coupled with the fact that my parents were home but not speaking to each other, made my decision way easier than I would have liked. So I let Hailey dress me up and do my makeup. The end result was that I looked a little on the trashy side and felt a whole lot uncomfortable.

"Do you want to walk a bit?"

Hailey and Link's lips were locked together. "Sure," I found myself saying. It's not like I was going to be missed here anyway. I felt like an idiot nursing a red Solo cup of Jack and Coke, and I don't care what Hailey said—it was just as gross cold as it was warm.

Caleb grabbed my hand, and we trudged in the opposite direction of Trevor and Drive-In Girl. We walked past a couple who were half undressed and pushed up against a tree and another couple whose moans made them sound like a bunch of wild animals caught in a trap. Seriously? Pride, people.

It didn't take long for the forest at the edge of the clearing to swallow us up.

"This is much better," Caleb said.

I wasn't exactly sure that *this* was, but so far, other than having an extremely high opinion of himself and his father's money, he seemed harmless.

"I don't think I've seen you at one of these bashes before." His hand was still on mine.

"Jason wasn't exactly a party animal."

Ha. That was an exaggeration. Jason had been into *Star Trek*, *The Big Bang Theory*, and books. Three things that had been totally fine with me. We'd sort of gotten into some heavy-duty touching and exploring one night after a movie, but I'd been kind of freaked out by my lack of wanting him to touch me, and I don't think I'd hidden it very well.

I guess it says something about our relationship that we

continued to date for nearly a year after that, and though he tried for more than a kiss a few times, we'd never progressed to anything beyond that.

"Your ex?"

I nodded.

Caleb's grin widened, and he reached for the Solo cup in my hand. "You're not liking this?"

I wrinkled my nose. "It's awful."

He tossed the cup, both of his hands suddenly on my arms. "So, you're like a party virgin."

"Um, I guess." He said *virgin* in a way that made me uncomfortable.

His breathing was different, and he leaned closer. "That's freaking hot." I could smell cigarettes and the sweet scent of whiskey.

"Caleb, maybe we should get back to the party."

"Sure, babe."

Babe? *Babe?*

"Are you for real?" I asked, trying to yank my arms from his grasp. "Guys still say babe?"

"Calm down," he said with a smile, and suddenly I knew exactly how he got girls to give him what he wanted. The guy had a great smile. I'd give him that, but his smile wasn't the one I wanted for myself. "Sorry." He murmured. "Got it. Mental note. Everly Jenkins does not like the word *babe*." He paused. "But maybe she likes a kiss?"

"Not gonna happen." Was there something wrong with me? Had I been sending out mixed signals and didn't know it?

"Everly likes to play hard to get. I'm cool with that. I'll take you out in my father's boat on Monday. You'll see. I know how to show a girl a good time."

Oh. My. God. This guy didn't get it.

"She can't," Trevor said, startling both of us, and I took the chance to yank my arms from Caleb.

Trevor stood about a foot away, alone and looking more adorable than he had a right to. He wore boots, jeans that fit him way too nicely, and a plain black V-neck T-shirt that showed off his chest, biceps, and abs. How that was possible, I don't know, but there you have it.

His hair waved to the tops of his shoulders, his eyes glittered, and there was a dusting of stubble on his chin. Like I said, adorable. And sexy.

And I didn't care because he was here with Drive-In Girl.

"Dude, who the hell asked you? Uh, the party is that way." Caleb had a smile on his face but his voice wasn't exactly sunshine. He squared his shoulders and faced Trevor, who kind of did the same thing. Total macho posturing, but it made me realize that they were sort of squaring off because of me.

For some reason I was kind of okay with that.

"Everly and I have a date on Monday," Trevor said softly.

Caleb's eyebrows shot up. "A date?"

That particular bit of info was news to me too.

"You guys are together?" Caleb asked, his eyes on me and his expression more than a little pissed off.

"No," I said.

"Yes." That was from Trevor.

"You could have said something." That was for me. "Dude, I didn't mean to chat up your girl. I had no idea you guys were hooking up." That was for Trevor.

"Oh my God, we're not hooking up."

Okay, so I shouted. And maybe half the kids at the party might have heard me. Whatever. My top was way too skimpy, my jeans on the low side of low rise, and the flats I wore pinched my toes. They belonged to Hales, so it wasn't surprising. I'd worn them because she'd insisted the sparkles would look great with my barely there top.

Most important, the guy I liked had been sucking face with Drive-In Girl, or at the very least, I'd watched her grind up against him.

"Everly," Trevor said. "Can we talk?"

I could have done one of two things at this point.

Who was I kidding? I was never going to do the second one.

"Sure," I said sharply.

Caleb muttered a bunch of stuff, and I'm sure none of it was nice, but neither Trevor nor I was paying any attention to him. He took off, and then Trevor and I were alone with only the echoes of the party and the flickering fireflies among the trees.

It was warm—June usually was—and the air was heavy. I

closed my eyes and dragged in great big gulps of it, trying to calm my butterfly-infested stomach.

"Everly."

He was close. So close.

Slowly, my eyes opened and, well, wouldn't you know… that big old lump of something was back clogging my throat. I couldn't swallow. Couldn't speak. I couldn't do anything but look up into the face of the most beautiful guy I'd ever seen.

Suddenly, I didn't want to do the whole "I'm going to play games and be mad at you" thing. Not anymore. I wasn't a kid. I wasn't some girlfriend who'd been wronged either, and I guess that was the problem.

Trevor was looking at me in a way that had all sorts of things zigging and zagging inside me. Maybe it was time for me to find out what all of this meant.

"Did you come with Drive-In Girl?" I asked, careful to keep my voice neutral.

"Who?"

Right. No more games. "Jess. Because that's fine, Trevor. I just…"

He stepped closer. "You just what?"

Could he hear my heart beating? Or the blood rushing through my veins like a tidal wave? Or how my breaths were ragged, catching on the emotion inside me as I exhaled?

"You just what, Everly?"

His hands were at his sides, and he kept opening and closing them. It was dark, so I couldn't be sure if the beating I saw at the base of his neck was his pulse or just a play of shadows.

"Everly."

Something in the way he said my name made my knees go weak, and I spoke in a rush.

"I just need to know what this is."

There. Good. I got it out.

"This?" His voice was low and kind of raspy. Of course it was. Because how sexy was that?

"Us. When you said we had a date on Monday, what did you mean by that?"

"I wanted Caleb Martin to back off."

"Why?"

"He's bad news, Everly. Caleb is a player, and he's only looking to get laid. He's not the guy for you."

My cheeks burned at his descriptive use of the English language. "And I suppose you know who is?" Wow, that wasn't leading or anything.

"Yes," Trevor said. "Yes, I do."

He moved closer, until there was only a whisper between us. I could smell his cologne, a light scent of woods and something else I couldn't put my finger on. But it was nice. It was more than nice. It was amazing.

Whatever this was between us, whether it was flirting or foreplay or something else entirely, it was exciting, electric, and scary.

I had to tilt my head because he was a lot taller than me, and this angle? Sheer perfection. The stars cast down their light, and the shadows on his face made him appear mysterious and more beautiful than he already was.

"So." I wet my lips because they were suddenly dry. "Who exactly is the guy for me?"

His hands crept up either side of my face, and I wanted to melt into them. Into him. Then Trevor bent low, his warm breath sending shivers across my skin. His mouth was at my ear, and I shuddered when I felt his lips move there. "Everly, he's standing right in front of you."

A pause.

"He's just not sure…"

I could barely breathe, and if you could ache all the way to your bones just from a touch, then I was there.

"He's just not sure that you want him."

Chapter Thirteen
Trevor

I don't think I've ever wanted to kiss a girl as badly as I wanted to kiss Everly Jenkins. Never. Not even Bailey, and she was the girl I'd dated for nearly two years.

With Bailey it had been about getting to the next level for the sake of getting there as fast as we could. There had been no finesse, not in the beginning anyway, so I guess it was easy to confuse love and sex. And kissing was just a prelude to what was coming next.

But this was different. Everly was different.

And this wasn't the closet at a birthday party in the sixth grade. This wasn't about boasting to my friends that I'd kissed the pastor's daughter. (Can't believe I'd actually done that, but then boys and hormones don't automatically make for smart decisions.)

I wanted to take my time. I wanted this first real kiss between us to matter to her, because it sure as hell mattered to me. Maybe it was the alpha male in me, or maybe I was just an arrogant dick, but I wanted this kiss to be the one she remembered as the best kiss she'd ever had.

I was setting the bar high, but I was cool with that. I had my fair share of practice, but with Everly, everything felt so damn natural. And anticipation rumbled through me, because man, I knew this was going to be good.

She was trembling, her body pressed so close that most of our parts were touching, and I had nothing to do with that. That was all her, and, holy hell, did it feel good.

I cupped her head and stared down at her, eyes resting on a mouth made for kissing. Man, if she knew some of the conversations that had gone on about her in the locker room, her cheeks would be as red as the polish on her fingernails.

Everly was uncharted territory for a lot of guys, but she was the kind of uncharted territory most of them dreamed about. Hot as sin with that sweet side we all dug. She wasn't the girl you scored points with. She was the keeper.

"Open your eyes," I whispered.

Slowly, they opened, and my hands sunk deeper into her hair. She was wearing more makeup than I was used to seeing, but her eyes…they were dark and mysterious, that mouth was shiny and soft, and her hair was all over the place, wild from the humidity. She was…

"You're beautiful."

She licked her bottom lip and smiled, a small half smile. "I could say the same thing about you."

"I don't think anyone has ever called me beautiful."

It took a second for my words to sink in, and just as the hot fingers of embarrassment worked their way up from inside me, she stood on her tiptoes, her hands now sunk into my hair. She offered up her hot, open mouth, and that was it. I was done.

I was a guy who wanted a girl so badly, and just like any other normal hot-blooded dude, all thoughts but Everly flew out of my head. I slid my mouth across hers. I accepted what she was offering, because right now, in this moment, there was nothing but this kiss. There was no embarrassment or awkward movements or anything that didn't feel right.

She was soft and smooth and pliant in my arms, and as I deepened the kiss, I thought I heard her groan. I cradled her head so that she couldn't move, and I tasted every inch of her mouth. Cherry gloss, spearmint gum. The more I tasted, the more she pushed against me, and I couldn't help myself—I let one hand travel down her back because most of it was exposed.

All that soft skin, naked and exposed.

I trailed fingers down her spine, and I knew that she wasn't wearing a bra because I felt her pressed against me, and by this point, I was pretty damn sure she felt all of me. Like *all* of me.

I pulled back a bit, because this was going way too fast and we were both breathing hard. Resting my forehead against hers, I struggled to get my shit together. When I thought I was okay to talk, I took a second and prayed that everything would come out right.

"That was pretty amazing," I said slowly, taking my time. And who was I kidding? My hands were still all over her. It was more than amazing. I don't think the right word had been invented to describe what I was feeling. Where was Nate the poet when you needed him?

In the distance I could hear the echoes of the bush party. Kids laughing and arguing and singing along to Nate, Brent, and Link. Funny, any other time, I would have felt left out. Like who did they think they were, jamming without me?

But right now, with this girl and the stars and the fireflies flickering along the ground, I felt like I was the king of the world.

Total chick analogy, but whatever.

"I think amazing doesn't come close," she said.

A smile crept across my face. Good to know I wasn't the only one who felt it.

"So, where do we go from here?" I asked, moving my head a bit so that I could see her. She gave a small shrug and was quiet for a moment.

"You're so not the guy that I…" Her eyes flew to mine, wide and more than a little embarrassed.

"The guy that you…" I prompted.

She exhaled and kind of shuddered. I felt it move down her body, and since we were still pretty much glued together from the waist down, I can't lie, I had a moment where I thought things might get dicey for me. Dicey in a way that wasn't cool for a guy in this situation.

Relax. Chill. Sure I might have been smiling, but on the inside, I was in pain.

"I just never expected a kiss like that."

I wanted to fist-pump, but I didn't think she'd appreciate that sort of display.

"It was pretty epic," I said.

A small smile crossed her face. "I'll have to agree with that observation."

"So what are we going to do about this? About you and me?"

Her eyes kind of clouded over, and she pulled away. It was a gentle maneuver, and I got the feeling that I should maybe give her some space. Truthfully? I needed a moment too.

She was quiet for a long time, and I was starting to get worried. Maybe she wasn't as into me as I thought. Maybe her idea of a boyfriend wasn't some brain-damaged dude who wasn't always the most eloquent.

"I've got stuff going on," she said softly. "I'm not in a real good place right now, and I'm probably not the best choice for someone to be with. Not exactly the most fun to be around."

I shoved my hands in my pockets because, God, I needed to do something with them other than what I wanted to do, which was put them all over Everly.

"If I was looking for fun and easy, I'd hang out with Jess. And I'm not dissing her, because there's nothing wrong with that. Hell, even though I feel older than my parents some days, technically we're still teenagers. We're supposed to be having fun, getting crazy, doing stupid things. But you and I are on a bit of a different path from most of the guys back there." I motioned toward the noise from the party.

She nodded but didn't say anything.

"So maybe we don't have to walk that path alone."

Okay, my mom would be all over this. How many times had she lectured me on being sensitive and treating a girl the way I'd treat my mother? (That was a bad analogy because, dude, who wanted to think about the girl they were getting busy with and their mom at the same time? That was kind of screwed up, even if I did get her meaning.)

I decided to go the whole nine yards, because by this point, what did I have to lose? Besides, chicks dug this sensitive stuff, didn't they?

"I want to know you, Everly." I took a step closer. "I want to know what your favorite movie is. What songs you sing. I know you dig Elton John, but what about Billy Joel? Mozart? Alicia Keys? I want to know what you think about at night just before you fall asleep." I paused, surprised at the tightening in my chest. "I want to know why sometimes you look so sad. I want to know who hurt you."

And I wanted to kick his ass, but I'd keep that to myself.

She pushed the tangle of hair off her shoulders and gave a half shrug, eyes wide and shiny. "My favorite movie is *The Last of the Mohicans*."

"Wow. I had you pegged for a chick flick. *Love Actually* or *The Notebook*. My sister Taylor watches them over and over again."

"I'm full of surprises."

"Good to know. What's your favorite color?"

"Blue."

"Song?"

"My Heart Will Go On." There was a hint of a smile there.

"*Titanic?*"

She nodded.

"Chick flick."

She was smiling now. "We're talking about music, not the movie. What's yours? Your favorite song?"

She'd moved closer, and I could see the stars reflected in her eyes, which made them seem mysterious. Kind of sexy.

"Simple Kind of Man," I replied.

She frowned a bit. "I don't know that one."

"It's Lynyrd Skynyrd. I'll play it for you someday." The words slipped out of me, but surprisingly, I didn't want to grab them back.

"Okay," she said.

Man, I wanted to kiss her again. I ran my hands through my hair because I had to do something with them.

"Why do you have a blue streak?" she asked. "In your hair, I mean. It's…I like it."

I paused. I'd always been into trying new things with my hair, and my parents had always seen this as an extension of my artistic side. Heck, my mom hadn't complained once, no matter the color. Not even the time I came home with a dark-purple Mohawk. Her only request had been that I leave it down while at home. Said she was afraid I'd poke someone's eye out. But the blue streak? "I was bored and Taylor had some extra dye so…"

"I like it."

Her hand slipped into mine, her thumb running over my tattoos, and then I pulled her in close for a hug. The girl fit against me perfectly, and I would have stayed like that the whole night.

Her nose was buried in my neck, her body relaxed against mine as I rested my chin on her head.

"Trevor?"

"Hmm?"

"I'm glad I came to this party."

"Yeah. Me too. I wasn't planning on it. Nate pretty much dragged me out of the house. I'll have to thank him later."

I could feel her heart beating, the warmth of her skin against mine, and I knew that if we didn't leave this secluded space, things would heat up again. Not that I didn't want them to, but there was something to be said for anticipation, and I was already anticipating more. So much more.

"Do you want to meet his girlfriend, Monroe? She's so cool. You'll like her."

Everly nodded. "Okay. Sounds good."

"I'm not letting go of your hand. Just saying."

A heartbeat passed.

"I wasn't going to let go either."

And she didn't.

Chapter Fourteen
Everly

Sunday morning was the same as always, except that it wasn't.

Sure I got up, went for a run, had my shower, and picked out an appropriate but cute outfit for church, but it wasn't the same at all.

On my run the birds were louder, their calls more intense. The flowers in Mrs. Mayberry's front garden had never looked so beautiful, the forest that skirted the old graveyard so lush, and the sun coming up over the horizon was more vibrant than any I'd ever seen.

I'd barely slept since Friday night, and yet I was good to go. I mean, I felt as if I could scale Mt. Kilimanjaro or run the Boston Marathon or…

Or run all the way to Trevor's house and just let him kiss me silly.

My cheeks stung with heat when I thought of the way he'd kissed me at the party and of the way I'd kissed him back. I'd thought about pretty much nothing else for most of Saturday and I'd been walking around all morning with pink cheeks, a big smile, and eyes that didn't look familiar. Yes, they were blue, but there was something else inside them. Something exciting and fresh and sparkly and…

I wasn't exactly sure what it was that I was feeling, but I sure liked it. I liked it a lot.

My cell pinged, and I scooped it off the kitchen table, humming a song as I did so. I was waiting for Mom to come down so we could leave for church, and Isaac was already outside, sitting in the swing on the front porch.

It was Hailey.

"Hey," I said, my voice barely above a whisper, sneaking a look over my shoulder.

"Why are you whispering?"

"I don't know," I giggled.

"Girl, you need to spill."

"Hales," I said, but then nothing else came out. I didn't know where to start.

"We need to hang out after church today, because I definitely need details about what happened with you and Trevor Friday night and…"

"And?"

She squealed so loud that I jumped. "I have something to tell you."

"What?" I asked a little louder. I hadn't spoken to Hales since the party, but by the tone of her voice she had something epic to share. I had a feeling Link was the reason. A creak sounded from the front hall, and I took a few steps out and glanced around, but Mom was still upstairs.

"This is definitely not an over the phone conversation."

"You sound like you're still in bed. Aren't you going to service?" Hailey's family didn't attend our nondenominational church. They went to Twin Oaks First Baptist on the other side of town.

"No." Now she was whispering. "I told Mom that I got my period and my cramps were brutal, so she brought me up some meds and told me to go back to sleep."

"Lying is a sin."

"Well, falling asleep in church is probably a sin too. I only got home two hours ago."

"If that's right, half of the seniors who go to my church are going to hell."

"Ha! True." She paused. "So come over after church?"

I chewed on my bottom lip and glanced at the clock. We were going to be late if my mother didn't get her butt downstairs. Dad had already left, the sofa in his office made up nice and neat with a blanket and a pillow.

That wasn't a good sign.

"Sure. I'll call you when I get back."

I tossed the cell into my purse and walked out into the hall. "Mom!" But she didn't come down. In fact, there was nothing. No creaks like old houses do when you move around, no water

SOME KIND OF NORMAL

running, and no music either. She liked to play her old bluegrass tunes when getting ready for church, so the heavy silence was weird. And come to think of it, I hadn't seen her when I got up or heard a peep out of her since I got back from my run.

I glanced out the front window and saw Isaac playing with one of his G.I. Joe guys. The doll was flying through the air like Superman and then crashing into his chair. We had maybe five minutes to spare or we'd definitely be late. And my mom was never late. Never.

I climbed the stairs, walked past my room toward my parents' bedroom, my stomach tumbling and diving as the utter silence in the house weighed on me.

"Mom?" I paused outside their door and then gave a small knock, this time speaking louder. "Mom. We need to leave for church."

There was nothing but more silence and the sound of rattling eaves as the wind blew outside.

You know that moment in a movie? The one where the heroine should leave but doesn't? The one where she heads into the house instead of runs for the hills? You know how freaky those moments are? How stupid she is?

Yeah. Well, I was having one of my own moments, because I had a really bad feeling about what was on the other side of her door. Like, really bad. But this wasn't a horror movie, and it was my mom, so I didn't have a choice.

Palms cold and clammy, I wiped them down the front of my skirt and carefully turned the knob. My parents' bedroom door

141

swung open, the hinges a little dry and creaky, so the sound echoed into the nothing that surrounded me.

Clothes were strewn around the room in a way I'd never seen, and my first thought was that someone had broken in and tossed her stuff all over the place. The window was open, large curtains billowing in clouds of gray from the early morning breeze. They twisted and arced, almost like fingers that pointed toward her bed.

Outside, the birds were still singing, the sun was still shining, and from what I could see, the sky was still as blue as a robin's egg. And yet as I took another step inside my parents' room, I knew that nothing about this morning was the same as it was less than five seconds ago.

Nothing.

My mother was in bed, turned toward the window, her long hair a tangle of chocolate spilling down her back.

"Mom?"

Nothing.

I don't remember moving to the bed. Or seeing her there, seemingly asleep and exhaling loudly as if it hurt to do so. The only thing I would remember later is the spill of pills on the floor, the half-empty bottle, and the realization that something was very, very wrong.

I might have screamed—in fact, I'm sure I did—but she only moaned, a soft sort of sound that bounced around my head, louder than rolling thunder.

Pills.

Oh my God, pills!

The summer when I was fourteen, my dad and I volunteered to work with street kids in the city. At the time I thought it was a way for me to earn some community hours and to hang with my dad. It was kind of depressing and a whole lot of eye-opening.

I learned that pills can kill, but more important, because of a twenty-one-year-old woman who'd taken too many, I'd learned what to do if something bad happened. And this was bad. This was really bad.

I slapped my mom. *Hard.*

Cell phone. Where is my cell phone?

Her eyes flew open, thank God, and I dragged her out of bed, yelling at her.

How many did you take?

When did you take them?

How many?

I pleaded with her as I hauled her into the bathroom, and God help me but I cursed her when I shoved her into the tub and ran the shower on the coldest setting possible. I held her when she clawed at her nightgown and spit out the water that ran down on her face. I made sure she didn't fall over when she managed to get to her feet, and I held her long hair away from her when she started to whimper.

"Don't tell your father. Don't tell your father. Don't tell your father." She repeated it over and over and over, until her voice gave out.

She sputtered. She cried. Great big gulping cries that made my heart pound even harder than it already was. Never had I seen my mother like this. Never. I was scared and upset and so mad that I wanted to scream in her face. I wanted to hurt her for doing this to me.

The water was still spilling over her, but she didn't seem to notice as she regarded me, eyes huge and glassy. We were both wet and shivering from fear and adrenaline and a whole bunch of stuff I couldn't name.

"Why?" I whispered. "I don't understand…"

But I did, didn't I?

She opened her mouth to say something, but before she could get any words out, she doubled over and moaned.

And then she vomited all over my shoes.

***

"Where's Isaac?"

The words were raspy, slow. I glanced up from my chair beside Mom's bed and tried to push back the anger inside me, but it was hard. The anger was heavy and hot and so damn eager to come out. I thought that maybe I should let it. Just this once. Maybe then it wouldn't feel as if a hundred-pound weight was pressed into my chest.

"Why?" was all I could get out.

Why. One lonely word, but a word that was bigger than it sounded, because it was packed full of things that would lead to dark places.

"Isaac?" she asked again, this time struggling to sit. She was still pale, still bedraggled from the shower, still pathetic and small and...

"Mrs. Ballantine took him to church." I tried not to sniffle, but that didn't work out all that well, so I took a moment to get myself together. See? This was me dealing with stress.

When I thought I could speak without sounding like a bumbling idiot, I continued. "I told her that you weren't feeling well and she said that she would let Dad know. She also said something about taking Isaac to a picnic in the park afterward, and since they're not back yet..."

"Oh," Mom said weakly. "That's good." A tear slid down her cheek, and I watched it navigate a zigzag path until she wiped her palm across her face.

I wasn't sure where to go from here. What to do or say.

"I didn't mean to," she said softly.

My eyes darted back to hers, and I struggled to keep my pain from showing. It wasn't too hard, considering I'd become the queen of masks these last few months. "How many did you take?"

Her bottom lip trembled. "A few..."

"A few."

"Everly." There was warning in her voice, like she was trying to tell me not to go there. Her. The woman who'd just had a shower in her nightgown.

"A few," I repeated. My voice rose as the enormity of what had just happened washed over me. The last hour and a half shot across my brain. Pills. Mom. Pills. Mom's hair all over the place. Pills. Vomit.

My body trembled. I was so cold. So far from where I'd been when I first woke up. I shot to my feet, teeth chattering even though it was warm and stuffy in her bedroom.

"*A few?*" I raged. "A few is like two or three. A few is less than four but maybe more than two. A few is…a few doesn't knock you out. A few…" I shrugged and tried not to cry, but it was no use, and tears stung the corner of my eyes. "Anything more is not an accident."

"Everly, I'm so sorry, sweetie, but you have to believe me. It was an accident. I would never…I never…"

I glanced at the bottle on her bedside table. It was half full.

"You're lying," I spat. "You're *lying* to me. I'm not Isaac. I'm not some little kid who will just believe whatever you tell me. Not anymore." I grabbed the bottle off her table and held it up high. "Since when do you take sleeping pills? Since when do you…since when do you take a *few too many*?" But I could barely finish my sentence, because my throat was closed up tight, so full of emotion and hurt and fear that I was nearly choking on it.

What is happening to my family?

"Don't tell anyone," she said, her voice breaking. "Please, no one can know."

Something was so wrong about the way this conversation was going. I was the kid here. Me. Seventeen years old. Since when did my mom beg me not to tell on her? When did that happen?

"Everly, please…"

"Why?" That knot in my throat loosened up, and suddenly the tidal wave inside rolled over and over until there was no stopping it. "Why are we hiding? Why are we pretending that everything is freaking A-OK in this house?" I took a step back. "Jesus, it's exhausting!"

My mom looked shocked, and I guess she should be. I'd never spoken to her like this before, but then again, I'd never scraped her up off the floor either.

"Everly." Her voice was stronger now. "I've already told you that it was an accident. I…I had trouble sleeping last night—"

"Trouble sleeping? Since when? Since Dad started sleeping in his office?"

Again, my mom looked shocked, which was ridiculous. What kind of bubble was she living in? Didn't she think I'd notice the blankets and pillow in his office?

"Your father and I are having a rough patch, but we're working things out."

Her face was blank. She'd found the mask she'd discarded last night, and she was firmly back in her camp of denial.

I thought of that conversation I'd heard a year ago. The

conversation I'd been trying to unhear ever since. And I thought about all of his trips to the city, all the times he was away.

I looked at the sad and lonely woman before me and I just lost it.

"Taking too many pills isn't working things out. Dad going to the city all the time and doing whatever it is that he's doing there isn't working things out. Lying to me, lying to Isaac, to your friends, and to God? That's not working things out. But the most pathetic thing of all is that lying to yourself sucks way worse than everything else. How can you think he's working things out? He's screwing around on you, Mom! He's in love with someone else!"

Her eyes were as wide as saucers, with papery thin smudges of blue beneath them. "Why would you... How can you..."

"Does it really matter?" I spat, tossing the capsule bottle onto the bed where it landed with a thud and then rolled onto the floor, spilling the remnants of the pills. I watched them roll away, under the bed, like little insects scurrying for cover.

I'm not sure how many seconds or minutes ticked by, but when I glanced up, my mother's face kind of crumpled in on itself. She blew out a long breath, smoothed her hair back, and spoke so quietly, at first I wasn't sure I'd heard her.

"I know about...about your father."

My jaw dropped. Like literally dropped open. She knew? I hadn't seen that one coming, and her admission became this heavy, meaty thing that punched me in the gut so hard I could barely breathe.

She knew. All this time I'd held this secret close because of her and Isaac…and she'd known all along.

"But it's so much more complicated than you know. There are things…there are things between him and me, and we just need some more time."

"You need more time," I said numbly. "Wow."

She was crying again, but there were no tears inside me. No need to comfort. There was nothing but that heavy, meaty thing, and it was cold and sharp and black.

Hands clasped over my mouth, I stared at my mother, hating myself for knowing. Hating her for knowing.

But most of all, I hated my father for letting us find out.

Chapter Fifteen

Trevor

By Wednesday afternoon I was pretty much fed up with our government, our laws, and our damn constitution. Pushing my laptop away, I leaned back in my chair and groaned. I had a nagging headache, hadn't slept well, and for some reason, Everly was ignoring me.

All kinds of questions crowded my brain, and that only made my head ache more. Had I moved too fast? Was *the kiss that rocked the world* too much?

She was a church girl, and not that I knew much about the church she went to, but maybe there were rules. Maybe she'd broken them. Maybe our kiss should never have happened. Maybe it was too early for that kind of stuff. Or maybe she'd figured out that I had a lot more problems than just learning the stupid constitution.

I was the freak on the floor after all. My eyes squeezed shut, and I knew my cheeks were as red as the apples in Mrs. Craddock's orchard. Man, when I was in bed trying to let go and sleep, that was the image burned into my retinas. Freak. On. The. Floor. So not cool.

I hadn't seen Everly since Friday because I'd had to help my dad out at his shop over the weekend. The only conversation we'd had was a text she'd sent Monday morning.

Stuff came up not sure when I can meet you. Will let you know.

That was it. After our amazing Friday night, that was all I got and nothing more.

I'd sent her at least ten text messages Sunday alone but had given up when I got the Monday morning wake-up call. Man, I couldn't figure her out. I know she'd felt it, whatever it was between us.

I'd held her hand all night, kept her tucked in my arms as the fire died down and the cooler air from the forest crept closer. She and Monroe got along just fine, and her friend Hailey was a cool chick too. Nate, Link, and I felt like kings.

And now nothing.

What. The. Hell.

I was at the library, same place Dad dropped me every day in the hope that she'd show up, but right now, I was so ready to bail. I'd only been here an hour and had four more to go. Dad wasn't done work until five. I guess I could have called Mom for a ride home, but I wasn't ready to be there yet either because I could never just relax. She still hovered. Still smoothed my hair back, rubbed where the incision in my skull had been. Still asked 101 questions.

How do you feel today?

Studies coming along?

Are you sure you're not pushing yourself too hard? (That one she asked a lot, and I was starting to get the feeling that she wouldn't be *unhappy* if I failed the stupid test. That meant I'd be stuck in Twin Oaks at least for a few more months.)

I poked at the edge of my laptop with my finger, sinking deeper into my chair as I eyed the tattoo across my knuckles. Courage. Huh. The word taunted me. Some nights, it was all I thought about. Courage to do what it was that I wanted to do, which was play guitar. Write some new songs. Do this stupid test and pass it. Move the hell on.

Then there was the other side to this whole mess. Courage to fail trying, though that was something I didn't like to think about. Right now, failure wasn't an option, but it was easier to say than to do.

A text came in.

Mom: Making your favorite. Invite Everly.

Me: Okay.

Mom: Okay to fajitas or okay to Everly?

I stared at her message for a good five minutes, aware that a few younger kids who were here for some sort of daycare program had left and I was alone. Well, except for Mrs. Henney, that is. I felt her eyes on me, and I knew it was only a matter of time before she came over and tried to chat me up. She was a nice lady but entirely too in your face. She didn't know the concept of personal space and liked to invade mine whenever she got the chance.

I mentioned it to my dad once, and he laughed. Told me that back in the day, she'd been one hell of a looker (I didn't see it but wasn't about to call my dad out on that one). Dad said that her first husband had been a rocker with long hair and tattoos. I wasn't exactly sure what my dad was getting at, but I had a feeling if I thought about it too long, the ick factor would gross me out.

Another text came in.

Mom: bad texting etiquette.
Me: what?
Mom: answer me about Everly.

I glanced outside once more, aware that Mrs. Henney was moving in for the kill. She always cleared her throat when she was about to pounce. I could stay here and play up to her teenage dreams, or I could…

Me: I'll let you know.

I scooped up my laptop and threw it in my bag, hiking it over my shoulders before sending Mrs. Henney a quick wave and escaping into the hot Louisiana sun.

It was a week until Fourth of July, and here in Louisiana, that meant hot. The kind of hot that leaves T-shirts soaked in minutes. By the time I reached Everly's home, my hair stuck to my neck, and I was dying for some water and seriously considering tossing my shirt.

Except her mom answered the door, and I didn't think it was appropriate, her being a pastor's wife and all.

"Trevor, I…" She seemed surprised and moved so that she could see around me. "Where's Everly?"

Wait. What?

Okay, this wasn't what I'd expected, but I played along because it was obvious that Everly had been lying to her mother and I didn't want to be the one to get her into trouble.

I pulled out all the stops, and according to my grandmother, I had a lot 'em. She'd told me once that I could charm the panties off a nun if I wanted to. (Her words, not mine, because the words *nun* and *panties* should never be in the same sentence.)

I smiled and gave a half shrug as I rolled back on my feet. "Oh, man. I guess I got mixed up and came here instead of the library. She's going to think I'm a tool."

Mrs. Jenkins looked relieved. "Oh, yes, she left for the library about an hour ago. You must be late."

"Sorry, I'll head over there now."

Mrs. Jenkins held up her hand. "How has she seemed these last few days?"

Huh. She'd been lying to her parents for three days?

"Okay," I answered, taking a step back. I didn't want to have a long conversation, because I wasn't exactly sure what else Everly had lied about.

"Just okay?" Mrs. Jenkins bit her bottom lip and her eyes got all big and shiny. That was a sign—of what I didn't know—but it couldn't be anything good. It was time to leave.

"Normal, you know…yeah, she's okay," I replied. "I should get to the library."

"Do you want a bottle of water? I could get one from the kitchen…" She seemed to be searching for words, like her mind was already somewhere else.

"Nah, I'm good. I'll see you later. Sorry to bother you."

I walked up the street, pausing long enough to take off my shirt, and after stuffing it into my bag, I took a moment to call Link. He'd been hanging with Hailey down at the pool after his shift at the bakery was over. But no luck. No Everly.

Huh.

I thought of Baker's Landing, but aside from the fact that it was out of town and would take nearly an hour to get to on foot, I didn't think she'd go there. That was my place.

It was then that a lightbulb went off and I crossed the street at a slow jog, ignoring the hoots from a passing car full of girls. I didn't stop until I finally saw the old mill, and by then, my knee was throbbing.

It hadn't been used as long as I'd been alive and probably for a long time before that. With shingles missing from the roof, chipped white paint, and broken windows that looked like large gaping wounds, the mill wasn't exactly postcard material. But if Everly was looking to disappear for a few hours every day, I could see why she'd pick this place, because who else in their right mind would hang out here?

I picked my way up the steps, careful to avoid the loose boards and the ones that were missing. The main door was locked, which was a joke really, considering the windows were broken. I looked inside, but it was dark and I couldn't see much, so I walked around to the far end of the building and continued out back.

And that's when I found her.

This part of the old mill faced the river, with the dam a few hundred yards away and the brush that clung to the riverbed giving her privacy. Everly had her earbuds in, so she didn't know I was there. I took my time and let my eyes roll over a whole lot more of Everly than I'd seen before. I can't lie—the view from where I stood was smokin'.

Her long hair was tied up loosely on top of her head, and she was on her stomach, feet up in the air, moving to the beat of whatever song she was listening to, reading a book.

My mouth was a little dry, and I thought to myself that lime green was my new favorite color. Especially when it was paired with a skimpy bikini, one that showed Everly's curves off in a way that made my chest tighten and my heart speed up.

Her skin was golden, and every time her legs bobbed, muscles moved. She was all smooth lines and smooth skin and a bikini bottom that showed a lot. I cleared my throat, but it didn't do anything.

Earbuds. Shit. I didn't want to scare her, but I couldn't spend the next two hours staring at a half-naked girl. (Well, I probably could but *could* and *should* don't exactly mean the same thing.) I took a step closer and then came up short when I realized her top was undone. All that smooth skin and no tan lines.

Okay, the little lime green bikini was one thing, but when a guy is presented with a beautiful half-naked girl, sometimes it's hard for him to keep his thoughts on the straight and narrow, if you get my drift.

I took a step back, wincing and swearing at the shooting pain in my knee. I'm not sure if it was the swearing or maybe she was just suddenly aware that she was no longer alone, but Everly glanced over her shoulder, hands across her chest, and for a second, our eyes connected in such a way that I felt it like a physical touch.

Keep your eyes above her shoulders.

I repeated those words more than a few times, because we were both kind of frozen. She was surprised, and I was unsure how to proceed without coming across as a pervert.

With one hand she slowly took out her earbuds, the other still holding her top in place.

"Hey," I managed to say.

Wow. Lame approach.

"You look hot," Everly replied, eyes sliding away when the grin I couldn't help opened up nice and wide.

"Thanks."

"I meant that…"

"I know." I glanced down at my bare chest, slick with sweat.

"How did you know I was here?"

"I remembered you mentioning this place a few weeks back when we were at Baker's Landing."

Her eyes were on me again, and damn if my heart didn't kick it up a notch. Man, if this kept up, I'd pass out, and it wouldn't be from heatstroke. What was it about this girl that touched me? The unanswered questions? Was that it? Was she a challenge? Or was it the way her eyes reflected deeper and darker things? Things that maybe I recognized.

My gaze dropped to her bare back. Or was it all that smooth, naked skin? The lime green bikini? Because, first off, I was dying to touch her, and second, I was, after all, a seventeen-year-old guy who hadn't been with a girl in months. Not since Bailey.

Maybe that's what all this was. Maybe I just needed to get laid.

As soon as that thought hit me, I gave myself a mental shake. What the hell? This was Everly. Who was I kidding? This here, whatever it was that I had with her, was so much more than hooking up with some girl. If all I wanted was a quick lay, I could have gotten that Friday night. Jess had made it clear that she was totally into the idea of the two of us getting physical.

Everly moved a bit and nodded at the space beside her. She didn't say anything, and I walked over.

"Could you?" she asked, her voice so quiet and low it took a few moments to sink in.

I swallowed, eyes glued to all that smooth bare skin. *Man up, Lewis*, I told myself.

Gingerly, I reached for her and grasped the two thin pieces of her bikini top together. And totally reverted to ninth grade when Melissa Byers let me touch her boobs. I was all thumbs, trying to tie the stupid thing together. Seriously, my youngest cousin could tie his shoes faster than what I was doing.

My knuckles grazed her skin—accidentally, I swear—the Sanskrit symbol taunting me as I looked down.

Strength.

Yeah. I was going to need a lot of it.

She shifted and her hip pushed into me.

Man. And then some.

Chapter Sixteen

Everly

I think a part of me expected Trevor to eventually show up, because as much as I was startled to see him standing behind me, it wasn't because I was surprised. It was because he was half-naked. Half-naked with skin that shone from heat and sweat.

I dragged my eyes away, but not so fast that I didn't notice a few things.

A scar on his right side that was jagged.

Abs that would make most athletes drool in envy.

Abs that would make most girls drool, period.

A thin line of hair that drifted from his belly button and disappeared beneath the top of his shorts.

Shorts that maybe he should hike up because they were dangerously low on his hips.

That indent guys get, you know, the one that girls talk about. The one that makes you think of things that you shouldn't be thinking about. It was there. Front and center. Taunting me.

So, yeah, I dragged my eyes away but still managed to take

him all in. And now he was sitting beside me. And my skin tingled where he'd touched my back. And I was nervous because we were both practically naked and I'd never been this close to a guy before without, you know, clothes on.

Ugh. I felt my cheeks get hot as I thought of him tying up my bikini top. But there'd been no way for me to get the job done without things peeking out that shouldn't be peeking out.

I sighed and pushed my sunglasses back over my eyes. How had I reached the age of seventeen without getting half-naked with a guy before?

Oh. Right. There'd been no Trevor Lewis up until a few weeks ago. No guy who'd ever tempted me the way he did. No guy who could make me forget. And right now, I was all about forgetting if I could.

I closed the book I'd been trying to read for the last hour and stretched out on the blanket, resting my chin on my arms. Trevor did the same, both of us looking out over the water, watching the birds that flew and dove for fish near the dam.

"I used to jump off the railway tracks just above the dam with Nate and Link," Trevor said after a few moments. "When I was, like, twelve. Man, we got in a lot of trouble when our parents found out. Especially after Daryl drowned."

I thought about that kid. "Daryl Mason?" I asked.

Trevor nodded and turned onto his side so that he was looking at me and not the water. "We were supposed to meet him that afternoon, but Nate had a family thing. I got into trouble for something, can't remember what, and Link just never showed. There was an undertow or maybe he got caught on something under the dam. I don't remember how he drowned. I just know he did." Trevor's eyes widened a bit. "I haven't been back to the dam since."

"He went to my church," I offered, not knowing what else to say. At the time it had been a tragedy the entire town felt. His parents owned the hardware store, but after Daryl died, they'd moved away.

"I know. His funeral was the last time I was inside a church. It was just hard, you know? We were young, stupid, and so… relieved it wasn't us. Seeing how broken up his parents were was awful. I remember his mom kept saying, 'He's gone to heaven now. I'll see him again.' But all I kept thinking was how do you know? How do you know life doesn't just end when we do?"

I considered his words. "My dad would say that's what faith is for."

My dad would say a lot of things, and now I wondered if my dad believed all the stuff he preached, considering the lie he'd been living.

Trevor reached over and plucked my sunglasses off the end of my nose. I wished he hadn't because now he could see the tears that sat in the corners. Tears that had haunted me since Sunday. Tears that had been falling on and off since forever, it seemed.

"Are you okay?" he asked. Three simple words, and yet so much meaning filled the cracks between them. He cared about me. I heard it in his voice. Most guys would have been up in my face, angry with the silent treatment I'd been doling out since Sunday. Wondering how I could let them touch me, kiss me, and then…nothing.

But not Trevor, and for that I was grateful. I was way too fragile right now to deal with anger.

"Everly? Did I do something?" He looked so serious. And more than a little unsure. "I mean, did I push you in a way that I shouldn't have Friday?"

That thing in my chest tightened again. The thing that was somehow connected to this boy.

"No." I shook my head. "No, Trevor. Friday was…amazing. This…" Would I ever be able to speak normally again? "The way I've been acting has nothing to do with you. I don't want you to think that."

God, his eyes were beautiful. A girl could lose herself inside them.

"Do you want to talk about it?"

I wanted to tell him everything. I wanted to so badly. But I couldn't vocalize the things in my head. Not yet anyway. Maybe never.

"I'm sorry I blew you off," I said instead. "I didn't mean to. I just didn't know how to be with anyone."

"At the moment you seem to be doing all right." His voice was light, touched with the slightest bit of something. It was that something that I needed, because I felt like I'd been holding my breath since Sunday and finally I was able to breathe a bit easier.

"I suppose you think that you have something to do with that?"

"That would make me an egotistical bastard, don't you think?"

"Yeah. It would."

"Then I guess I'm an egotistical bastard." There was that smile again. "Because I think it has everything to do with me."

I found myself smiling in return, and I nudged him with my shoulder. "You're pretty full of yourself, Trevor Lewis."

He didn't answer because his eyes were on my mouth.

And suddenly the air between us got heavy. Or maybe I couldn't breathe because I was too busy hanging on to this moment, thinking that Trevor had the longest lashes I'd ever seen on a guy. That his sweat-slicked skin was so different from mine, taut over muscle and somehow stronger.

I saw his tattoo, the one along the side of his neck, and I couldn't help myself. I traced it with my forefinger, following the strange pattern until it crept up over his shoulder.

I moved closer to him, loving how the sun reflected in his beautiful eyes. I think he groaned. Or maybe it was me.

Either way, that sound tugged at something hot and heavy inside me, and I pushed him back, sliding up along his body until I was on top of him. His hands moved up over my hips, pressing in on my lower back before gliding up to my waist, where he held me so that I couldn't move.

Not that I wanted to.

In a world that had felt wrong for so many days, everything about being here with Trevor felt right.

We were both breathing heavily and hadn't done anything yet. Not really. But I felt his heart beating beneath my chest, and my fingers dug into the hair at his nape.

"Kiss me," I whispered, closing my eyes when I heard the need in my voice and hoping he didn't.

His hands moved up, slowly, fingers on skin sending little shock waves through my body. He cupped the back of my head, brought me closer, and then his mouth slid across mine. If ever there was a little piece of heaven on earth, it was somehow tied up inside Trevor Lewis.

The kiss was fire and heat and pulsing pleasure. I'd never been kissed like that before. If I thought Friday night was amazing, this here, right now, blew that out of the water.

Sure, it could be because he had no shirt on and I was practically naked. It could have been because every single inch of me was pressed against him. It could have been the sun shining down on us, warming already heated skin. Or it could have been the call of the birds as they flew over the dam, making us feel alive.

It could have been all of those things that made me squirm and want to get so close to Trevor that I was willing to do things I'd never contemplated with anyone else.

But it was more than that.

I kissed him fiercely, wanting him to feel what was inside me. Wondering what it would feel like to have *him* inside me.

He finally pulled away and smoothed a long piece of my hair back from my face and tucked it behind my ear. He shuddered and pulled me in close, so close that his heart sounded as if it was going to beat right out of his chest.

I knew that this was something more than just a summer fling. A hookup.

I thought of what Hales had told me only a week ago.

Do you believe in love at first sight?

Was that what this was? Love? The beginning of love? Was it possible that I was falling in love with Trevor Lewis? Or was this just plain old lust?

Startled, I moved slightly because I needed to see his eyes. Needed to see what was there.

Needed to see if I'd recognize whatever it was.

"Hey," he said gruffly, hands still in my hair, though his expression was kind of pained. "I'm not kissing you again."

Okay. That's not what I'd been expecting to hear.

"Why?" I asked without thinking.

He attempted a smile. "This might be the ego talking, but I'm pretty sure that if I kiss you again…"

He shifted a bit, and suddenly I was aware that his body had changed. That things might not be so easy for him, you know, being a guy and all.

This was the moment where I could have said *Screw you, universe. I'm going to do what feels good and right and…*

"What if I want you to kiss me again?" I asked, watching him closely.

We both knew that I wasn't talking about just a kiss.

"Right here? Right now?" he answered. "That's what you want?"

We stared at each other for a long time, and then I shuddered, letting him pull me back into a hug.

"We've got all summer," he said, voice a little rough. "To figure things out."

"Thanks," I murmured.

He kissed the top of my head. "For what?"

"For not thinking I'm a total freak. For not being pissed at the way I've been acting since Sunday, and for coming out here to find me."

"You might not thank me when you find out the diabolical reason I came looking for you."

"Diabolical. That sounds serious."

"Dinner at my house can be a pretty serious thing, though that usually depends on Taylor's mood, and since she's still grounded, it's not looking great. But," he said, arching his back slightly so that I could see him, "my mom's famous fajitas?"

That was pretty much all it took. That and the fact that I wanted to float in this boy's orbit for as long as I could. Trevor Lewis was exactly what I needed.

"Fajitas sound perfect."

Chapter Seventeen

Trevor

"She's a nice girl."

"She's…yeah."

I waited a beat and watched Everly wave from her porch, and then when she disappeared inside her house, I exhaled loudly. I'd been wound tighter than Link's snare drum ever since she'd climbed on top of me out at the dam.

I'd had to sit across from her at the dinner table when what I really wanted to do was jump over the stupid thing and kiss her until she made those sexy noises again. It was hard, trying to maintain some kind of control.

"Yeah," I said again, turning to my dad. "She's nice."

Wow. That didn't sound anything like what I really thought, but I hadn't talked girls with Dad in a while, and this particular one had kind of thrown me for a loop.

"Nice," Dad repeated.

I shrugged.

His face split wide open in a grin as he put the Mustang in reverse. "Nice," he said again with a laugh.

"Well, what do you want me to say?"

"You guys dating?"

Were we? I glanced in the mirror and watched her house disappear from view.

"We're hanging out."

"Huh. Serious hanging out or just hanging out?"

"I'm not sure yet," I replied honestly.

"Well, you just make sure you're careful is all."

"Got it covered, Dad."

He glanced at me sharply. "You guys having sex?"

I shook my head and groaned. What was this? We'd had the birds and the bees talk years ago, and it consisted of Dad buying me a box of condoms and telling me to "use them, goddammit. Your mother and I are too young to be grandparents."

"No, Dad, we're not having sex." *Not yet, anyway.* "And can we talk about something else? Gee, way to kill the mood."

Dad steered the car with the palm of his hand—something he would have given me shit over—and turned off of Everly's street before heading toward Main.

"Where we going?" Obviously in the wrong direction.

It was early yet, just after eight, and we had at least another hour and a half of sunlight.

"Thought we'd hit some balls."

Surprised, but in a good way, I shrugged. "Sounds good, but we don't have our clubs."

"Threw them in the trunk when you were showing Everly how the dog plays dead."

"Okay," I replied, wondering what this was all about. He was a pretty crappy golfer. My mom was the superstar in our family, and I don't think I'd ever gone to hit balls with him before.

"I'm probably going to suck," I said.

Dad snorted. "It's like riding a bike, Trev. You're way too natural of an athlete to forget how to line up a ball and hit it."

Yeah, but the last time I'd been on a golf course, my knee hadn't been screwed up. I didn't think I was going to be all that stellar, but the thought of spending an hour or so hitting balls with my dad was a good one.

The driving range was still fairly busy, but we managed to find two spots side by side. I changed my shoes (Dad had thought of everything), grabbed my clubs, and set up shop by a couple of older ladies who gave us the stink eye as we walked by. Didn't blame them. Dad looked like he could ride with the Hells Angels with his sleeved tattoos and shaved head. And me? I guess they weren't exactly used to dudes with blue streaks in their hair.

I gave them a wave, smiled that smile my grandmother liked to boast about, and asked them how they were doing.

That was that. Ice was broken. They smiled in return, said it was a perfect night to hit balls, and then complimented me on my clubs.

I saw the way my dad rolled his eyes when he brought over a

couple of buckets of balls, and I tried not to laugh. As much as the whole charm thing seemed to have landed on me in spades, apparently it skipped a generation, and he'd never been hit with that particular stick.

I grabbed my seven iron and took a few practice swings. Felt good. Got into the groove. Sent the ball flying. Once I was warmed up, I took out my driver and lined up my shot. My knee was starting to throb a bit, so I adjusted my footing. I took a moment and then, with gentle wrists (the secret, according to my mom), sent the ball straight down, well over 250 feet. Heck, practically 300.

The ladies beside me gushed about my form and asked if I belonged to the local country club. I'd had a junior membership years ago, but music had kind of taken over, and other than football, I'd pretty much given up on sports.

I laughed, shook my head, and said no. They were shocked when I told them I hadn't picked up a club in nearly two years. The tall, thinner lady gave me a second look, her eyes softening a bit as she placed her club back into her bag.

"Are you that boy who was in the bad car accident last summer?"

I nodded, not knowing what to say really. It had been a long time since anyone had brought up the accident with me.

She glanced behind me. "I recognize your daddy from pictures in the paper." She winked. "How wonderful to see you out here. You're looking good as new."

I shoved a tee into my pocket. Looks could be deceiving.

"Thanks," I said, giving them a wave as they headed back to their car. We were losing the light and maybe had twenty minutes left.

Dad moved over just then. "I'm outta balls."

I snorted. "Yeah, half of them are in the trees."

"True," he said. "But golf's never been my strong suit. It's more your mama's game."

I glanced in my bucket. "You want some of mine?"

"Nah. You're doing good. I'll watch."

I shrugged. "Your call."

I grabbed some more balls from the bucket. After sending them straight ahead, all within ten to fifteen feet of each other, I paused, aware that my dad was watching me in that way that told me there was something on his mind.

I set up another ball.

"I heard you playing your guitar this morning."

And just like that, any ease that I'd had slipped away like water down the drain. My muscles cramped, my knee throbbed like hell, and, well, the gentle wrists went the way of the dinosaur.

I swung my club, angry he would bring something like that up out here. Golf was sacred—what part of that didn't he get? I chopped at it and the ball hopped to the left, jumping a few feet before coming to a standstill.

Glaring, I turned around because I wanted my dad to know I wasn't impressed with his choice of conversation. But his eyes were dark and I saw the concern. It was a look I'd seen way too many times, and even though the anger was still there, rumbling beneath my skin like his Harley, I couldn't act on it.

"I sounded like crap."

I would be lying if I didn't say that I was waiting for him to tell me the opposite. You know, butter me up a bit. Inflate the ego when it was sagging. But that wasn't my dad. The guy had no tact, but you had to give him points for always being honest and direct. He'd told me once that anything other than the truth was a waste of time. That time wasn't always on our side, so why waste it?

"Can I do anything to help?" he asked gruffly.

I placed another ball on the tee. "Nope." And sent it sailing up the green.

"Are you worried?"

"Jesus, Dad. Are we really going to have this conversation here? Now?"

"Is there a better time?"

"Yeah," I replied.

"When?"

"Never," I whispered to myself.

I stared down into my bucket and fought the urge to send the stupid thing flying. I was in the mood to hit something, but it sure as hell wasn't balls.

"Trevor."

I cut him off. "Of course I'm worried and pissed off and a whole lot of other stuff that I can't even name."

Something let loose inside me, something nasty, and I tossed my club. It hit my bag and sent it flying, and I watched my dad bend over to straighten it.

"I haven't told Nate that I suck. He has no idea that the thought of performing in front of a bunch of kids scares the crap out of me because I'm not so sure that I can remember half the notes to a simple AC/DC song. They're, like, three chords. And even when I do, sometimes my fingers won't do what I'm telling them to do anyway, so why even try?"

The driving range was now empty, so there was no one out here to hear my tirade. No one except my dad, who stood a few feet away, his eyes intense as they studied me.

"You're getting better, Trevor. But it's going to take time, and your mother and I, well, we..." He cleared his throat, and I knew this was just as hard for him. Must suck to look at your kid and know he's defective.

"What?" I asked, but I knew where this was going.

My dad ran his hands over his head, big beefy hands that had no hair to smooth. It was a nervous gesture. I hated seeing him like this.

"I know we had a deal. Pass your government test, collect your diploma, and you could leave for New York with our blessing, but Trevor, the seizure changes things."

Something ticked behind my right eye as I clenched and unclenched my hands. I hated that word almost as much as I hated those three little letters, the ones I saw when I closed my eyes: *TBI*. "It was one seizure," I finally got out.

"There could be more."

"You think I don't know that? It's all I think about. The only time it goes away is when I'm with Everly." My right eye was throbbing as much as my knee, and I dragged in a big gulp of air. "Music is my life, Dad. New York and Nathan was my plan. It still is my plan. How do you expect me to get to where I'm supposed to be if you take New York away from me?"

He took those few steps until he was inches from me, and my throat tightened when I saw his eyes. They were glassy and shiny. Geez, I wasn't sure if I could deal with this right now. How could I keep it together when he was about to lose it?

"I'm not taking anything away from you. Trevor, I would give my right arm if it meant that you could have your dreams. Hell, I would cut both of them off if that's what it takes to give you everything you want. Everything that you deserve. But we gotta be realistic here. It might be time…" He scrubbed at his face. "Ah, hell."

"Time for what?" I could barely get the words out.

"It might be time for a plan B, Trevor. Time to maybe find another dream."

I couldn't believe he was saying this to me. I squeezed my eyes shut and struggled to keep my shit together.

"I don't have another dream, Dad. Music, that's it. That's all I got."

I felt empty saying it and kind of sick to my stomach too. Because the raw truth of it was exactly that. Music *was* everything to me. Always had been. What was I going to do if I couldn't get it back? Who would I be?

Nobody.

Pain stretched across my chest, and before I could help myself, I bent over and vomited into the grass. I heaved until there was nothing left inside me, and when I finally wiped my hand across my mouth and slowly straightened, my dad was there.

His massive arms wrapped around my shoulders, bands of steel that were hard and safe. I let him hold me and felt his body shudder as he tried to keep his grief inside, but it was impossible. As much as my dad was tough on the outside, he could cry at the drop of a hat. It's where he got his nickname, Teddy Bear. But that's who my dad was…he was that guy. The one who cared so much, his feelings had a hard time staying inside.

I let him hold me just like he used to do when I was a kid and was hurt or upset. He probably needed it just as much as I did, because I knew that if he could, he'd chop his arm off and offer it up to whatever god he thought would make things right.

But out here under a blanket of stars that lit up a hot Louisiana night, I think we both realized that there was no easy answer. No easy way. That's the thing about action and consequence. You have to learn to deal with it or you'll go crazy.

My deal? I knew the odds were against me. Most people never made a complete recovery after a TBI, and now with the seizure sitting pretty on my résumé, things were worse than they were a week ago.

A year ago, I'd felt extraordinary, on the verge of something big. Nothing could touch me. Nate, Link, Brent, and I were kings.

And then we weren't.

Now, I was less than ordinary, and for the first time since I'd come out of the coma, it hit me. Really hit me. *Less than ordinary.* Three words that carried some heavy weight.

They weren't words that floated around in my head like clouds moving across a lazy summer sky. Words with no tangible meaning. They were words that hit hard. They burrowed beneath my skin and penetrated the screwed-up brain inside my head.

I might be stuck at less than ordinary for the rest of my life, and less than ordinary was now some kind of normal for me.

At seventeen. How the hell do you deal with that?

Chapter Eighteen
Everly

The crap thing about floating on a cloud is that eventually the cloud dissipates and there's nothing left to keep you up there, suspended above a life you no longer recognize. There's only the fall and the hope that nothing gets hurt on the way down.

I'd been falling since Wednesday night, and so far the ride down had been gentle enough, but this is my life we're talking about, so I should have known things would get rough.

Friday started off okay. I managed to score the last of the strawberry freezer jam for my toast. Win!

The sun was shining. Double win!

And the kiss that rocked my world was still percolating in my brain, summoning sighs and smiles when it wasn't exactly appropriate. Case in point. The night before at dinner, while my parents went about their charade, Mom making small talk and Dad looking like he actually cared, my mind drifted to the old mill. I closed my eyes and could practically feel the heat of the sun, Trevor's sweat-slicked skin, and the ache his kiss left me with.

"Why is your face all screwed up?" That was from my little brother, who was in the process of making an epic smiley face out of his mashed potatoes.

"It's not."

"It kind of is," Dad said.

"No," I said, digging into my food. "It's not." My tone said "don't bother me," and I tuned out the rest of their conversation. The good thing about all the tension at home was that it was a lot easier for me to get away with being a bitch. Mom was afraid to say anything because she was guarding her secret and didn't want me to spill, and Dad was just confused. I guess he thought if he left me alone, I'd eventually morph back into the girl he knew.

Funny how lies do that to people.

But now it was the Friday of the long weekend, and there was a world of possibilities before me.

Trevor hadn't asked me to go to the Fourth of July celebrations with him. Or the cookout down at the park. Or the overnight trip to Link's parents' cottage near Baton Rouge. There was still time…right?

Dad had already left for his part-time gig at the used car dealership in town. I know. But he was surprisingly good at it, mostly because everyone trusted the pastor. If only they knew.

Mom came down for breakfast already dressed, which surprised me. She'd taken some time off work since her *episode*, and as far as I knew, she wasn't due back to her office job until after the long weekend.

She didn't say a word about the crumbs left on the table or the fact that I'd put the empty jar of jam back in the fridge. She even overlooked the coffee grounds smeared across the garbage container.

Something was up. I wasn't sure it was a good up or a bad up, but when she took a sip of coffee and cleared her throat, I knew right then that I wasn't going to like what she was about to say.

"I hear they're calling for rain this weekend."

Okay, opening with the weather wasn't a good sign at all.

"What's going on, Mom?" I so didn't want to play games with her. Not now. Not when I knew that she played by a whole set of rules I knew nothing about.

She opened her mouth to say something but sighed instead and took another sip of coffee, her eyes settled on me over the rim of her cup. She looked tired. Sad and maybe a little scared. She finished her coffee and set her mug on the counter, pushing at it with her forefinger until it was a safe distance away from the edge.

She was starting to freak me out a little bit.

"Mom?"

"The weather looks good in New England," she said softly.

Wait. What?

"For the long weekend, I mean."

I stared at her for so long that she shifted, her eyes sliding away from mine.

"Maybe longer."

I shook my head. "No."

"Everly…I can't…I need some time away to think things through."

"I'm not going with you."

"I thought I could stay here and things would just go back to the way they were before but—"

"I'm not going with you." My heart was beating nearly out of my chest, and I took a step backward, legs crashing into a chair and sending it skittering across the linoleum floor until it rested against the pantry door. New England? With her brother and his five kids? No. Way.

"I just can't. I need to be away from your father, because I can't breathe when I'm around him. I can't function. I can't think."

"You seemed to do a good job of it last night." My voice rose as anger clogged my throat. "Both of you. Acting as if everything is great and wonderful and, you know, *normal*."

"Yes, well, pretending is hard."

"No kidding. I've been doing it for over four hundred days. Do you know how long that is? Four. Hundred. Days. It's like an eternity. My entire senior year was a big fat lie."

She smoothed her hands down the front of her skirt and tightened her ponytail. Was that gray I saw threaded through her dark hair?

"I understand this has been hard on you, and I can't apologize enough for my lapse in judgment, for what I put you through, but…" She frowned. "You never did…the other day… you didn't tell me how you knew." She sniffled. "About your father, I mean."

"I didn't tell you because you didn't ask. You didn't ask because you'd just overdosed on sleeping pills."

"I didn't—"

"Jesus, Mom. Cut the crap. You can lie to yourself all you want, but don't lie to me." I shook my head. "Not anymore. I mean, what else is there for me to know?"

Something in her face changed, and my stomach dipped at the look in her eyes. I was cold, which was ridiculous because it was hot in here. So. Freaking. Hot.

"What else is there?" I asked angrily.

But she was all closed up tighter than a locked box. She cleared her throat again and grabbed the rag from the sink. Guess my crumbs were finally getting to her.

"You will not take the Lord's name in vain again. Do you understand me?"

Unbelievable. That's what she was going to focus on?

"I need you to pack your things," she said briskly.

"I'm not going with you," I said again, the tears in my eyes sitting heavy in my throat as well. "Trevor…he needs me."

I need him.

"I need you," she said firmly.

"You need your husband," I shot back, and if I could have taken the words back, I would have because she looked small. Defeated. And I knew I had done that. "I can't fix this for you, Mom. I just can't, and it's not fair of you to expect me to."

Her bottom lip trembled, and she leaned back against the

sink. "Everly, I don't know how long I'll be. Isaac will be at Bible camp for two weeks and then we'll be at my brother's place. Right now, our plans are indefinite."

"You're just going to run away?"

She didn't have an answer for that one, so I pressed on.

"Are you getting a divorce?"

Wow. Imagine the scandal. Pastor Jenkins cheats on wife and drives her out of town. His flock would diminish overnight.

"No," she said, shaking her head. "I mean, I don't know. I love your father, you know…" She shrugged and tried to smile through her tears. "Even if we don't end up together, I'll always love him. I just hope that he can find his way back to me. I hope he can forgive himself for his sins and find a way to fight for us." She blew out a long breath. "That's why I need you to hang on a little longer, and please keep this to yourself. It's not as cut-and-dried as you think. If word gets out, he'll be destroyed. We'll go on and survive, but your father won't. He won't come back from this."

Holy. Cow. I so didn't understand adults, but then again, I guess I wasn't supposed to.

"I'd better say good-bye to Isaac."

She tossed the rag into the sink. "I told your father you'd be coming with me."

Huh. So that's why he'd lingered in the kitchen this morning. He'd been trying to say good-bye without saying good-bye.

"I'll send him a text later. Give him the heads-up."

For a moment I thought Mom was going to force the issue. Her lips thinned, and if she kept frowning like that, she was going to have perma lines between her eyes.

"You're sure?" she asked.

"I am."

"Okay, I'll leave some cash for groceries, and there's always your dad's debit card." She worried her bottom lip and attempted a smile. "It will be good for you and your father to spend some time together."

I snorted.

Her frown deepened. "He's your father, Everly. When all is said and done, there is still that, and he deserves your respect."

I wanted to shout at her. To scream and tear out my hair. I wanted to tell her that respect is earned. That just because you're an adult doesn't mean you get to break the rules and get away with it. That being a liar and a cheat isn't something to look up to.

I got what she was saying. But love and respect are two different things. I would always love my dad, but right now, the respect thing was more than a little iffy. It was pretty much nonexistent.

"Okay." She pushed away from the counter. "I think it will be good for you and him to have some alone time."

"Sure."

Not a chance in hell, but I wasn't about to tell her that. I had plans for the weekend, but they sure as heck didn't involve my dad. In fact, I was contemplating doing something so out of character that I was surprised Mom didn't see it plastered all over my face.

I let her hug me. Kiss the top of my head. I said my good-byes to Isaac, who looked confused as ever, the poor kid.

"You're not coming?" he sniffed into my neck.

"Buddy, I'm too old for Bible camp."

"I don't mean camp."

I knew what he meant. When had Mom ever gone away without all of us?

"Not this time."

"Dad's not either," he whispered.

I hugged him. Hard. "I know, but you'll have a blast at camp, and just think of all the fun you'll have with your cousins."

He wrinkled his nose. "They're all girls."

"I know." I gave him one more kiss. "You won't have time to miss me, and I'll see you before you know it, okay?"

I watched them load bags into her car, and after one last hug, they drove down the street and disappeared from sight.

And then I dug out my cell, scrolled past my dad's name, and called Trevor. He answered on the first ring.

"Hey," he said, all husky scruff that told me he'd just rolled out of bed.

"It's Friday," I replied.

A pause.

"Yeah. I think you're right about that."

I smiled at the teasing note in his voice.

"Friday, July 3."

"Huh. You're two for two."

"So are you taking me to Link's cottage for the long weekend or what?" Holy cow. What was wrong with my mouth? Run on much?

A pause. A long, painful pause as my cheeks flooded with heat. I sank down to my knees and pulled a pillow off the sofa to cushion the fall. Oh God. What had I just done?

I squeezed my eyes shut and tried to stop my heart from beating, because it was making me dizzy. Or maybe it was just the *stupid* that was making me dizzy. The *stupid* that ran through my veins. I wasn't good at this whole seduction thing. If that was even a thing.

"Are you offering to be my roomie?"

"Maybe." I barely got that out. "I mean, I suppose I could be persuaded." That was an epic line. *Epic.* Gonna have to remember it for future use. Not.

"Are you flirting with me, Everly Jenkins?" he asked so softly I had to strain to hear him.

"The fact that you have to ask reiterates my lame attempt, but yes."

"Good to know."

Another pause.

"Everly?"

"Yes?"

"It's working."

"The flirting?"

"The flirting," he replied.

I exhaled. "So that means…"

"It means that we blow off study session. It means that Link will scoop up his girl, and he and I will be there to pick you up at noon. Are you sure about this?"

I was off the floor and already heading up to my room, so yeah, I was pretty sure.

"There are only two bedrooms up there, and Brent has already claimed the sofa."

This was obviously his way of warning me that we'd be sharing a room, which was sweet. But I was kind of done being sweet. I wanted something more.

I thought of my father. Of how he was living a lie. Pretending to be happy when all he was doing was destroying what little bit of happiness his family had. What was the point in living like that? What was wrong with being true to yourself and being honest?

I wanted Trevor. That was my truth. That was my honesty. I wasn't exactly sure how far I was willing to go, but I trusted him enough to know I'd be safe. He was the one who'd pulled back at the old mill, not me.

"That's okay," I said when I reached the top of the stairs. "You can sleep on the floor."

He laughed, and I felt a bit of the heaviness in me lift. "Now you're being cruel."

"See? I suck at flirting."

"Actually you don't."

"Don't what?"

"Suck."

"At flirting?" God, Everly. Just. Stop. Talking.

"Yeah." I could picture the grin on his face. "At flirting."

Good to know.

I went in search of luggage and tried to ignore the little voice in the back of my head. The one that kept asking me if I knew what I was doing, because I was pretty sure that Trevor Lewis didn't go away for the weekend with a girl and not expect a few things to happen.

Namely sex.

I knew Hales and Link had already done it. They'd barely waited a week after the drive-in, but then Hailey had never been the kind of girl to wait for something that she wanted. I kind of admired her for that.

Besides, no guy ever was going to turn down sex. They're not wired that way. So where did that leave me? Where did that leave Trevor? I wasn't even sure what we were exactly. Was he my boyfriend? Did he think of me as his girlfriend? Could we spend the weekend together and not do anything? Like anything naked?

I reached into my closet for my weekender bag.

Guess I was going to find out.

Chapter Nineteen

Trevor

Link's cottage was on the Tickfaw River, not far from Baton Rouge. When we were younger, we'd hang on the dock, go fishing, eat as much junk food as we could stuff down our throats, and stay up late watching cheesy horror movies. One year, Link scared the crap out of us when he jumped on our bed, yelling at the top of his lungs and wearing a white goalie mask. You know, of the Jason variety. Funny now, but not so much back then, because Brent crapped his pants. Like literally.

I'd been coming here since I was a kid, tagging along with Link and his parents, but over the last couple of years, a few things had changed, namely the lack of parents. Now we come up on our own, and as long as we don't get stupid and trash the place, Link's dad is okay with us using it.

Man, that first time, we'd felt like kings. On our own with no adults to tell us what to do. I'd only been fifteen but had told my folks we were going with Link's dad. A total lie, and I eventually got caught, but Brent (who was the oldest and had a license) drove us up. We were serious musicians, and it was just guys, and we were gonna write hit songs and get drunk and eat as much crap as we could. We weren't going to worry about girls and the drama they brought with them. Except, you know, girls do add a certain flavor, and after the second night, we knew we were missing something. Girls and guitars just seemed to go together.

I glanced up at the place as Link pulled his truck in behind Brent's car. We'd had some pretty intense parties up here, a lot of good times, and it felt good to be back, even if some of the gang was missing.

Everly had fallen asleep on the ride up, and she was curled into my side. She was soft and warm, and I could have stayed holed up with her in the back of Link's truck all afternoon. Pretty hard not to think along those lines, because she was so damn sweet with her long lashes touching the tops of her cheeks, and she was going to hate this, but the girl snored softly. It was kind of adorable, although I had no plans to tell her.

I couldn't help myself. I let my finger trace the contours of her top lip and then slipped my hand into her hair so that I could kiss her.

There's something to be said about how amazing it feels to wake up a girl with your mouth. Especially when she tastes as sweet as Everly Jenkins.

She moved against me, turning slightly, and I thought I should pull back. Hell, we were in the back of Link's truck, and

Brent stood a few feet away, leaning against his car. But she was so soft and warm and...

I deepened the kiss, wanting more, needing to feel her wanting the same thing. Her eyes flew open, and she stilled, her hands already buried in the hair at the back of my head.

"Hey," I said, voice a little rough, because man, there were zings and zongs going off in my body. Things had heated up pretty fast.

"Sorry," she breathed. "I didn't mean to fall asleep."

"It's all right. You can sleep on me anytime." Her eyes slid away, and her cheeks got all rosy. It took everything I had not to kiss her again. Like I said. Adorable.

"We should go help get our gear in," I said.

She never looked away. Her eyes were dark, like liquid navy, and I thought they were the most amazing eyes ever. "Okay. Sounds like a plan."

I waited for a few moments and then cleared my throat. "You might have to move a little." The girl was snug between my legs, and I was hoping she was gonna move to the right, because if she moved to the left, well, let's just say I wasn't prepared for that.

"Oh." She glanced down and then her eyes shot back to mine. "Oh. I'm sorry. I..."

I had to laugh. "Everly, don't worry about it. It's my deal, not yours." I bent forward and kissed her nose. "You can't help it if the sight of you makes me crazy."

"Does it?" There was that soft, slow smile that I dug.

191

"Do you want me to show you right here?"

She glanced out the window. "Um….no!"

We both rolled out of the truck and followed Hailey, Link, and Brent up the stairs with our bags. The guys went back a few more times for the coolers that were stuffed with food, beer, and—

"Who the hell packed two club packs of Popsicles?" I eyed Brent, but he shrugged.

"Not me."

"I did," Hailey said, grabbing them from me and heading to the kitchen with them. "They're, like, my Kryptonite."

I made a weird face, and Everly tried like hell not to laugh.

"So, they'll kill you?" I asked, following her into the kitchen. She was stuffing them into the freezer.

"Huh?"

"Kryptonite. It was the one thing that made Superman weak."

She grabbed a cherry Popsicle but didn't bother to offer me one. "Superman?" she asked, tearing off the wrapper. "What does Superman have to do with me?"

I opened my mouth to answer, but Link was already there, biting off a huge piece of her Popsicle. "Mmm," he said, moving in for a kiss. "Cherry is my new favorite flavor."

He pushed her back against the kitchen cabinets, and the two of them started to make out like porn stars. Time for me to leave. I glanced at Everly, but she was already moving back toward the family room that overlooked the river.

"Our bedroom is this way." I grabbed her bag and she followed me down the hall. The cottage wasn't big, but the bedrooms were a good size. Link was taking his parents' room, which overlooked the water and had an exit to the hot tub. The guest room had a view of the shed and not much else, because it was tiny. I was okay with that because the bed was a huge king-sized monstrosity that took up most of the space, *and* we had our own private bathroom.

Win.

"Wow," Everly said softly, eyes on the red and white plaid blanket. "It's…big."

I tossed my bag. "And squeaky. The springs are shot."

"What?"

I tried to keep a straight face but lost it when she took a step toward me. "Kidding," I said, hands up in surrender.

"That's not funny." She tried to punch me in the shoulder, but I ducked and grabbed her around the waist.

We both fell onto the bed. Again, win.

And she ended up on top of me. Double win.

I was laughing, and she was trying not to laugh. And my hands were on her hips and then she was leaning over me, her hair tickling my nose. She was bare legs, exposed stomach, and summer sweet smell.

God, she felt great.

Our laughter slowly died and I couldn't tear my eyes away. I exhaled and tried to get my head screwed on straight, but it was damn hard. The air was different. It was thick and heavy, with a need that I didn't think we were ready for. At least, not yet.

I tucked that piece of hair that teased me behind her ear, shifted a bit because, well, she was on top of me, and cracked a smile.

"See? No squeaks."

I sat up, Everly still straddling me, and wrapped my arms around her. What was it about this girl that had me all fuzzy and warm, acting like a damn teddy bear?

"I should unpack," she said.

"Yeah," I said slowly, pressing one last kiss on a mouth that was pretty much perfect. Her breath hitched, and that did all sorts of crazy stuff to me. More than a little unsteady (when had a girl ever made me this freaking crazy?), I pulled away.

"We've got all weekend."

Chapter Twenty
Everly

The summer I turned eight, I went through a phase of jumping into situations without thinking. Like literally. One afternoon in particular, my parents took Hailey and me to a park on the river. There were waterslides and sprinklers and a wave pool. But as soon as we got there and with no hesitation, because I'd been planning my move since I found out we were going, I ran for the river, ignoring my mother's screams, and I dove in. With my shoes and everything.

At the time I was convinced that I was a mermaid, and *everyone* knew mermaids didn't die in the water. Apparently everyone except my mom. She practically had a heart attack, waded in (yes, in her shoes), and hauled me out of the river. She caused a scene and didn't seem to care that everyone and their mother was watching. Which totally isn't my mother, but that's how mad she was.

And I wasn't allowed to play on the waterslides as my punishment for not listening and, as she said, "pulling a stunt like that."

She didn't get that it wasn't a stunt. I begged. I pleaded. I cried. I told her I was a mermaid. She threw her hands up in the air and told my father I wasn't allowed to watch Saturday cartoons anymore. I had to spend the entire afternoon watching Hailey make new friends as she went up and down the water-slides. I was mad and resentful and thought that my mom was the meanest lady on the planet.

Of course, my teenage self knew that she was only trying to protect me from getting hurt. That she'd been scared, and I know that it had been a reckless thing to do. And sure I could argue that most eight-year-old kids would have done the same thing, except I was pretty sure that they wouldn't.

That summer, I'd been hit with "the crazy stick," as my father called it. I was a little adrenaline junkie who jumped in with no thought of the consequence, because that feeling, the one that hits just before you're about to do something out of this world, *that* feeling was worth the punishment.

That feeling meant that I was alive. Really alive. Not all that smart, just alive.

It took some doing, but after endless chats and groundings and threats of how sinning wasn't a great way to stay on God's good side (because not listening to your parents was a sin), I eventually calmed down. Or maybe I just got older and outgrew the crazy stick stage. Who knows?

And yet I couldn't forget how standing on the edge of some-thing unknown made me feel more alive than accepting things that just were. It seems as if that hasn't changed. It was still scary and thrilling and probably ten more adjectives (at least).

We have all weekend.

Here I was again, about to dive into the river, and there was no Mom to rescue me or Dad to preach at me.

I splashed my face with cold water, scowling at my reflection in the mirror above the bathroom sink. Big eyes stared back at me, bluer than ever. My skin was pale, but my cheeks, seriously? Blushing sucked.

"Hey, you."

I loosened my hair from its ponytail and let it fall down my back, grateful that Hailey had popped in because I needed her right now. I hugged her tightly, then let her go.

"I hate you. We've just spent most of the night on the beach, in the wind, and your hair looks freaking amazing." She glanced at herself in the mirror and stuck out her tongue. Grabbing my tie off the sink, she secured her hair on top of her head and then leaned against the sink, eyes on me. "The guys are putting out the fire. Brent's already passed out on the sofa."

He'd been hitting it pretty heavy, so I wasn't surprised. "I saw that."

"Okay," Hailey said, twirling a long piece of hair that hadn't made it to the top of her head. "Spill."

"What?" I asked.

"How did you convince your parents to let you go away for the weekend with Trevor Lewis?"

"What did you tell your mom?" I asked instead.

"The truth."

"The truth." I didn't believe her.

"Well, yeah. I'm almost eighteen, and she knows Link and I are...well, that we've been having sex." She giggled. "Lots of sex."

"Hales. TMI. I don't need to know the details."

She squealed and hugged me again. "Lots of sex!"

I couldn't help but laugh and told her she was a nympho.

"Just wait," she replied. "You'll understand."

My laughter died at the same time my stomach decided to take a nervous dip.

Hailey didn't notice, because she was doing her best selfie poses in the mirror, contorting her lips into smooches and smiles. "Mom told me not to rely on just the pill and to use condoms, because you know." Her eyebrows rose and she whispered "STDs."

"Huh."

She whirled around and made a face. "She even bought me a box so I've got lots of them if you..." She paused, eyebrows scrunched something fierce. "Am I making you uncomfortable?"

"No."

Yes.

But I didn't know why I was uncomfortable. It's not as if Hales and I hadn't discussed sex before or talked about boys and all the stuff you could do with them. Even when she actually started doing the things we talked about, I was okay with it. I wasn't a prude. I didn't judge.

Maybe sometimes I hid behind the whole "pastor's daughter" thing. It was a good way to keep guys away when I wanted to, but the plain truth was that I just hadn't met the right guy. Jason wasn't the right guy.

Maybe that was it. Maybe I was hypersensitive because Trevor was *the one*. Why else would I come here with him? Why else would I be thinking about the things that I was thinking about, namely getting naked with him.

If we did it, would people know? Would I be different? Would they be able to tell? I bet Mrs. Hannigan from church would. She had some weird internal radar when it came to that stuff and was always talking about teens and how wicked they could be. Would she look at me and *just know*? I heard that she wouldn't let her daughter ride a bike because she thought she'd hit a bump or fall and somehow lose her virginity. Can you imagine?

"So," Hailey said. "Let me guess. You lied to your parents and told them you were spending the weekend at my house?"

"Nope." Well, not really.

I pushed past Hailey, and she followed me into the bedroom. A lamp was on near the bed, but it was small and barely cast any light. I guess some people might think it set the mood or something, but I was just glad that it made the bed seem a little smaller. Not so overwhelming.

"Damn, that's a big bed."

I groaned. "Hales."

"I'm just saying. Link's is smaller."

"Do you want to switch rooms?" Yeah. I was now irritated.

"Chill," she said, testing the mattress out with the palms of her hands. She giggled, pushed up and down a few times, in an exaggerated motion. "Good. It doesn't squeak."

"Oh my God, Hailey."

She stepped back. "Just teasing, though you should know the walls in this cottage are paper thin."

"Okay. Got it. Are you leaving?"

"Like, I can hear Brent snoring from here."

I paused. Oh. She was right about that one.

Hailey took a step toward the door and paused. "So what did you tell your parents?"

"Nothing."

She frowned, and I had to marvel at how her one eyebrow rose while the other didn't. "What do you mean nothing?"

"They don't know."

"What do you mean they don't know?"

"Hales, they don't know I'm here."

"But..." She made a weird face and threw her hands into the air. "Okay, don't take this the wrong way, Everly, but in what world does that happen? Not in Everly Jenkins's world. Aren't you going to go, like, straight to hell or something?"

I made a face. "Ha. Ha. Ha. You always throw the religion thing in my face."

"I'm being serious. Since when do you pull a stunt like this?"

Did I want to get into it? No. But I knew Hailey wouldn't leave it alone, so I decided to give her a little recap. "Mom and Isaac went to New England. He's going to camp and then joining her at my uncle's for a few weeks. My dad thinks that I went with them."

"So he has no idea at all that you're here? You didn't leave him a note or anything? Like he thinks you're in another state with your mom?"

I shrugged. "I don't know what he thinks. I haven't seen him yet."

"Wow. If anyone else had the balls to do this, I'd say that I was impressed." She took a step toward me. "But Everly. This isn't you. It's not even me. I tell my mom everything. What's going on?" Hailey knew me better than anyone, and I knew that she was concerned. I saw it in her eyes. "Look, I'll be the first to admit that Link's taken up a lot of my time. But you would tell me if something was up, right?"

"Hailey. Stop. It's okay."

"But it's not. You've been weird for weeks, and I guess I was just hoping you'd come around. You used to tell me everything."

Man, I so didn't want to do this.

"Hailey. I'm good."

She didn't believe me.

"Trevor isn't, like, making you do something you don't want to do, is he?"

"No! God no."

"Well? Are you going to tell me what the problem is? Because I know something is going on."

"Nothing. Everything." I sighed. "I don't know. I didn't want to go with my mom, and I really didn't want to stay home with Dad so...I just sort of ended up here."

"That's it?" she asked. I could tell by the tone of her voice she wasn't going to let this go, but a soft knock sounded behind me, and we both turned as Trevor walked into the room.

"Do you guys need a minute?" he asked, his arms above his head. The edge of his T-shirt lifted, exposing enough taut skin to get those butterflies dive-bombing again.

"Yes," Hailey said.

"No," I replied at the same time.

"Okay, so what am I doing?" Trevor asked, eyes moving from Hailey to me.

Hales sighed. "You're gonna tell me, right? Eventually?"

I nodded, afraid to talk because my throat was so tight.

She glanced at Trevor. "I think we're good. I'm heading to bed." She gave me a quick hug and whispered. "I love you, idiot girl. And I'm here for you when you're ready to talk, okay? Be careful."

And then I was alone with Trevor.

He closed the door and shoved his hands into the front pockets of his shorts before turning to me, and that was it. I was done. The guy took my breath away. With his amazing eyes, that slow crooked smile, and that five o'clock stubble on his chin, he was all kinds of intensely yummy. And the hair…man, I wanted to run my fingers through those thick waves.

"So," he said, moving forward. "Tinker Bell?"

The ends of his hair were damp as if he'd just had a shower. "What?" Man, I sounded like a dork. A dork who was running out of breath, because seriously, it was as if he was sucking up all the air, leaving me weak and helpless. I stared at the pulse that beat at his neck. It was beating fast. As fast as mine, and that made me feel a little better. His index finger slipped under the strap of my tank top, and I think that maybe the floor moved beneath my feet. Not kidding.

"Your pajamas. Tinker Bell."

"Oh," I managed to say. He was so warm and he smelled so nice. "I have a thing for…ah, Peter Pan, and you know…"

But he'd moved on, and I inhaled sharply as his fingers moved along the top of my shoulder until they found a spot at the base of my skull.

"Tinker Bell, huh?" he asked.

"Yes." I closed my eyes and felt his warm breath along the top of my head.

"I'm more of a Wonder Woman kind of guy, but I'm willing to overlook your Disney addiction."

I attempted a smile but had no idea if it passed muster or not. As it was, I was lucky to be articulate enough to speak. "It's not an addiction. I don't own the Disney princess line of pajamas or anything."

"Good to know," he chuckled and then pulled back. "Are you ready to go to bed?"

I nodded, because I couldn't speak. That big old lump was back, clogging my throat. I'd never shared a bed with anyone other than Hailey. Like ever. And here I was, alone with Trevor Lewis and an Olympic-sized mattress.

He tugged off his T-shirt, tossed it, and then his eyes were on me, a wicked glint in them as his fingers went for the zipper on his shorts. I scrambled for the bed, pulling back the covers so I could climb inside, but snuck a quick peek just to make sure he wasn't, I don't know, naked or anything.

He wasn't naked, but he may as well have been. He wore a pair of black boxers, but not the kind that I was used to seeing in my house. Nope. His were the kind that athletes or actors or hot guys wore. They were the tight kind, the kind that showed off a very male and very well put together body.

Oh. My. God.

I turned on my side and felt him slide in behind me. He moved around a bit, punched his pillow, and then…

I held my breath, not wanting to breathe. Not knowing what to do.

Because then his arms were around me, and he pulled me in as close as two people could be. His hands were warm, just below my breasts, and his mouth was near my ear.

I'm pretty sure my heart was beating so fast and hard that he could not only feel it but hear it too.

"So you know," he murmured, "I should probably warn you that I'm the king of cuddling."

"Cuddling?" I managed to say without sounding like too much of an idiot.

"Cuddling," he repeated. "King."

"Okay," I whispered, not really sure where he was going with this, but I relaxed a bit.

"Nice?" he murmured, snuggling closer.

Nice? He felt amazing. His body was hard and lean and so different from mine.

"Yes."

A heartbeat passed, and then I asked a question that had been buzzing around my brain since we got here.

"Can I ask you something?" I whispered.

"Anything."

"Have you brought other girls here?"

Trevor was silent for a few moments, and when he spoke, I felt his warm breath on my skin. "Not a lot or anything, but Bailey's been here a few times."

"In this bed?" Oh. My. God. Like where else would they be?

Again a pause.

"Yeah."

"And you guys…" I don't know why, but suddenly tears poked the corners of my eyes. Hot, prickly tears. How inconvenient. "Never mind."

"Hey," he said, voice low. "It's okay. I'm not hiding anything from you. I'll tell you anything that you want to know."

"I just…I've never…and you have and I don't know if I can…" Ugh. I was making a mess of this.

He kissed my cheek and rested his head on my shoulder. "I don't mind going slow, Everly. I don't mind at all."

When I could speak again, I whispered, "Thank you."

"You're worth waiting for."

The tears, oh those stupid, silly tears, fell silently down my cheeks, and it took everything I had not to sniffle or shudder or let him know how affected I was by him. By the way he was with me.

Trevor Lewis had just knocked my world off its axis. He was the river.

And boy, I was glad that I jumped.

Chapter Twenty-one
Trevor

Our plans to spend the day out on the Tickfaw were ruined by a couple of things. First off, no one dragged their butts out of bed until nearly one o'clock in the afternoon. And well, the rain. It was coming down in buckets, and I'm not talking about a nice, soft, summer rain. This was a full on Louisiana sorry-about-your-luck kind of rain.

Whatever. Didn't bother me at all. I could have spent the entire weekend in bed with Everly. Even if all we did was cuddle, because the girl was soft and warm and she smelled amazing.

Also. *Everly*. Nuff said.

If it weren't for the other three people in the cottage, we might have, but Brent was a total douche and kept banging on our door, making inappropriate noises, the kind that made Everly's cheeks go rosy and adorable. After the fourth or fifth time, we realized he wasn't giving up. The guy couldn't help it. He'd always been a bit of a dick.

And apparently he wasn't staying either. Said the rain was

depressing as hell and that hanging out with two couples was even worse. I knew he was not digging the fact that Link and I weren't interested in getting loaded with him, and drinking seemed to be the only thing he liked to do these days.

After he ate a crap ton of eggs, he packed his stuff and took off for home. Said he'd catch up with us later, but I wasn't so sure I'd see him before he left for Texas again. The guy was different. But then again, I guess we all were.

So, the way I saw it, Everly and I had a couple of choices.

We could stay in the cottage, maybe play cards (strip poker? not likely), and cuddle on the sofa while Link and Hailey disappeared into the other bedroom. And in the space of two hours, they'd disappeared at least three times.

Or we could head to Baton Rouge on our own.

We opted for Baton Rouge, because the thought of trying to act like we *didn't* know what Hailey and Link were doing, while we kept busy doing *everything but* what Hailey and Link were doing, kind of sucked. We were taking it slow, and I was cool with that, but still, the cottage had paper-thin walls and our roommates weren't exactly quiet.

Everly drove and I tried to ignore the tic behind my right eye and the dull headache that wouldn't seem to go away. Wasn't hard to do. She looked hot in a dress that showed just enough leg to get a guy thinking. Tight jeans or short shorts were great, but there was something about a girl wearing a dress that I liked.

By the time we reached Baton Rouge the rain had stopped,

and we decided to eat dinner at an outdoor place on Front Street. It was family owned, and according to my parents, had the best Creole and Cajun food in the city, which is why I suggested it. Turns out Everly had never been to Baton Rouge.

After digging into a plate full of crawfish-stuffed beignets, I had to agree. The food was top-shelf, and the company, well, I could have stared into Everly's eyes all night. I know. I was the guy in the chick flick. Sue me.

"What?" I asked, wiping the corner of my mouth as I settled back in my chair.

Everly shrugged and twirled the straw in her glass of soda, that slow smile creeping over her face. The one that made my stomach tighten. The one that made me think about lying in bed with her the night before.

"You sure can eat a lot," she said softly.

"I'm a growing guy." I laughed. "With a big appetite." There it was. The blush I'd been waiting for.

"Good to know." She tucked a loose piece of hair behind her ear. "I, uh," she said slowly, so slowly that her slight southern drawl was accented. "I'm just happy to be here with you. Away from Twin Oaks and everything."

"Ditto."

She smiled then, a full-on one-hundred-watt smile, and man, it felt like I'd just won the lottery. It was amazing that a smile could do that.

"Do you think this is weird?" she asked suddenly.

"Weird?" I wasn't sure where she was going with this, and damn, but my head was starting to throb again.

"Us. I mean, I just didn't think that we'd…that you and I…I'm…" Her cheeks flushed again and she blew that piece of hair back. It was humid and kept curling onto her face.

"You're?" I reached over and tucked that piece of hair back where it belonged. I heard her breath catch. It was a soft sound, but it hit me hard, and I leaned back in my chair again, heart racing in that way that's part excitement and part, I don't know, fear?

"I'm not like the girls you've dated. I'm not…super outgoing or into big parties or clubs." She made this noise, like she was frustrated. "What do you see in me, Trevor?"

I tossed my napkin. She really didn't get it.

"What do you think I see?" I asked, because I was curious to know what was going on inside her head, even though the conversation had taken a sharp turn toward serious. Not usually my gig, but I *wanted* to know everything about the girl sitting across from me. Any guy looking at her would see someone with big blue eyes and an amazing mouth. He'd see rosy cheeks and hair that hung down her shoulders in dark, shiny ropes. He'd see a beautiful girl.

I saw a beautiful girl.

I wanted to know what was underneath all of that. I wanted to see it. To touch it. I wanted to be the guy she shared everything with. And maybe she was right. Maybe that was weird, considering we'd only been together for a few weeks.

But I also think that you can be with someone forever and not really know them. Not really love the parts that matter. (Did I really just use the word *love*?) A lot of guys get caught up in the physical stuff. I mean, we're guys. We're wired for that shit. Heck, most of the time it's all we think about when we see a girl. Getting laid and moving on to the next good time.

But this was different, and Everly Jenkins had somehow burrowed underneath my skin. She was like an invisible tattoo, and I wanted to show her off to the world.

She took a sip of her soda and exhaled.

"Truth?" she asked. "You really want to know what I think you see?"

"Truth."

"I think you see a girl who might be a bit of a challenge."

"Challenge?" Okay. That wasn't what I'd expected.

"Sure. I live in the perfect house, with the perfect family. God, we even have a white picket fence. Some kids think I'm a snob. Other's think I'm driven to get straight As, to be the best at everything."

"You got straight As?" I was trying to joke, but she didn't take the bait. In fact, her eyes got darker, like she was angry.

"I know what they say about me, Trevor. A lot of guys think it would be cool to nail the pastor's daughter, and a lot more think that *because* I'm a pastor's daughter, I must be a raving sex maniac. So guys are either scared to approach me or they're in my face, and not in a good way."

"Nope."

"What?"

"You're wrong."

I waited a beat, because I needed to get this right. I needed for her to know. It was just hard, making the right words come out sometimes. And that damn tic was getting worse.

"I see *you*, Everly. The real you. The one that no one else gets to see. She's beautiful and she's sad and when she thinks no one can see her, she's kind of broken. I get that."

She blinked, her eyes wide and shiny. "No one has ever said anything like that to me before."

"It's because you've never let them." I scooped up my napkin, fingers nervous now. "Why is that?"

"Why is what?"

"You dated that guy, Jason what's-his-face, for a while, but other than him, I don't remember seeing you around with anyone."

"Trevor, you didn't know I existed until this summer."

"Wrong again. So damn wrong."

She looked surprised at that. "But we've barely talked since grade school."

"Everly. Come on. Twin Oaks is a small town. Everyone knows everyone, and everyone knows everyone's business."

She shook her head. "That's not what I mean. Tell me you didn't think I was a stuck-up snob. Tell me that you weren't dreading spending every day with me at the library. Tell me you didn't think it would be a total drag."

She kinda had me there. "Truth?"

"Absolutely. Truth," she replied.

"You've never been part of my crowd, so I wasn't sure what to expect. And I'm not…" Okay, this was getting personal, but hell, we were in the middle of something that felt big. I had to be honest. "I'm not the guy I used to be. I'm not one hundred percent. Not after the accident, and that's been kind of hard to deal with." I was quiet for a few moments. "I was nervous to be around you because I thought you would think I was just another loser, you know? Some metalhead with scrambled brains and looking at a road leading nowhere. Not even Nathan knows…"

Her hand crept across the table, and she covered my fist. She was warm. And soft.

And when I glanced up, the look in her eyes took my breath away. Like literally. I couldn't breathe.

That's what this girl did to me.

"What doesn't Nathan know?" she asked. It took a bit for me to push away the lump in my throat. For me to be brave enough to share. I don't think I'd ever been this freaked out by a conversation before.

"For as long as I can remember, music has been everything to me, Everly. *Everything*. It kind of defined who I was. Who I want to be. And I'm scared. Nathan's expecting me to come to New York this fall, and I don't think I have what it takes anymore." I looked away, chest tight. "Jesus, I haven't played in front of anyone since our last gig. I'm afraid to, because I screw up. A lot. I forget things. Play the wrong notes, screw up the lyrics. It really sucks to be seventeen and to know that the one thing you're good at, that thing that is your dream, is gone."

"Then maybe you need to find some new ones," she said so softly that it took a moment for her words to sink in.

"But what if I don't want a new one? What if I can't get past this?"

She stared at me for so long that my vision began to blur and that annoying tic in the back of my head began to press in hard.

Everly pushed her chair back and stepped around the table until she was beside me. Until she was kneeling on the floor. Again, this girl surprised me. We were in the middle of a restaurant.

"Then make it work," she said, reaching for me.

I met her halfway, her mouth close to mine. "When you say that, it sounds easy," I murmured.

Her hands were on either side of my face, and I couldn't look anywhere other than into her eyes.

"It kind of is, Trevor. You have two choices. You can accept the way things are without trying to change them, or you can do everything that you have to do to get to where you want to be. Where you're meant to be. It might be a different version of what you wanted, but that's okay. We're kids. We're supposed to adapt." Her mouth grazed mine. "I'll help you," she whispered.

I would have scooped her into my arms and kissed her until I couldn't breathe, but someone cleared their throat and Everly began to giggle. She looked up at the waiter, but I couldn't take my eyes off her. For one perfect moment I saw the girl who completed me.

But then her expression wavered, and she slowly stood up, her eyes on the street behind me.

"Everly?" I followed her gaze, but there were so many people in the street heading down to the river for the fireworks that I wasn't sure who she was looking at.

"Everly?" I asked again, standing up beside her.

"I…I have to go," she said hoarsely.

What?

I barely had time to drop enough cash on the table to cover our bill and follow her out into the crowded street. By then, big fat drops of water were falling from the sky, the kind that splashed back up at you when they hit the ground. Everly was just ahead of me, and when she glanced back, I saw what was inside her. I saw it clear as day.

Hurt. Confusion. And fear.

It was the part of her that was broken, and it made me crazy to know that someone was responsible for it. I glanced at the hundreds of people around us with only one question in my head. Who could it possibly be?

Chapter Twenty-two

Everly

It was raining. Of course it was raining. My whole world was about to freaking explode, and we wouldn't want the sun shining down on that, now would we? Nope. Just doom and gloom.

I wiped at my eyes and tried to see past the gray mist, but it was no use. Where was he?

By the time I reached the opposite side of the street, the crowd had thinned a bit, and I turned in a full circle, eyes darting everywhere, but again I came up with nothing. How can someone vanish like that? He was nowhere. And maybe he'd never been. Maybe I was crazy. Maybe I was like the crazy lady who sat at the park sometimes, talking to ghosts that only she could see.

Maybe I hadn't seen him leaning toward another person. Maybe I hadn't seen his arm around that someone else. Maybe. Maybe. Maybe.

"Hey, Everly. Hold up."

Trevor strode toward me, cutting through the crowd, his

eyes heavy with concern. I saw it there, and it made me more emotional than I already was. This was all so wrong and not the way I'd thought our night would be. Why had we come here?

"Everly, what's wrong?"

I shrugged, a small pathetic sort of thing, but I knew that if I tried to talk, I'd start to cry. Emotional crier. That was me. My throat was so plugged that I knew it would be a big ugly cry too, the kind that you don't want the guy you're hung up on to see.

Trevor's arms slid around my shoulders, and the next thing I knew, my nose was pressed up against his shoulder.

His T-shirt was damp from the rain, but his skin was warm and I felt his heat through the fabric. It felt so good to just be there, in his arms, taking in his warmth and strength. I don't know how long we stood there, the two of us entangled in each other's arms, but I do know that when I finally pulled away, my face was wet and it wasn't from his clothes.

"Can we just walk?" I managed to say.

His hand engulfed mine, and we followed the crowd toward the Mississippi where there were supposed to be fireworks. Fireworks that I'd been looking forward to. Fireworks I no longer cared about.

Where was he?

I craned my neck, eyes searching and searching. I suppose I should have asked myself what I was going to do if I actually ran into him, but at the moment, I wasn't doing the question thing. I was just *doing*. I was reacting.

"Everly."

I was reacting badly, because I knew that I was going to cry again. Dammit.

"Hey." Trevor's hand was underneath my chin. "What's going on? Why is the sad girl back? What happened?"

I stared up into eyes that I could lose myself in. Eyes that made me believe I could finally unload some of the burden. Did I do it? Did I trust Trevor with my secret? I exhaled and lowered my gaze, staring at the stubble on his chin. It was easier than the eyes. So much easier.

And eventually my heart slowed enough for me to speak.

"There's been stuff going on at home." My eyes squeezed shut on their own, and I saw it again. The back of his head. The way he tilted to the left when he was listening. His familiar shoulders. His favorite blue shirt.

All the pain and anger and disappointment that had filled me for the last year threatened to come crashing down like tidal waves slamming against the rocks. It was big and painful and raw, and I knew that if I let it take over, I would break down completely. Right here in Baton Rouge on the Fourth of July.

Awesome.

So I fought it. I fought it with every scrap of strength that I had, and finally I managed to get some more words out, but none of them made any sense.

"Things with my parents. I heard a phone call. My mom, she took pills, and my dad is lying to all of us." Trevor squeezed my hand but remained silent. "I thought I saw him here with someone." My voice faded to almost a whisper. "Someone who isn't my mom, because my mom's in another state, visiting my uncle."

We were just inside the alley, so the noise from the street was muted a bit, but my heart was still pounding so hard that it didn't matter. Everything was loud and noisy. Everything hurt. My heart hurt.

"Maybe it wasn't him," Trevor finally said, sliding his arms around me again. "Everly, there's, like, thousands of people here. You might have seen someone who looks like your dad."

Doubt crashed in hard. Maybe Trevor was right. Dad was always going to New Orleans, not Baton Rouge. Maybe I was just seeing things because I wanted to see them. Broadcasting or whatever they called it.

"Can we just keep walking?" I asked.

"Sure." Trevor's hand slid back to mine. "Whatever you want."

We continued down the street and eventually ended up near the banks of the Mississippi. I kept glancing around, my eyes constantly searching, but I didn't see my father. Was I relieved? Kind of. Disappointed? Not sure. Probably a bit of both.

"Hey, we don't have to stay for the fireworks," Trevor said. "It's your call."

"What do you want to do?"

He smiled and kissed my cheek. "I want to do whatever is going to make sad girl go away."

Trevor moved so that he was in front of me. His hand still held mine, and I glanced down, reading the tattoo along his knuckle. *Strength.* That's what he'd said the symbols meant. Or was it…

I ran my thumb across his skin. "Which one is this?"

"Courage," he answered.

Courage.

I traced the symbols on his other hand. *Strength.*

"I want to get a tattoo," I blurted.

"What?" He was smiling now. "You're crazy. You don't just get a tattoo. I mean, I guess some people do, but ink is personal. Ink means something, you know?"

"So you don't think I'm cool enough to get a tattoo?" I don't know if I was annoyed or hurt, but I was something.

"I think that a tattoo on any part of your body would be very, very cool." His hand grazed my shoulder and then up along my neck. "Like right here," he murmured following his fingers with his mouth. "But it needs to be right. It needs to be you, and well, until you turn eighteen, you'd need your parents' permission anyway."

Oh. Right. Downer.

"Do you want to go back to the cottage?" I asked. The rain had stopped, but still, I was done with this place. Done with Baton Rouge. The only place I wanted to be right now was with Trevor back at the cottage, preferably under the covers.

"Like I said, I'm up for whatever you want to do." His tone

was teasing, but the look in his eyes was anything but. The look in his eyes told me that he was as affected by this connection that we had as I was.

I thought of his tattoos. Strength. Courage.

Maybe it was time for me to stop living a life that was a lie. To have the courage to stop hiding behind the secrets and sins of my parents and worrying about what everyone else thought. Maybe it was time for me to just be me and to let myself experience the things that I wanted to experience without any of the guilt. Without trying to be someone other than me.

I wanted to be with Trevor. I wanted to kiss him and touch him and see him. I wanted to experience all of him.

Could he see that in my eyes? Did he know?

"Let's go," I said before he could change his mind, or maybe it was more like before I lost the courage that I'd just gained and changed mine. I tugged on his hand, but instead of following me, he kind of stumbled to the left.

"Shit," he said roughly. "Hold on."

He looked up at me, and I knew that something was really, really wrong. "Trevor?"

But he was shaking his head, and oh God, his eyes were wonky. I was scared out of my mind, so I couldn't imagine what he was feeling.

"Trevor!"

He bent over, hands on his knees, and the fear in my gut shot up so fast and so hard that I thought I was going to be sick.

The crowd around us suddenly moved back, like they knew something was about to happen. Like there was a disease among them and they didn't want to touch it.

He glanced up one more time, and I barely managed to grab him before he pitched forward. He half landed on me and the wet muddy grass, but I had him. *I had him.* His body was shaking, his hands twisted, and I shouted for someone to call 911. I tried to remember what Mrs. Henney had done in the library.

Nothing. She'd done nothing.

So I did the only thing that I could do. I held him and tried not to cry, pushing his hair out of his face and trying to protect him from the crowd that had gathered. I didn't want them to see. Didn't want them to be anywhere near him.

I kept shouting "move back" until my voice was hoarse, and then someone shouted that the EMTs were on their way. Okay. I could do this. I could hold on until they got here. But it seemed that the minutes were hours, and when I felt a hand on my shoulder, I wrenched back, ready to fight or I don't know, do something, but it was a uniform.

They were asking questions, and some of them I knew, others I didn't. I told them about Trevor's brain injury and the seizure he'd had a few weeks earlier. They asked about medication, and I thought of the small bottle I'd seen at the cottage, but again I wasn't sure. They wanted to know where we were from and where his parents were, what his blood type was, his age, any other pertinent medical history.

He was a boy I liked. A boy I thought that maybe I was falling in love with. I knew that and not much else. Pretty pathetic.

And then they said they were taking him to the hospital.

By this time Trevor was coming out of it, but nothing he said made any sense, and that terrified me. Alone and afraid, I scooped my cell from my purse and hit the first saved number.

When he picked up on the second ring, I could barely speak. My teeth were chattering, and I was shivering so badly that I nearly dropped my cell. "Dad, are you in Baton Rouge?"

There was a long pause, and by this time I was crying again. I was crying so hard that I could barely see, and I scrubbed at my face, tearing hair from my eyes as I tried to keep up with the EMTs.

"Everly, are you okay? Where's your mother?"

But I wasn't okay. I was so far from okay that I didn't think I'd ever find my way back. "No, no, I'm not. I'm in Baton Rouge, and I need you."

"Calm down." He didn't hesitate, and his warmth crept through the phone. "Tell me exactly where you are, sweets. Everything is going to be all right."

"I'm down near the river, by the Buffalo Bakery. They're taking Trevor to the hospital, but I can't ride in the ambulance and I don't think I can drive and I think he just had another seizure and I don't…I don't know what to do."

"I'm less than a minute away, Everly. Hold on."

And he was. His warm arms were around me, and he gathered

me in close, murmuring things I couldn't really understand. By this time I was nearly incoherent, so I didn't take the time to ask the questions. Or wonder about the fact that I spied Kirk Davies, his old college friend, watching us from a few feet away.

I would wonder about them, but those things could come later.

Chapter Twenty-three

Trevor

I woke up in a hospital. I knew this for a couple of reasons.

First, the smell. It's horrid as hell, and no matter what hospital you're in, it's the same. It's a smell of death and sickness and puke, and the heavy disinfectants they use to try and cover it all up just makes it worse.

Second, I heard my mom crying. Well, I heard my mom sniffling like she was trying to hide the fact that she was crying, which was almost worse than just getting it all out. I guess she thought that the softer her cries were, the better it was for me, but honestly, the fact that she was there at all made me feel like crap.

Also? My mouth was dry and I would just about kill for an ice chip.

I lay there for a few moments, not opening my eyes, wanting those few seconds to get my thoughts straight in my head. I wish that I could say I remembered what happened. But I don't. I don't remember a damn thing other than a pain in my head and...and Everly.

I must have groaned or made some other pathetic noise, because the sniffling stopped and then my mom was there, hovering over me like she used to do back in the day. Back when I was somewhere in that place between life and death.

I used to hate that. Waking up and seeing her there. Knowing it was all my fault, and right now, I felt exactly the same. God, she must be sick of this, because I sure as hell was.

"Trevor?"

I tried to sit up, but her hands were on my chest and she was smoothing hair from my face. "Water?"

She knew the drill, but then I guess there're some things you can't forget no matter how much you try. She grabbed a cup from beside the bed, unwrapped a straw, and once I was elevated a bit, held the cup in front of me like I was a baby with no idea how to hold the stupid thing.

But I wasn't a baby. I was a pissed-off seventeen-year-old, so I acted like one. I grabbed the cup from her and managed to spill half of the damn thing before I got it to my mouth.

"Be careful," she said.

Once my throat was lubricated, I decided to try and speak. This was always a bit tricky, because I wasn't so sure that what came out of my mouth would even make sense. But I had to try. I had to know.

"Where's Everly?"

My voice sounded rough, but I got the right words out. Another win for the pathetic Trevor Lewis.

"She's outside with her father." My mom's bottom lip started to tremble. "Thank God she was there when it happened."

Yeah. Awesome that she got to see that.

"We're in Baton Rouge, at the hospital." She was fussing with the blankets. "Daddy and I came as soon as Everly called, and Taylor, she's here too."

My head still felt fuzzy, my eyes were sore, and my tongue felt like it was ten times too big for my mouth. I was pretty damn sure I looked like hell, and I found myself reaching for my hair, just to be sure, because after my initial prolonged hospital stay, I had nightmares in which some big-ass orderly shaved my head and kept all my hair.

"It's nearly three in the morning, but the doctor says if things look good, we can take you home after he checks on you. About eight, I think. He says the seizure happened because your medication needs to be altered, so once that's fixed, you'll be good as new."

I felt like laughing, because really, that was a joke. Good as new was the old Trevor. The one without a TBI. But I didn't want to think about that, because it was just depressing as hell.

"Can Everly I see?" I asked instead.

My mom kind of pursed her lips, like she wanted to say no, but then her eyes softened a bit and she nodded. "I'll get her, but you need to take it easy, okay?"

I nodded, and that was exhausting. God, it felt as if I'd been to football practice ten times over, and I was the douche who got tackled every single play.

Man, I hated hospitals. I thought the day I walked out of Twin Oaks Memorial, I'd never be back. Pretty naïve of me, I know, but still. A guy can only hope. What a joke to find out that all the hard work I'd done over the last year had been for nothing. I was defective, and it looked like I would always be defective. Trevor Lewis. Freak of nature.

"Hey."

Her voice was soft, and there was a bit of tremble in there. I sat up straighter and tried to crack a smile, but I'm sure it came off as more of a lopsided grimace.

"Bet you never thought you'd see me in a dress," I said, voice hoarse and not really sounding like me at all. Man, if I looked as bad as I sounded, she should be running away as fast and as far as she could.

But she didn't, and I felt something like hope flare inside me.

Everly's eyes were huge and her skin was pale and her dress, that hot little dress she'd worn to dinner, was covered in mud. She crossed the room and sat on the bed beside me, a smile on her face that didn't quite reach her eyes. She looked tired and sad and so damn beautiful that it made me crazy. I wanted to grab her up and hold her. I wanted to touch her hair and smell that spot at the base of her neck. I wanted to kiss her until she made that sexy little sound at the back of her throat.

I wanted to do it all, and yet I did nothing.

"You kind of rock a dress," she said. "Especially a pink one."

I glanced down. Wow. The shame just wouldn't go away.

"Good to know," I managed to say. "I'll make sure and wear one the next time...we are, uh...together." What the hell was I doing? Where was I going with this? What girl in her right mind would want to hang out with a dude whose brain wasn't quite right and who'd had two seizures in the space of a few weeks?

She reached for my hand and brought it up to her face. "I just might hold you to that, Trevor Lewis."

I shook my head. She was so soft and warm and perfect. "Why are you still here? I don't get it."

"You don't have to get it, because it doesn't really matter now, does it? I'm here because I want to be. I'm here because I care about you." She leaned close and kissed the corner of my mouth. "Trevor, I'm here because you're here. Where else would I be?"

I rested my forehead against hers, mostly because I was wiped out, but damn, the girl felt good.

"Oh, man. Even here you're sucking face? Jesus, Trevor, is that all you think about?"

I glanced around Everly and spied my sister Taylor standing at the end of my bed. She must have been crying, because she looked like a raccoon with her Goth eyes and smudged liner. But her attitude, it was all there, and I was kind of glad to hear it. That was normal. She was normal.

"What else is there to think about?" I joked.

Everly fake-punched me.

"Hey," I said. "Next time you do that, I'll have to think up some form of punishment."

"That is, like, the lamest line ever." Taylor was now sitting on the other side of the bed, inches from me and Everly.

And Everly was smiling. "Yeah, but it just might work."

"Not surprised," Taylor said slowly. And then she pinned me with a look that wasn't easy or light. It was all Taylor and all 115 pounds of attitude. "If you ever do that again, I will hunt you down and kick your effing ass."

"Language, Taylor."

"Whatever, butthead."

Taylor got up. "Your dad says that you have to go, Everly."

Everly's eyes were on me when she whispered, "Okay. Can I have one more minute with him?"

When the door closed behind Taylor, Everly collapsed on the bed, curling up against me. It felt amazing to have her there, even though I was tired as hell and hating everything about where I was.

"Are you okay?" I asked.

"He was there," she said softly. "In Baton Rouge. I called him when you fell. When the paramedics came. I was just so scared, like I was frozen or something, and it was automatic, you know? I just…wanted my dad."

A heartbeat passed.

"But now…"

I hugged her. She was delicate and small, and I hated that sad girl was back. Hated that I couldn't make things okay for her.

"Now I have to go home with him, and I don't want to,

because after all this time, there's no more hiding, and I know it's crazy, but I'm not ready. I thought I was, but I'm not." She blew out a ragged breath. "He knows that I know. He wants to talk."

"But isn't that what you want? No more lies?"

"I thought so, but right now, I'm more scared of the truth than I am of being angry at his lies, and I wish…I wish that I never called him. All I wanted was the truth, for him to stop lying to all of us, but now…now I don't know what I want. I'm afraid of the truth. How screwed up is that?"

"It's not screwed up. It's just real. It's how you feel."

"I have to go, Trevor," she whispered.

"I know."

"Call me when you get home tomorrow?"

I nodded. "First list on my thing."

She bent over and pressed one last kiss on my mouth. "Okay," she breathed against me.

And then she was gone.

It took all of two seconds before my words went around my brain again. I thought about how her eyes got all shiny and how she'd smiled at me in a way I recognized. Because it was the same way my mom smiled at me when she didn't know what else to do or say.

The thing is the part of my brain that controls anger got damaged in the accident, and right now, I needed some kind of control, but that wasn't happening. I could feel this wall of emotion sliding over me like a hot, wet cloth, running from the top of my head all the way down my body. I clenched my hands into fists and slammed my head back onto the pillow, because I knew it was going to be bad. And then I pretty much lost it.

Chapter Twenty-four
Everly

We drove home in silence, the two of us acting as if everything was fine, as if we were strangers sharing a ride home. As if the last twelve hours hadn't happened. As if the last year hadn't happened.

I should be so lucky, I thought.

For miles I watched the road, that anger that had been buried inside me growing as fast as the weeds in Mr. Harrison's backyard. It got so big that my hands shook because I couldn't keep it contained.

But I wasn't ready. Not yet. So I gritted my teeth and squeezed my eyes shut, as if not seeing him would help. What a joke. Nothing helped, and nothing would ever be the same again.

By the time we rolled into our driveway, the sun was peeking up over the trees behind out house, and our five a.m. sprinklers were up and at 'em. Dad pulled his car as close to the garage as he could and cut the engine. Some country song was playing on the radio, and just as the guy was about to belt out the line about his cheating wife, the song was gone.

Kind of ironic, if you ask me.

And there it was. The big silence that I'd been dreading since we left the hospital. This silence was different from the one that had followed us back from Baton Rouge. This silence was full of heavy, dark things that would hurt, and as angry as I was with him, I just couldn't do it. At least not right now.

Maybe it was because I needed to believe that my father wasn't about to rip our family apart, at least for a little while longer. Or maybe it was because I was just too tired.

He cleared his throat, so I knew that I had maybe two seconds.

"I'm not doing this with you right now," I said, opening the door and practically throwing myself out of the car. Like literally. If not for my dress catching on the edge of the door panel, I would have fallen on my butt. As it was, the seam split, but I didn't care. I just wanted to get away from him.

"Get some sleep, Everly, and we'll talk after I get back from service."

The tears were already starting, so I didn't look back. I ran across the wet grass and up the steps of the porch and didn't stop until I fell into bed. Until I grabbed my pillow close and let everything out. And there was a lot to get out.

I cried for Trevor, because I knew he was freaking out. I cried for the fear and pain I'd seen in his parents' eyes. I cried for my mom and for Isaac, because they had no idea what was coming their way. I even cried for my dad, because no matter how much I thought I hated him, I didn't. *If I hated him, I wouldn't hurt so much.*

But most of all, I cried for myself, because…well, just *because*. I had a year of stuff inside me, and it seemed like the only way to let it out was to soak my pillow with tears. That was hours ago, and my eyes were still puffy. Not even slices of cucumber had been able to make them look better.

I was in my bedroom, fresh out of the shower, and had just dragged on some clothes. My cell buzzed for, like, the twentieth time in the last half an hour. Hales had sent a ton of text messages and left me three voice mails. She was threatening to come over unless I told her what the hell was going on. She knew about Trevor, of course. They'd had to take a cab from the cottage in Springfield all the way to Baton Rouge to grab Link's truck. But she also knew that something big was up, and I loved her for caring enough to threaten me. Even if there was no way she could take me down.

Hales: I will beat the crap out of you unless you spill.
Me: I'd like to see you try. Also I'm fine.
Hales: Okay I won't beat you up, but call me asap. I'm worried.

I heard a car door slam, and my cell slipped from my fingers. I scooped it up and typed a quick reply.

Me: will do. ttyl
Me: have you heard from Trevor?
Hales: Link's here and no. Call me when you can.

I heard our front door close and then my dad's voice calling for me. *This is it*, I thought. My stomach was a mess, and I felt like crap and looked even worse. I pulled my hair up into a tangled ponytail, wiped my palms along the top of my legs, and headed for the stairs.

By the time I got to the bottom, all the anger that I'd bottled up this last year, well, that anger was in me. It was like a living thing, pulsing hard and fast, and I was out of breath by the time I found him.

He was waiting for me in the kitchen, standing just in front of the sink where the sun came in. Figures. He was about to tear my world apart, and yet here he was, bathed in sunlight, like a god or something.

"Do you want a cup of tea?"

"Really? We're going to act like everything is okay? You're going to be that guy?"

He looked shocked, and I guess I shouldn't have been surprised. I'd hardly conversed with him this last year, and when I did, I'd always been polite. Detached but polite. I'm sure he put it all down to teenage female hormones or some other kind of crap, but he wasn't used to this side of me.

God, it was cold. So, so cold. I shivered and shoved my hands into the front pockets of my jeans, wishing I'd grabbed a sweater instead of the thin T-shirt I had on.

Dad stirred his cup but didn't drink, and I thought that maybe he just needed something to keep his hands busy. I had my pockets; he had his cup.

He sighed, this sort of, I don't know, denial kind of sigh, if you can picture what that would sound like, and then he actually looked at me.

"Does your mother know you went to Baton Rouge with Trevor Lewis?"

For a moment I didn't answer, because I was too pissed off that he wanted to talk about me instead of what he'd done. I guess he wanted to ease into the whole thing. Heck, I only had one lie to hide behind. He had hundreds, maybe thousands.

"Nope," I answered.

"That's all you have to say for yourself?"

Okay. That stomach thing was getting pretty bad (I felt like I was going to puke), but the anger inside me was so much stronger, and I didn't care one bit that he saw it.

"You asked the question. I gave you an honest answer." The fact that I stressed the word *honest* wasn't lost on him. He flinched. Score one for Everly.

Dad set his mug on the kitchen table and ran his hands over the top of his head.

"This is serious, Everly."

"Damn right, it's serious."

"Are you and he…well, are the two of you…"

Wow. He was going all in on this one. I considered adding one more lie to my short list, but in the end, I was just too damn tired and emotional to play games.

"I haven't slept with Trevor Lewis, if that's what you're trying to ask me. And even if I had, it's really none of your business. I'm almost eighteen."

I moved to the other side of the kitchen table and leaned my hip against it, going for the calm and composed look, but the real truth was that I needed something between us. Something hard and solid. Because this right now? This conversation felt surreal.

"It was wrong of you to lie to your mother, Everly. Wrong of you to go away with a boy and not tell us. If anything had happened to you…how would we know?"

Okay, this wasn't going at all the way I'd envisioned. Why were we talking about me? Did he think I'd just forget? That I wouldn't ask the questions that were right there, hiding in my head?

I took a moment, a good long moment, and studied the man in front of me. The man who'd always been my rock. My hero. There's something heartbreaking in knowing that the person you've idolized your entire life isn't the Superman you'd always thought him to be. He's not made of steel. He's flesh and blood, and his Kryptonite is his humanity.

"Can I ask you a question now?" I asked softly, watching him closely.

Dad's eyes got all shiny, the way mine did just before I was about to have one of *those* moments. You know, an ugly one. He dropped his head for a second, as if the stupid mug was going to somehow help him, and then he nodded.

"Sure," he said, his voice so low I barely heard him. I think he knew what I was going to ask before I even opened my mouth.

"Why were you in Baton Rouge with Kirk Davies?"

Kirk Davies. The guy who'd been coming around our home since I could remember. He'd been at my birthday parties, at family gatherings, and he'd even spent a few Christmases with us. He was funny and charming and hot in a CW kind of way. He liked to draw, told funny stories, and had the most beautiful smile that you can imagine. He was my parents' oldest friend, a guy they'd gone to college with, and he was totally, unequivocally, one hundred percent gay.

No one had ever said it out loud, but I knew.

Dad cleared his throat, took his time just like I had, but there was nowhere to run. No place to hide in this kitchen. There was the pantry, the fridge, and the table. There was the heavy silence full of dark and painful things.

There was him and me.

And now, finally, the truth.

"Kirk and I… We were there for the celebrations."

Celebrations. Did he think I was stupid?

"I don't believe you." My heart was beating, fast and hard, but I didn't waver. This was too important. Too hard. But I had to know.

Dad's mouth tightened, and his gaze slid from mine, which spoke volumes to me.

"He lives in New Orleans, doesn't he?" I asked. "Is that why you're there all the time? Is he the reason you go?"

"What is this? I counsel a—"

"You're lying!" Something broke apart inside me. My voice was shrill and loud, and that cliff I'd been standing on forever it seemed, was suddenly right there. My toes were over the edge, and I was going to fall, but I didn't care anymore. "Can you just be honest with me? I know, Dad." My voice broke, and dammit, there were those tears again. *"I know."*

And I did. It was suddenly clear as day to me. His secret.

But my heart wasn't breaking because of what he was going to tell me. It was breaking because I was afraid. Afraid because my family was already cracked, with gaping wounds that couldn't be fixed, and when the dust settled, I wouldn't have him anymore. Not like before. Not like I was supposed to have him.

"This is hard for me, Everly." His voice was shaky, his hands fisted. That place inside me, the small soft spot where my heart was…that place expanded and then constricted so tight that I could barely breathe.

"It's hard for me too," I said hoarsely. "And for Mom."

He made a weird noise when I said that and exhaled a long, shaky breath.

"I've never broken my marriage vows. I want you to know that. Never."

I didn't know what to say to that. I mean, it was so personal, and there was a part of me that couldn't believe I was hearing this stuff.

"But I'm…" He cleared his throat again and leaned onto the table, his hands spread, his long elegant fingers thumping nervously. I swear it was the only thing keeping him on his feet. "Things between your mother and I haven't been good for a long time."

"And that gives you the right to lie to her? To us? For over a year? How is that dealing with a problem?"

"I was trying to protect...to..."

"How is lying protecting your family?" I butted in. "I'm seventeen, and I know that lies only make things worse. Just because it's easier to lie doesn't mean you should do it." My voice was shrill. "You taught me that."

He was silent for a few moments. "No. No, it doesn't, and I'm sorry for that."

"Are you gay?" I blurted before I could stop myself.

"What? No, I..."

But I saw the truth in his eyes.

"You're lying," I shouted. "This right here is going to change my life. Can't you at least be honest with me now? There's no one here but us."

"It's complicated," he said carefully, eyes falling from mine.

But it was enough. I saw a truth that was quickly overshadowed by fear. I got that. Fear could make anyone do stupid things. But this was my life too, and he needed to own his shit. Not bury it.

"Are you gay?" I asked again, moving so that he had to look at me.

I didn't think it was a sin or anything. I mean, I don't think that I did, but staring across the table at my father, I couldn't deny the fact that along with anger, disappointment, and fear, the only other emotion inside me right now was shame.

I loved this man. I hated this man. I was proud of him, and I was ashamed.

How screwed up is that?

Chapter Twenty-five

Trevor

I stared at the acoustic guitar in my room for a good hour before I picked it up. My dad had worked hard to make enough cash to buy it for me on my fifteenth birthday. He'd got it off some old guy out in the swamps, a poor bastard whose talent had been stolen by arthritis. The guitar was battered, beat-up, and used, just like a Gibson should be, and it was worth a small fortune.

I had, like, six guitars, but this one was my favorite. Partly because it was a '56 Gibson, but mostly because my dad gave it to me.

I use to play it all the time, but I hadn't touched it since the accident. Sure, I practiced scale runs on my electric because it was easier. The strings were lighter and the action was low. But that wasn't the only reason I avoided this acoustic. The Gibson reminded me of that night.

The only reason it had survived the accident was because I'd left it behind at the party, too wasted to care about this special thing my dad had given to me. Brent had scooped it up for me. He'd kept it for months, and when I finally came out of the coma, it was the first thing he'd brought to the hospital. I think he thought it would make me feel good, you know, to see it. Touch it even.

But it didn't. Something about the guitar triggered a kind of blackness in me, and truthfully, setting it in the corner of my room was almost like a punishment. Maybe one I deserved. A screw you for the stupid mistake that had landed me right where I was. On a road to nowhere.

I held the guitar in my hands, and it didn't even feel right. Didn't feel like there was anything there. No connection. No passion. There was nothing.

And if that wasn't scary enough, I sat on my bed and played a few chords, but nothing sounded good. Nothing sounded *right*. And that blackness, well, it was still there. Still invading every space inside me, falling into every nook and cranny that made up Trevor Lewis.

I'd just had an epic meltdown, and hiding in my room didn't make me feel any better. Nothing did. I was going to be eighteen, and I knew I was acting like a damn eight-year-old, but I couldn't seem to help it.

We'd been home from Baton Rouge for a few hours, had just finished dinner, and Mom said something about studying and the stupid government test and I just…I lost it. I don't think I've ever seen Taylor speechless. And my dad, man, when he could speak, he told me to disappear because he was this close to hurting me.

He said that, and my mom burst into tears.

I told my mom to go to hell. *My mom.* What the hell is wrong with me? Kind of a rhetorical question, because I know exactly what the deal is.

Epileptic.

Jesus, the sound of the word made me sick, and now it was something tangible. Something real. It was a label I couldn't hide from. Not only was I the stupid bastard who'd scrambled his brains, now I was an epileptic to boot.

Awesome. Great thing to add to my résumé.

Fuck.

I'd started this summer with pretty low expectations, but even I hadn't seen the freak-on-the-floor thing happening.

Someone knocked at my door. I considered saying nothing. Doing nothing. You know, 'cause that was the easy way out. *The immature way out.* Though I guess immature and Trevor were kinda one and the same these days.

The knock sounded again, and I swore, wincing when I stood, 'cause along with everything else, my knee hurt like hell. I considered pulling on a T-shirt but then thought *what was the point?*

It was probably my mom, though I hoped that it was my dad. Hell, I wanted it to be him just as much as I wanted him to kick my ass. Maybe then I'd feel better about things. Maybe then I'd *feel.*

I was nearly there, my hand on the doorknob, when I heard her.

"Trev?"

For a moment I faltered. I wasn't ready to see Everly yet. God, would I ever be? I kept thinking of how stupid I'd sounded in the hospital, messing up my words. And of the shame and embarrassment that wouldn't go away. That's not what a guy wants to feel when he's thinking about his girl. Worse than that even was the thought of that freak on the ground. When I thought of Everly, I pictured myself on the ground, with a bunch of strangers staring at us. How was I ever going to get used to that? Bad enough that it was me on the ground, but even worse for Everly to be there with me. That was pretty hard to take.

"Trevor? I…I really need…to talk."

Huh. Maybe she wanted to break up with me. Maybe she'd finally figured out that I was a lost cause. That I was never getting back to the way I was before. Fired up at the thought, I was motivated to get this over with.

I whipped open the door and…

She fell into my arms, her body shaking and her fingers cold on my back as she dug in and burrowed against my chest. I was kind of shocked and, if I was honest, a little grateful, but mostly a lot confused.

I wasn't allowed to have girls in my room. Not since my mom had caught me feeling up Brooke Smith. I'd been fourteen, and she'd been a year older. It had totally been worth it because, you know, boobs, real live boobs. Still, my mom hadn't shared the joy that a fourteen-year-old boy feels when that first time happens, and she hadn't been real happy to find a braless Brooke in my bed and me in my boxers. So the no-girls-in-my-room rule had been firmly established, and that was one the parents were pretty much in agreement on. You don't want to know how many times I'd been warned about what would happen to me if I made them grandparents before their time.

After the stunt I'd pulled earlier, this had to be pretty damn important for my parents to let Everly in.

"You never called me," she whispered.

I wanted to tuck that stupid piece of hair behind her ear. I wanted to hug her back and smell her shampoo. I wanted to hold her head and kiss her mouth, taste the cherry gloss that she used. God, there was so much I wanted to do, but something held me back. Some invisible force field that said *back the hell off.*

So I did nothing. I said nothing. I just stood there like an idiot (which I sorta was) and listened to her sniffle until there was no more sniffling. Until her body stopped shaking and her fingers were warm.

Finally she pulled away, and I couldn't look at her. It wasn't because I didn't want to see her. I mean, that would be stupid crazy. She was the most gorgeous girl I knew. I just didn't want her to see me.

So I turned around, feeling that familiar spike of anger hit when I spied the Gibson lying across my bed. I stomped across the room, grabbed it up, and placed it back in the corner where it belonged. Where it would stare at me in silence, a reminder of everything I'd lost.

"Are you okay?" Everly asked.

"Never been better." My answer was clipped, but at least I got the words right. Score one for the freak.

God, I was a prick.

I heard her move and knew that she was standing just behind me. When her fingers touched my side, I nearly jumped out of my skin. But I stayed still, hands fisted at my sides, anger churning for no reason. It just churned and burned and made me crazy.

"How did you get this scar?" If I was paying attention, I would have known that her voice was scratchy and used up. It was sore and painful. But I was so focused on me that all I thought about was getting her out of my room so that I could wallow in my own private pity party.

"I got it jumping from the dam. Jumped in the river just behind Nate and got snagged against a tree that was under the water."

"Must have needed a lot of stitches."

"Thirteen."

"Oh."

Her hand was still there, running up and down the scar, and a sudden urge to rip her hand away from me had me breathing heavy and clenching my teeth together so tightly my jaw ached.

"What do you want, Everly?" I sounded like a cold bastard.

I think she must have been shocked, because she made this sharp sound, like a gasp or something. The weird thing was I kept hearing a voice in my head, a voice that sounded like it was under water. It kept repeating, *do it, do it, do it,* over and over again.

Do what?

I felt the tic behind my right eye, and the band of pain that circled my head throbbed so hard that I wrenched away from her and took a few steps. I didn't want to hurt her, but I sure as hell wanted to hurt something.

I couldn't explain any of this. The thoughts in my head. The pain in my chest. It was just a big jumbled mess of stuff, and I didn't want to deal with any of it anymore.

"I wanted to make sure you were okay. I wanted to see you and I wanted to…" Her voice broke. "I wanted to talk."

"That's a joke," I muttered.

"What?" Her hand was on my arm.

"Let go of me, Everly."

"What's going on, Trevor?" Her hand fell away, but she didn't back off. She moved a few inches so that I had no place else to look but at her. I thought I looked like hell? She looked like she'd been to hell and back.

Her hair looked like she hadn't brushed it for days, and her eyes looked bruised and overly glassy. If I didn't know her better, I'd think she was high. Her cheeks were pale and her lips even paler.

"Why are you being like this?" she asked.

I shrugged. "I just can't do this. I mean, what's the point?"

"What's the point?" Her voice was loud, and little spots of red appeared in her cheeks. "What's the *point*?" she repeated even louder. She pushed me, both hands to my chest, and I rocked back on my feet, which considering she was so small told me that the girl was pissed.

"The point is that I need to know you're okay. The point is that I care about you. The point is that I've been worried all day because you didn't think to call me. *That's* the point." Her voice broke and she took a step back, but the back of her knee met the edge of my bed and she fell onto it, barely managing to keep herself up. Her hair fell out of her ponytail and covered half of her face. Angrily, she yanked it back and glared up at me. "The point is that I needed you and I thought that you cared enough to be there for me, but I guess I was wrong." She bit her bottom lip, and I could tell she was on the verge of tears.

I've done some shit things before, but this here, this stupid roller coaster that I couldn't seem to get off, this had to be the worst. I'd hurt her, and I couldn't figure out how to make it better.

"God, you haven't even asked about my father. About what happened, and you know how much…" She blinked her eyelids fast, as if trying hard not to fall apart. "Trevor, you knew that I was freaking out over that."

I wanted to say something to make her feel better. I really

did. But I couldn't find the words. I had nothing. I was nothing. Couldn't she see that? Why was she pushing so hard?

She jumped to her feet. "What the hell is wrong with you?"

The fact that Everly Jenkins had just cursed me should have told me that she was walking that tightrope. And that maybe she was going to fall. But I didn't pay attention to that because I had other stuff going on.

I don't know what it was. The tone of her voice. The actual words that she used. Or the image of me on the ground twisted up and helpless while all around us, a bunch of strangers watched me. That was an image burned into my brain, and when I closed my eyes, it was all I saw.

Whatever it was, something dark lit up inside me, and finally I found my voice.

"You want to know what's wrong with me? Have you got all night? Because I've got to tell you, Everly, the list is impressive."

She flinched, like I'd slapped her or something, but I kept on because now that I'd found my voice, there was no stopping me.

"Let's see, I can't drive anymore. You know, because of the whole epileptic thing. I doubt I'll pass the stupid government test, which means I'm stuck here for a lot longer than I want to be, and that sucks more than you know. Um, I have trouble sleeping, my head hurts, and well, as you've seen more than once or twice, my vocabulary isn't always stellar."

"I don't…just shut up," she said.

"You started this, Everly. You came here. You need to know that I can't handle my shit and deal with your crap too."

"I can't believe you just said that."

"Yeah, well, believe it. I'm a dick. I know it, and now you know it, and I think that whatever this is that we have is done."

"You're breaking up with me?"

The dark fire, it just got hotter and hotter. I let it spread, and being the bastard that I am, I kind of enjoyed the feel of it.

"Were we an official couple? I guess I missed the memo on that one. Jesus, Everly. We made out a few times and went to a cottage. That's about it."

The hurt in her eyes was something I'd never forget, and I don't think it was possible for me to feel any more like the stupid bastard that I was. But being a stupid bastard was easier than letting her see the real me. She didn't know it yet, but I was doing her a favor.

"You're an asshole."

"Been told that before, so now that you know, it makes things easier, doesn't it?"

For a few moments she said nothing. I was already coming down from wherever the hell I'd been and feeling sick to my stomach. My head hurt. My body hurt, and my *heart* hurt.

"I can't believe that after everything," she whispered, and her voice broke, "after Baton Rouge, you can be like this." She wiped at her eyes. "What did I do?"

I needed to make her understand.

"You didn't do anything. It's not you, Everly. It's me. It will always be me. Don't you get it?"

She sniffled. Wiped the back of her hand across her damp cheeks. "No," she said hoarsely. "No, I don't get it." She paused for a moment, her eyes dark. "I would have been there for you. I would have done whatever you wanted. Been whatever you needed me to be."

"Yeah, well, I don't need you," I said.

Liar.

Everly moved toward the door. "That's too bad, Trevor." Her voice shook. She opened it and paused. "Because I need you."

And then she was gone.

Even though I wanted to run after her, to scoop her up and hug her and to be there for her, I didn't. I sat on my bed and stared at the floor until darkness fell. Until my dad came into my room and sat down beside me.

He didn't say anything for the longest time. He didn't give me shit for the stunt I'd pulled at dinner or ask about Everly. He just sat with me, his massive shoulders touching mine, his beefy hands folded together on his lap. And when I couldn't take it anymore, I broke the silence.

"I screwed up."

A pause.

"I know."

"Like I think I just lost everything that matters." I thought of Nate and our plans. Of my guitar that had been silent for months. I thought of Everly and the hurt in her eyes and the fact that I didn't think I could fix her, or me for that matter. I felt something hot prick the corner of my eyes.

I scrubbed my face and tried to hold it back, but when my dad's arms crept around me, I couldn't stop that thing inside me. The one that was hot and heavy and full of pain. My dad pulled me in close, just like he used to do when I was a kid, and I cried like a baby. Me. Trevor Lewis.

The weird thing was? It felt so damn good to let everything out. To let my dad take away some of my pain. And as I squeezed my eyes shut, I heard a voice in my head, and the words made my insides twist even more.

Who was taking away Everly's pain?

Chapter Twenty-six

Everly

Two weeks passed, and my life, such as it was, returned to some kind of normal. I emailed Trevor a bunch of notes I had on government. I sent him links that I thought he should check out. I even went so far as to send him a practice test *and* I cc'd his mom as well. (I'm sure he loved that one, but whatever.)

I did all the things that I thought I needed to do, or at least the things I thought I *should* do. Trevor Lewis might have hurt me, but that didn't mean I had to let him know it. It was bad enough that I'd gone to his house. Even now, my cheeks burned when I thought of how his mom had looked at me when I came running out of his room, trying to keep from crying.

She'd taken one look at me and threw her arms around me like I was hers. She'd stroked my hair and told me that I needed to go slow with Trevor. He had issues to work through. His brain injury. His seizure. It was a lot, and he hurt people without meaning to.

After a few moments I pulled away, and I told her that everyone had stuff to deal with. Everyone had scars that didn't show.

She'd asked me if I was going to keep working with him, and I said that I didn't think so. I was being honest, and I could tell it wasn't the answer she'd hoped to hear.

That was the last time I saw Mrs. Lewis.

A few days ago, I'd gotten an email from Trevor, but it was obviously an accident since there wasn't anything in it. No "hello," no "hey, I miss you, how are things?" There was nothing. And yet I couldn't help but wonder, had he been thinking of me? Did I care? Stupid question, that, because I cared a lot. Pathetic, I know.

When I was alone at night, huddled beneath the covers, I cared a whole lot. I'd cried so many tears over the past few weeks that I swear my tear ducts were in danger of malfunctioning. I mean, if that was possible.

Trevor had pretty much broken my heart, and my dad had definitely broken my faith, but at least he and I were working on it. Not that it was a slam dunk or anything. Not even close. There'd been days when I couldn't even look at him because of all the things I didn't understand. Like, how could he love my mother and have feelings for someone else? It didn't matter that it was a guy. What mattered was that he'd made a commitment to my mom. A promise. And he'd broken it.

He'd broken it, and he'd been dishonest about the whole thing. That right there had me all kinds of twisted up inside. To me, honesty equals love and respect. So what did that say about my father? What did that say about our family?

I know that love is love. I truly believe that. I also know that I can go to church and believe in a God who understands that. It's my God and my faith. I mean, how could a God pick and choose who he loves? How does that even make sense?

Sure, my father being gay was a shock. How could it not be? He's married to my mother. But it's not the gay thing that makes me angry. And maybe it doesn't make sense, but I still can't forgive him for *allowing* himself to have those kinds of feelings for someone other than my mom.

Right or wrong, that's what was inside me. That's what makes things so hard.

He told me everything. How he'd been in love with Kirk Davies since college. How he'd always thought he was different but hadn't realized it was because he was gay until he met Kirk. He'd just thought he wasn't into girls or that he hadn't met the right one yet.

He even told me of the night he'd shared his realization with his parents. Of how his father had beaten him so badly that he'd ended up in the hospital with his jaw wired shut. (I don't remember my grandparents because they died in a car crash when I was three.)

My dad had lived a lie his whole life because he thought it was what he had to do in order to survive. He wanted to lead a parish. He loved God, and he wanted to help people. To counsel them and be there for his community. But how could he do that if he was outed?

He told me that he loved Mom. Like really loved her. But that there were all kinds of love, and it was different from what he felt for Kirk. It didn't lessen it or anything, but it wasn't what she deserved. And still he struggled with the thought of destroying our family, because he loved me and my brother more than life.

He was at a crossroads and wasn't sure where to turn or what path to take, and I guess I wasn't much help. Some nights I screamed at him for destroying everything that I loved. And other nights, we talked like real adults. He was honest with me, and I was honest with him.

It didn't mean that things were fixed. In fact, they were far from it, and it was only going to get worse. But what it did mean was that his honesty was the first step toward healing, and I hoped, it would be enough.

I guess only time would tell.

Just last night, he'd asked me my thoughts on his sermon today. I knew that he was planning on putting himself out there and that it was going to be the hardest thing he'd ever done. I might only be seventeen years old, so, you know, my opinion wasn't exactly worldly or anything, but I told him that I thought living a lie (which is basically what I'd done for the entire year) was kind of cowardly. And that being honest was the bravest thing a person could be.

"Hey, you almost ready?"

It was Sunday, and Hailey had slept over the night before. We'd spent most of it watching *Friday Night Lights* on Netflix and talking about nothing besides Tim Riggins (most tragic dude ever) and the bitchy Julie (how could she break Matt's heart?). Hales made me laugh, and we'd drank enough soda and eaten enough chips to feed a small country.

She didn't mention Link, even though I knew they were still serious, and she sure as heck didn't mention Trevor. She'd done what she always did; she'd just been there for me.

Today Hailey was breaking code and coming to church with me instead of sleeping in because, well, life as I knew it was about to change, and I was pretty sure it wasn't going to hit that upward curve we all dreamed about.

"Yep, we should head over soon," I answered. I leaned into the mirror and applied some gloss before stepping back.

"So, your mom, she knows what your dad's gonna do?"

I nodded. "She was home with Isaac a few days ago but decided to go back to my uncle's. She just thought this was going to be too hard for Isaac, and well, she's pretty devastated, you know? She's not doing very well."

"Was she mad that you stayed here?"

"I don't think she's mad, but she wanted me with her. She's confused and hurt by everything, and I think she just wishes it was all over. She's supposed to be coming back next week, but I'm not sure that's going to happen. And poor Isaac, he's like this little confused puppy dog. This is going to be hard on him. Hard on everybody."

I missed her so much. I swiped at my eyes. *Don't cry.* Not today.

Hales walked up behind me, slipping her arms around my waist and staring at me in the mirror as she leaned her head on my shoulders.

"Well, I think it's great that you're supporting your dad the way you are. I don't know if I could…I mean, I love my dad even if he's the biggest grump on the planet, but if he came home and told me he was gay, I'd freak the hell out. I'd eat at least one hundred cartons of ice cream and end up in the hospital or something."

"Um, impossible to eat one hundred cartons of ice cream. Besides, that's a little bit of an overreaction, don't you think?"

"I don't know, Everly. The gay thing is worth at least eighty cartons."

I made a face in the mirror. "Maybe seventy-five."

She giggled but fell silent as soon as our eyes met in the mirror. "It's going to be tough, you know that, right? Like, people are going to talk and they might say some really awful things. Not everyone is forward-thinking in this town. Heck, in this country. It's just the way it is."

"I know, but I've got you in my corner, right?"

She stood back. "Yep. You do. So, we gonna do this or what?"

I blew out a long breath. "Thanks for everything, Hales."

"No problem. I'm the sunshine to your KC."

Okay. "Um, what?" We were heading down the stairs.

"You know. KC and the Sunshine Band? They're, like, older than retro so I'm not surprised that you've never heard of them. Your taste in music is pretty pathetic."

"You're crazy."

"Yep, that's me. The rock to your roll. The snap and crackle to your pop."

By the time we reached her car, I was laughing, though that didn't last long, because when we reached the church, the parking lot was packed. Like sardine packed, and I glanced at Hailey nervously as we pulled in behind my dad's car in our family spot. I spied Mrs. Henney walking up the steps, and she hadn't been to service in at least six months.

"Go figure, everyone's decided they need to worship today," I said woodenly, staring at my hands. At the chipped blue polish I'd meant to replace.

"You don't have to do this, you know. Your dad will understand."

I knew he would. He'd told me to stay home, but how could I? He needed me, and even though a part of me was still confused and upset, he was my dad and I loved him. All of him. Even the parts that I didn't know all that well. The ones he'd kept secret.

"I'm going in," I said quietly, reaching for the door.

"Okay, Captain," Hales said. "I'm right behind you. Just don't expect me to sing or anything, because we both know I can't carry a tune. Like seriously. Remember in fifth grade when Mrs. Yancy told me not to sing the national anthem? Remember?"

"I remember."

"I mean, she had no right, but she totally called it. Honestly, I love you, Everly, but I have to draw the line somewhere."

"Noted."

"I mean it, Everly. If things go bad in there and you decide that you want some comic relief, do not look my way. I tell a joke worse than I sing."

"Okay." I was grinning again, and once inside the church, I tried to keep my spirits up.

"I mean, it's not like I wouldn't try or anything. You know, in a pinch if you, like, *really* needed me. I could, you know, pretend I'm in *Glee* and break into Gaga or Britney. Or, oooh, I know, I could sing an Adam Lambert song if you think that would help. You know, hit them over the head with the whole gay thing instead of easing them into it."

Ah, Hales. The girl always knew how to make me smile.

"I think we're good."

Dad was already at his pulpit, arranging notes, his fingers shuffling them nervously. I walked up to him, and my first inclination was to give him a hug. He looked like he needed one badly.

I hesitated, and when I would have stepped back, he scooped me into his arms. He held me until the stiffness in my limbs and muscles faded.

And I let him.

I was cold, and my stomach felt pretty bad, so I could imagine what he was feeling.

"You came," he whispered near my ear.

"Wouldn't be anywhere else."

He stared down at me, and I saw the new lines around his eyes, the dark circles underneath, and the magnitude of what he was going to do hit me so hard that my knees buckled.

"Hey, sweets. Are you okay?"

"Yeah," I said, a little shaky. "I'm good. I just…do you have to do this? I mean, can't we…can't you just, I don't know, be yourself without having to make an announcement?"

He was silent for a few seconds as he glanced over my head at the people gathered behind us. "No," he whispered. "I've been hiding and lying my whole life, and if I'm going to lead and counsel and be there for these people, I need to be honest about who I am. I need to show them that…"

"Love is love?"

He kissed my forehead. "Yes. Love is love. Things are going to get rough."

"I know. That's why I'm here." I gazed up at him and hoped he saw what was in my heart. "No more lies. Be brave. All in." Wow. I was starting to sound like Coach Taylor.

"You're amazing, you know that?"

"I do," I quipped and attempted a smile.

He paused. "Have you talked to Trevor? Is he going to be here for you?"

I shook my head, lips tight. "No. We're still not... We're not together."

"Oh Everly. I'm sorry. You're sure this has nothing to do with me?"

I heard his concern and tried to smile. "I'm sure."

"Okay." He glanced over my head. "Okay. It's time."

I smoothed the front of my dress and walked around the pulpit, bypassing the piano that I normally sat at for opening hymn. I spotted a few kids from the youth group, which I'd pretty much ditched over the last few weeks, and I gave a small wave. Two of them waved back, the Charnish twins, but the other girl, Joanne DuPonte, did the whole "I'm going to pretend I didn't see you" thing. I had no idea if she was mad because I'd ditched youth group or had some other reason for being so high school. Whatever. I had more important things to worry about. I crossed over to where Hailey sat in the front row and squeezed in beside her. Mrs. Gentry, our treasurer, was in her usual spot, and I gave a small smile as I settled back and tried to relax. Kind of hard when every muscle in my body was tight.

My dad cleared his throat into the microphone, there was some feedback, and the entire congregation went silent. Like you could drop a pin in the choir box and everyone would have heard it. There were no crying babies or shuffling of feet. There were no whispers or giggles from the little kids. No coughs or sneezes. It was like someone had pressed the mute button.

There was nothing. There was my dad and the congregation.

Hailey's hand found mine, and we held hands like we used to when we were little. I exhaled slowly and looked up at my dad.

His eyes were on me, those electric blue eyes that I'd loved since I could remember, vibrant and alive. He smiled, a reassuring warm smile, and I noticed the sunbeams coming in, bathing him in the light that I'd missed for so long.

He was everything that was good. Everything that was kind and compassionate. Things would be okay, wouldn't they?

I mean how could these people not see the beauty and kindness in front of them? Why should they even care about who he loved in his private time, when it was so obvious that he loved them all?

My heart swelled, looking up at him, but when he started speaking, I didn't hear his words. I was too caught up in the sunbeams, too hypnotized by their magic as the light moved around him like it was alive.

I thought of my mother and my heart constricted, because I knew hers was broken. I just hoped that one day she'd find someone who could love her the way that she deserved to be loved. All in and full of bravery.

It's what all of us deserve. Pretty simple, really.

Even someone who thinks that they don't deserve it. Someone like Trevor Lewis.

Chapter Twenty-seven

Trevor

I'd sent Everly at least twenty text messages in the last twelve hours, and she hadn't returned one. Seriously, I was that pathetic, and even Link told me to cut it out. Said that I was turning into a pussy and that girls don't like guys who try too hard.

"She hates me," I muttered.

"Who hates you?" Taylor asked with a yawn. It was ten o'clock Monday morning, and the parents were gone to work. Taylor had just been hired at the local Dairy Queen and was up early (for her at least—she was never up before noon most days).

"Oh, never mind," she said, reaching for a box of pasta, the breakfast of champions, according to her. "Everybody hates you because you've been an A-hole for the last few weeks."

Guess I had that one coming.

"So have you talked to Everly?" Taylor asked as she filled a pot with water.

"No."

"Really? She still hates you too?"

"Yep," I replied darkly.

"Can't say that I blame her. I mean, you did blow her off like she didn't matter."

"Is there a point to this?"

Taylor made a face. "So did you know? I mean, that her dad was gay?"

"No."

Word had spread fast in our small town of Twin Oaks. There was gossip and then there was *gossip*. A pastor confessing he was gay? That was the feeding frenzy kind of gossip.

"Well, I think he's the bravest person I know. I mean, who does that? Like, he just put himself out there, and he had to know that not everyone in this town would like what he had to say."

"Yeah," I mumbled.

"You should call her."

I glanced up sharply. It wasn't like Taylor to be all cheerleader for anyone. But she was right. The only problem? I was pretty sure Everly would blow me off, because that's pretty much what I'd done to her.

"I think that I'm the last person Everly wants to hear from."

"I heard their house got egged."

"Who told you that?"

"Megan Chambers. She lives beside then and posted a bunch of crap on Facebook. Said he deserved it. Said Mr. Jenkins was a creep and that he was going to hell. But then, she's such a bitch.

I mean, who deserves to get egged? Freaking Megan Chambers, that's who."

I'd barely managed to process that when there was a hard knock on the back door and Link walked into the house. He worked part-time for a landscaper, and by the looks of him, he'd been mowing a lot of grass. My mom was gonna have a fit when she saw the amount of clippings he'd just tracked onto the floor.

"Dude, watch where you're walking," Taylor said.

"Sorry." Link's eyes were on me. "Have you talked to Everly today?"

"No," I said sharply and maybe a little defensively.

"So you don't know."

My head whipped up so fast I was surprised I didn't get whiplash.

"Don't know what?" That was Taylor.

Link rolled back on his feet, and I could tell it was not good. "Man, the church was vandalized, like bad, and uh, Hales is over there with her."

He paused for one second, but I was already on my feet. I had to do something. Anything to make up for my epic fail as a boyfriend. Or whatever we'd been to each other.

"Hey, wait up," Taylor said as she ran to the stove and turned the burner off. "I'm coming too."

We hopped into Link's truck, and about ten minutes later, we pulled over in front of the church.

"Shit," I muttered, because really, there wasn't anything else to say.

The three of us stared up at the white clapboard building. The church had been there for as long as I could remember, but it had never looked like this. Words had been spray-painted across the front doors. On either side of the main windows. I could see stuff written down the one side.

They were words meant to hurt.

Faggot

Kill the gay

Sinner

Gays burn in hell

"Who would do something like that?" Taylor asked.

I didn't even care. Not really. I mean, the guys that did this? Bunch of lowlife dickheads with nothing better to do than spread their own small-minded kind of hate. All I cared about was Everly.

I hopped out of the truck and jogged up the steps, Taylor and Link following behind me. I pushed open the front doors, and for a moment I couldn't see shit. It was dark, and my eyes were still blinking out the sunlight.

When my eyes adjusted, I almost wished they hadn't, because it was more of the same in here. Awful stuff spray-painted every-where, and a couple of the pews looked like someone took a sledgehammer to them.

I saw Hailey and a group of girls up near the pulpit. She

looked up when we walked in. Even from here, I could tell she'd been crying. I spied the sheriff talking with Pastor Jenkins to the right. I saw Mrs. Henney and a few other ladies I recognized gathered in a small group, speaking quietly.

But I didn't see Everly.

"Thanks for coming, guys," Hailey said when she reached us.

"Where is she?" I asked. "It's just so…so… I don't even have a word for it."

"I know. It's awful." She exhaled and glanced behind me. "Did you get the stuff?"

I didn't care about stuff or anything else. All I cared about was Everly.

"Where is she?" I asked again, stepping forward and nearly tripping over the paint cans that Link brought.

"Out back. She needed some air, and I told her not to go out front because, well…"

But I was already moving past Hailey. I ran to the back of the church and took the side door out. There was a small parking area here, and I followed a worn footpath that led around back. And that's where I found her.

She was staring up at the building but turned when I rounded the corner. The girl literally took my breath away. I couldn't speak, and even though all I wanted to do was walk up to her and fold her into my arms, my legs were suddenly made of cement and I couldn't move.

She sniffled and pushed back that piece of hair that I loved and tucked it behind her ear. For a few seconds there was only silence filling the space between us, a heavy, sad silence.

I shoved my hands into the front pockets of my jeans, because I didn't know what else to do with them, and for those few seconds, I felt like the biggest loser on the planet. Why hadn't I been there for her? Had I screwed things up so badly that she didn't want to talk to me?

"Hey," she said, her voice hoarse and barely above a whisper.

My chest tightened, and I had to force myself to swallow this big-ass lump that was all of a sudden blocking my throat.

"Everly, I'm...I'm so sorry for your dad and the church and... everything else." I cleared my throat. "Shit, I don't know what to say."

Wow. Pretty much the most pathetic apology ever.

"Yeah," she said. "So am I."

"Is there anything...I mean, I..." What the hell? Just say it.

I found my legs and strode toward her, eyes focused, my heart open and my head finally clear. When I reached her, I didn't hesitate. I just folded her into my arms and held her. She started to cry right away, and damn, my heart felt like it was going to break into a million little pieces.

She went real quiet, and for a moment I was scared that I'd totally screwed this up yet again. She wriggled a bit, and even though I didn't want to, I let her go.

We stared at each other for a long time. How long? I have

no clue. But it was long enough for me to know that things weren't going to be easy. And long enough for me to know that I didn't care.

I'd do whatever it took to make it up to this girl.

"I'm glad that you're here," she said softly. "My dad will appreciate it. But Trevor, shutting me out because you felt sorry for yourself was selfish and wrong."

My heart felt as if it was twisting. "I know. I didn't mean to. You gotta believe me. I couldn't see past my own pain."

"We all have pain."

"I know. I just…I was embarrassed about the seizures. It's totally uncool, you know? For a guy to just lose it in front of his girlfriend? I hated that you saw me like that. Hated that it will probably happen again. You deserve someone who's…"

"Who's what?"

Uncomfortable, I shifted my feet. "You deserve someone who's not screwed up. Someone who's normal. Not some freak on the floor."

"I get it," she said softly. "But you hurt me, Trevor, and I can't just forget how that felt. It's up to me who I want to be with. If we're going to be anything. If we're going to be an 'us,' then you can't run when things get tough, and you can't push me away. If we're going to work, then you need to be all in. I'm not settling for anything less. I deserve at least that. We all do. Even my dad."

"I'm all in." And I was. God, was I ever.

Her eyes were huge, her skin pale. But she looked fierce as she gazed up at me.

"Maybe you are. Maybe you're not. Maybe you like the idea of being all in, but the idea is a lot less complicated than the reality. The reality is hard. The reality can suck sometimes. But the reality can also be amazing."

My heart was pounding. Couldn't she hear it?

"You have to believe me, Everly. You believe me, right?"

She glanced up at the building, and I followed her gaze, wincing when I saw the ugliness there. Guess the bastards had decided to spread their hate all over the place.

"What I do know, right now, in this moment, is that this wall needs to be painted. What I do know is that the hate that's up there? That hate needs to be obliterated. That's about all I have right now. That's all I know."

I stared at her for a long time. I saw her pain, and I knew that it was going to take time to get her trust back. The old Trevor might have said, "screw it," because he would have been afraid of rejection. But this new me, the one who wasn't perfect or normal or anything of the sort? Well, this new me was willing to put this girl ahead of himself.

She was the one, after all. The one my dad had warned me about. The girl who'd knocked me on my ass. And it was up to me to make her realize that even though I'd been a douche bag, she needed me as much as I needed her.

"We should get started," I said.

"Started?"

"Link brought some paint." I nodded to the wall. "We should get started."

"You don't need to do this," she replied.

"I know I don't need to. I want to. If you'll let me."

She chewed her bottom lip for a few moments and then spoke so softly, I barely heard her. "Okay."

We went back inside, and after I shook her father's hand and offered whatever support I could give, we grabbed a can of paint and a couple of brushes and headed out back. Taylor, Link, and Hailey were already busy out front.

We painted in silence for a while, and then she nudged me with her elbow. "You've been studying?"

"Been trying. It's just not as much fun on my own."

"When's your test again?"

I scowled. "Next week."

"I could be persuaded to help you do a last-minute cram."

"Really?"

"Yep." She slapped her brush against the wall and finished off her section. "If you play your guitar and sing me that song that you told me about, I will give you one hundred percent of my tutoring capabilities, and you're guaranteed to pass."

"Song?"

"The Lynyrd Skynyrd one. 'Simple Kind of Man.' Your favorite."

God, this girl. She remembered.

Could I do it? Could I pick up that guitar and finally sing? Could I try?

"It's a date."

"It's not a date."

"No?" I slapped on some more paint.

"It's a beginning, Trevor."

"I'm good with that."

We worked in silence for the rest of the afternoon. Sure, we made small talk and stuff, and even though things weren't all tied up in a pretty bow, I needed to believe we'd be all right.

So even though the thought of playing guitar and singing a song in front of a crowd scared the ever-lovin' crap out of me, I would do it.

I was either going to rock it or I was going to crash and burn, but at least I'd have Everly with me. And failure didn't look so bad when the prize was the girl I loved.

Chapter Twenty-eight

Everly

"You ready yet, girlie?"

I pulled my boots on and glanced up as Hailey walked into my room. She gave a low whistle and I blushed, because I was already considering changing. She caught my look and shook her head.

"Uh-huh. No way. You look way too hot, and Trevor is going to be drooling like a sick dog."

I stood and glanced at myself in the mirror. "I don't know. Are you sure?"

She gave me the look, the high eyebrow, are-you-even-kidding-me look, and I grabbed my gloss and shoved it into my purse.

I'd dug through my closet and found a denim skirt that may or may not have been on the short side. I'd pulled on a pair of spandex shorts because, well, you know, the bending-over thing could be dicey. Paired with an indigo-colored halter top and my boots, I was kind of rocking some weird sort of country/rock thing.

"The guys are waiting. Let's go."

I followed her out of my room. "Do you know where we're going?"

"Yes, I do," she said with a giggle. "But I'm on strict orders not to say a word."

It was Friday night, and my week had been full of highs, mostly because of Trevor, and a few lows. The highs kind of balanced out the crap that my family was dealing with, and I was grateful for that.

I spied Trevor before he saw me, and just like every single time I saw him, he took my breath away. He was chatting with my father, arms crossed over his chest as he nodded to whatever Dad was saying. He wore a plain black T-shirt, faded jeans, and a pair of Docs. The ends of his hair were damp, as if he'd just showered, that blue streak fading a bit, and he was sporting the unshaved look (which I totally adored).

I stepped off the last stair, and whoop, there went my stomach again. His eyes were intense, and the smile that lit up his face when he saw me made me feel like I was the only person in the room. Stupid and kind of cliché, but there you have it.

It was hard not to let him know how twisted up inside I was. And as much as he'd apologized and told me that he'd never push me away again, there was still a part of me that was afraid. That kind of pain wasn't something I ever wanted to feel again.

"Hey," I said.

He smiled and shook my father's hand. "We won't be too late, sir."

"It's Eric, and I'm going to hold you to that."

"Okay," Link said, reaching for Hailey. "We better go or we're going to be late."

I slid in beside Trevor but made it a point to keep some distance between us.

"You look beautiful," he said, voice a little rough.

I didn't answer, because I wasn't really sure what to say. Did I tell him that he looked so gorgeous it made my heart ache? Did I tell him that when his eyes met mine, some little piece of me melted?

Hailey cranked the tunes, and that filled the silence between us until Link pulled over to the curb several minutes later.

"We're here," Link said.

I peered out the window and saw that we were downtown. I spied the Coffee House across the street, and even though it was hot as sin, the patio was full. Groups of kids milled around, and there was a steady stream of teens moving inside.

"What's going on?" I asked.

"Word got out, I guess." Link was grinning like an idiot as he and Hailey started forward. I didn't have a chance to say anything else, because Trevor grabbed my hand and we followed them across the street.

A few kids yelled out to Trevor and he nodded, a smile on his face and a lightness in him that I'd never noticed before. It was packed inside the Coffee House, and as soon as I saw the two guitars up on the small stage at the back, I knew.

Heart pounding, I let him put his arm across my shoulder and guide me through the crowd. We had to stop a few times, guys wanting to high-five him and slap his shoulder. He was polite and introduced me to every single person he talked to. Several of them mentioned what had gone down with my dad, and the cool thing was that every single one of them was supportive.

We finally made it to the front where Hales was already seated, and Link winked at us. "So we gonna do this or what?"

Trevor was nodding, his eyes on me, his hands on either side of my face.

"I wouldn't be doing this if it wasn't for you," he said, voice a little rough. "And I don't even know if I'm going to be all that good, but for you, I'll try." He cleared his throat. "I'm all in, Everly. You have to know that."

I took a moment. I ignored the scared voice inside me—the one that said he might hurt me again—and I nodded.

I reached for his hands, my fingers caressing the tattoos on his knuckles. Courage. Strength. I stared at them until the symbols blurred. Until my heart was pounding so hard and loud, I was sure he could hear it.

I was either all in or I wasn't. There was no more figuring this out.

I leaned into him. "I know." And then I stood on my toes and kissed him. And I mean, kissed him. There were catcalls and whistles, and when I finally broke away, we were both breathing heavy.

"I love you," I whispered.

Trevor rested his forehead on mine. "You know that I love you too, right?"

"Show me," I said with a smile. He took a step back and nodded. He knew. That was enough.

He turned and hopped onto the stage, striding across it like he owned it. He grabbed a guitar, and Link grabbed the other one, and then they were sitting right in front of us.

Trevor flexed his fingers and then started strumming, but his eyes were on me and they never left. He cleared his throat a couple of times and then started to speak.

There's this extra cadence that you can hear when someone is on a mic, like, it picks up all the warm parts and makes them larger than life. Trevor's voice was like that—I had the whole goose bumps thing going on. I had it huge. And man, it felt great.

"It feels good to be back," he said to a chorus of cheers and *we love you*. "Yeah," he said with a grin that melted my heart. "I love you too."

He kept strumming his guitar, and Link joined in, the two of them filling up the place with something that was perfect.

"I've had a shit year, you know? But ah, this girl right here." He pointed to me, and the place erupted into more catcalls and whistles. "I know, right?" He laughed. "Well, this girl taught me a few things over the summer."

Someone shouted something that I didn't quite get, but Trevor laughed and shook his head. "No way, man. Some stuff is just for me, got it?"

More catcalls and whistles.

And then his playing got softer, more intimate, and I thought that if I wasn't careful, I'd drown in his eyes.

"I haven't played this particular guitar in over a year and, uh, I'm glad that my dad's here to see it put to good use again."

I cranked my head around and spied Trevor's parents near the coffee bar, along with his sister Taylor. His dad raised his chin, and his smile was so huge I could see it from where I sat.

"I'd try to play my old Epiphone, but my chops, well, they weren't up to snuff. I almost gave up, and the only reason I'm here tonight is because of this girl right here. Everly Jenkins." His eyes were on, intense, and beautiful. "I love you."

Okay, I was blushing and blushing hard.

"This song is for you."

And then something magical happened. Trevor closed his eyes and started to sing a song about a man who loved his mother and loved his God. It was a beautiful song. A simple song. It was a song about love, acceptance, and listening to your heart.

I don't know if he screwed up, got the words wrong, or played the wrong notes. If he did? It didn't matter, not to me anyway. He was up there for himself, and he was up there for me. Singing to me. Singing a song that made my throat tight and my heart ache. A song that I would never forget.

It was Trevor's song.

And for that one perfect moment, it was my song too.

After
Trevor

It's funny the things that you think are important when you're invincible. When you think that nothing can touch you. Music. Parties. Girls. Getting laid. Two years ago, that was me. I was that guy. The one who had it all.

Until I wasn't.

But the thing is? I don't care anymore. I'm okay with the fact that I'm not the guy I used to be. Not even close. But whatever I am is some kind of normal, my version of normal at least, and that's all that matters.

I was glad that Everly let me in. Glad that she gave me a chance to prove that I wasn't always gonna be a dickhead. And let's face it, I'd acted like a total douche toward the one girl who made me want to be a better person. My dad had been right. She was the one. And I was willing to do whatever it took to be the kind of guy who deserved her.

I wrote my government test and got a C. Everly helped a lot, and I don't think I would have snagged my diploma without her. Without her I wouldn't be in New York City. I wouldn't be living my dream, writing music with Nathan, and living in this awesome loft that Monroe's parents own. Our rent is doable, and well, the acoustics, man, they're out of this world.

I still have things to work on. I still mess up my words, and sure, the whole epileptic thing sucks. But who needs to drive in New York City anyway? My meds are working, and I haven't had an episode since the summer.

So yeah, life is good. It still has its challenges, but with a girl like Everly in my life, I can believe that things will only get better.

I miss her. She's at college in another state, but we Skype and we'll both be back in Twin Oaks for Thanksgiving. I'll get to hold her, inhale that sweet scent that is all her. Everly Jenkins. The girl who knocked me on my ass.

And for now, that's all I need.

After
Everly

If someone had told me at the beginning of the summer that (A) I would fall in love with Trevor Lewis, and (B) my family would be broken and fractured, I would have told them they were full of crap.

The Trevor Lewis thing came from nowhere, and sure, I'd known my family was hurting, but as it turns out, I just didn't know how badly.

Funny how things work out.

My dad lost half of his parish, but the ones who stayed were amazing. They were supportive and nonjudgmental, and well, it was exactly what he needed.

I'm not going to lie. Things were tough at first. Hell, they still are. As much as I wanted to accept who he was, who he'd been all along, it's hard getting past the broken family his truth had destroyed. I got it. I really did. But it still hurt. In a perfect world my family would be whole and intact.

We're working things out, and for now that's enough. I'm

happy that he's found some kind of happiness. He's on his own. I think he's seeing his first love, Kirk, but it's not like he shares that stuff with me. And for what it's worth? Not like I want to hear the details of my dad's love life anyway.

I've learned to accept things and move on, because really, there's no point in living in a past that was a lie. Mom moved to Maine with Isaac to live with her brother. I hate that Dad doesn't get to see Isaac all that often, but I get why she did what she did. My dad hurt her, and in a way, he destroyed parts of her. I just hope one day she finds someone who can help put those pieces back together.

She deserves to be loved. Everyone does.

We talk all the time, and I Skype with Isaac, who I miss more than anything. But we'll be together again, and for now, I know that his life is settled.

As for me? I'm loving college, although I miss Trevor so much sometimes that I ache. At first I wanted to come to New York City with him, but then I realized that was his dream and he needed to do it on his own. Prove to himself that he could.

But that doesn't mean that I don't still love him. I think about him every day. About the way his eyes get all dark when he's about to kiss me. Or the way he holds me, touches me.

I miss every little bit of him, even the imperfect parts.

But that's okay. I'll see him in a few weeks when I go home for the holidays. And in the meantime? I'm working on me. Working on happy.

Working on some kind of normal.

And right now, in this moment, it feels pretty awesome.

Acknowledgments

This book was partially inspired by a true event and partially inspired by my daughter and her big heart. Her mantra, that love is love, is one we should all aspire to live by. Our world would be a much kinder, gentler place if we did so.

I'd like to thank Kristen and her friends Hailey, Mariah, Maggie, Abbey, and Danielle for being bright, compassionate, funny individuals. I so enjoyed all the "BAE" conversations I overheard while you were all gathered around the kitchen table. I wish all of you much success and hope that no one ever breaks your heart. Ever.

I also need to give a shout-out to my wonderful agent, Sara Megibow, my editor Aubrey Poole, the team at Sourcebooks, and all my author buddies who are in this crazy world of publishing with me. It's a crazy ride, but hey, I wouldn't want any other job in the world!

About the Author

USA Today bestselling author Juliana Stone fell in love with her first book boyfriend when she was twelve. The boy was Ned, Nancy Drew's boyfriend, and it began a lifelong obsession with books and romance. A tomboy at heart, she split her time between baseball, books, and music—three things that carried over into adulthood. She's thrilled to be writing young adult as well as adult contemporary romance and does so from her home somewhere in Canada.

Two shattered hearts are about to collide in

small-town Louisiana.

Don't miss Juliana Stone's

BOYS LIKE YOU

Chapter One
Monroe

My gram told me once when I was eleven that I could do anything. She'd been very matter of fact as she poured us each an iced tea on a steamy afternoon.

It was the kind of afternoon when the air sizzled and stuck to the insides of your clothes. The kind of afternoon that made your skin clammy and your muscles lazy. I remember that the birds were quiet but the locusts chimed like mini buzz saws.

Funny, the things that you remember, and the things that you can't forget no matter how hard you try.

On that particular afternoon, we'd sat on her front porch in the rain, Gram's hyacinths bent over from the weight of the water, her two cats Mimi and Roger curled at our feet. I'm sure I wore some trendy New York outfit that was totally inappropriate for Louisiana in August, and Gram Blackwell was dressed in what she liked to call "genteel southern attire," which basically meant cotton instead of linen or silk.

We settled back in our chairs and chatted about the soccer

team. I told her how much I wanted to make first string, and she told me that anything was possible as long as I applied myself. Of course I believed her with all the enthusiasm an eleven-year-old who has never been hurt or disappointed feels.

Why wouldn't I? This was Gram, and she was never wrong.

I tried my hardest and made the team.

But that was before Malcolm. Before the awful year that had just passed. That was before I learned that my charmed life could bleed. That pain could become an everyday kind of thing, and that happiness was just a word that didn't mean anything.

And now, at the ripe old age of sixteen and a half, I don't know what I believe in anymore, and I don't know if I'll ever be fixed.

It's not like I haven't tried.

I went to private therapy. I went to group counseling. I read the books that I was supposed to read, did the relaxation exercises that I thought were stupid, and took the meds that they gave me.

In fact, I loved how those little blue pills made me feel nothing—which isn't very different from the way I feel most of the time—but medicated nothing is so much better than the real, hard nothing I had been living with.

I suppose it's why they weaned me off them. "Addict" wasn't exactly a label my mom wanted to add to the impressive list of everything else that was wrong with me.

My point is…I did it all. I tried.

It's just hard to succeed at something when you don't really care, and as much as I want to get better for my parents, I can't *make* myself care. Not even for them. My therapist says I need to care for myself first.

And therein lies the problem. The catch-22. I just don't care anymore. Not really.

Yet there are moments where, if I try real hard, I can close my eyes and smell the rain. Not just any rain, mind you, but *that* rain. From that long-ago afternoon.

Gram's rain.

"Monroe, I'm heading to town in a few minutes. Do you want to come along?"

I turned as Gram walked into the kitchen. It was nearly noon and I had been sitting at the table for about an hour, trying to decide if I was going to eat the bowl of pears she'd put out for me earlier or if I was going to put them back in the fridge.

I liked pears. I liked them a lot. I just wasn't all that hungry.

"Uh, I think I'll stick around here, if that's okay with you."

Gram put her purse on the table, and I pretended not to notice how her eyes lingered on my hair. I'd pulled it back in a ponytail yesterday—or maybe it was the day before—because I couldn't be bothered with it. I'm pretty sure I hadn't brushed it since.

She pointed to the bowl in front of me and raised her eyebrows, waiting half a second before grabbing it and setting it on the counter. She pulled plastic wrap from the drawer and covered the pears before putting them back in the fridge.

Gram turned and leaned against the counter, and for a moment, we stared at each other in silence.

I'd arrived a week earlier and we hadn't had a real chat yet— the one that I sensed was coming—and my stomach churned at the thought.

Gram's long hair was swept up in a clip at the back of her head, the silver strands glistening in the sunlight that poured in from the window above the sink. She wore pink lipstick, a casual cream skirt—cut to an inch above her knee—a moss-green blouse, and low open-toe heels to finish off the outfit. Pearls were in her ears, and the matching pendant lay at her neck. A classy choice that was totally Gram.

She was beautiful.

My gram had turned sixty last year and still carried that simple elegance that set her apart from a lot of women. She'd been a real hottie in her day, and though my mother said I was her spitting image, I didn't see it. But then I suppose beauty is more about your state of mind, and since mine was all dark and gloomy, that's what I saw when I looked in the mirror.

"All right," she said after a while and glanced at the clock above the stove. "I have someone coming by the house anyway, and I'll need you to show him where the job is."

Great. I thought of my bed and the nap I'd planned.

"Who is it?"

I didn't really care, but I could at least be polite and ask.

"I've engaged the services of a local contractor for some repairs and maintenance around the plantation. Today the fence around the family crypt and burial plot will be painted."

Gram's ancestors had lived in Louisiana for generations and this place—Oak Run Plantation—had been in the family for just as long. Years ago, Gram's father had turned the family home into a successful bed and breakfast/museum, which Gram had inherited, because according to my father, Gram's brother, Uncle Jack, was a no-good drunk who couldn't find his own butt if he needed to.

My grandmother even stayed on after her husband died, but instead of living in the big house, she moved into what used to be the carriage house. And that's where I'm staying this summer.

Everyone—which would be my parents and my best friend Kate—was hoping the hot Louisiana summer and laid-back atmosphere would somehow fix me. They think that the city and the memories are too much, and I don't have the heart to tell them that the memories will never leave. That much I've learned.

So location doesn't really matter, but I was glad to be away from my mother and her large, expressive, puppy-dog eyes. She looks at me a lot when she thinks I won't notice, and every time she does, I feel like the biggest failure on the planet.

I don't know how to react to her anymore—do I pretend I'm better to make her pain go away? Do I ignore her? Do I tell her to get out of my face?

And my father, God, he's the total opposite. He acts as if everything is normal. As if the last year and a half never happened—as if each one of us is whole—and that makes me angry. And kinda sad.

Gram grabbed her purse, bent low, and gave me a hug. "I love you, Monroe."

"I know," I whispered.

She grabbed her keys and paused. "Barbecue sound good for supper?"

I shrugged. "Sure."

"All right then." She moved toward the door but paused, her hand on the ivory handle. "He'll be here in an hour. Why don't you brush your hair?"

"Okay," I answered, though I'm pretty sure we both knew it wasn't likely to happen.

Chapter Two
Nathan

The crap thing about not being able to drive is that I do a lot of waiting around for rides, and I hate waiting. Doing nothing makes me crazy, and crazy Nathan isn't exactly the kind of thing I'm going for these days.

But mostly I hate waiting because it gives me too much time to think about the reasons I'm waiting in the first place. About how one stupid mistake changed everything. About how I screwed up so badly that now, the summer before my senior year—the one that I should have spent hanging with Rachel and Trevor and the rest of the guys—is going to suck.

Though it won't suck as much as Trevor's.

I wiped sweat from my brow and scooped up my bag from the porch. I hate waiting. I hate thinking.

In the fourth grade, Alex Kingsley tripped Trevor in the hallway, just outside our classroom. We had been in line waiting to head into the gymnasium, and Trevor tumbled into me. Long story short, we both wiped out, and the entire row of girls laughed their butts off. So did Alex—until we cornered him in the schoolyard at lunch.

Trevor and I taught the little turd exactly what happened to dickheads. After that, Alex pretty much left everyone alone, and though Trevor and I were punished—we had to stay after school every day for an entire week—it solidified our friendship.

We bonded over our mutual dislike of Alex Kingsley and our love of music and sports. Eventually, I forgave Trevor his thirst for all things country—he couldn't help it, his parents were true hicks—and he learned to like my progressive ear. He was into country music, bluegrass twang, and he also had a soft spot for the New York Jets. I was all about the old classics my dad loved, hard rock, and loud guitars. I also preferred the Dallas Cowboys, but he was cool with that.

Somehow we gelled, and our band is, or rather *was,* the hottest act in the area.

One mistake. One stupid-ass mistake and I ruined his life.

I would switch places with him in an instant if I could. Maybe then the guilt would go away. Maybe then I could look in the mirror and that empty hole in my gut would fill up with something other than loathing.

It should have been my future in the gutter. But I was Jack and Linda Everets's son, and around these parts, that meant something. Around these parts, it meant special treatment or a second chance, even when you didn't deserve it.

I'd gotten off easy and I knew it. Everybody knew it, except they used all kinds of excuses to cover up the fact that Trevor was lying in a hospital bed and I should be locked up.

Nathan is a good boy.

He's never done anything like that before.

They can't be perfect all the time.

They all make mistakes, even the good ones.

Blah. Blah. Blah.

None of it changed the fact that I'd screwed up huge, and I wasn't sure what made me more bitter—the fact that I should be riding a bench in juvie and wasn't, or the fact that I should be the one lying unconscious in a hospital bed with broken bones that would never play a guitar and a brain that might be scrambled for life.

My cell buzzed and I grabbed it from my pocket, frowning when I saw my uncle's name pop up.

Shit. I knew what this meant.

I started walking.

"Nathan, I'm going to be late."

The Oak Run Plantation was about thirty minutes down the road, and though the air was thick with humidity, anything was better than sitting on my front porch, staring at a car I couldn't drive and thinking about stuff that made me more depressed than I already was.

"I'll head over," I answered.

"It's hot as hell out there, boy. I don't want you to have heatstroke. Your mother will tan my hide if that happens."

My parents had gone north for the week in a bid to escape the heat, so at the moment, I was stuck home with no wheels and no one to take me anywhere. I could die of heatstroke and they wouldn't know until Sunday night when they returned, because they never called when they were away—and I knew not to call them unless the house was on fire.

I could say it was because cell reception was bad, but the simple truth was, my parents really dug each other—still—and they kinda forgot about the world when they went away.

I used to think it was gross—the way my dad would paw my mom—but now I realize they have something special, and that's a hell of a lot more than I could say for a lot of my friends' folks.

"I'm good." I grabbed a bottle of water from my bag and emptied it over my head. It soaked through my hair, which hung down to just above my shoulders, and splattered drops of water across my white T-shirt. My dad hated my hair, but Mom and my girlfriend, Rachel, loved it.

Rachel had told me once that if I ever cut it off, she'd dump me—she was joking, of course, but for a while there I wasn't so sure.

It was hair; I didn't see what the big deal was, but Rachel thought it made me look like some guy on TV, and Rachel was, if anything, all about looks. I guess when you are a hot little blonde, it's not surprising.

"Thanks, Nate. You're a good kid."

Tell that to Trevor, I thought.

"The paint and brushes are already there, so you just need to get started and knock off around five, or earlier if need be. It's Friday, you got plans?"

Rachel had left for the lake about an hour ago with a group of friends we hung out with, including one of the guys in my band, Link.

I could still taste her cherry gloss in my mouth. She'd come by, wearing the skimpiest bikini top you can imagine, along with the shortest jean shorts she owned. If I cared enough, I would have given her crap about it, but since I didn't anymore, I said nothing.

She'd jumped from the car and into my arms, wrapped her legs around my waist, begging me to reconsider and come with them. She seemed almost desperate—as if she knew something that I didn't.

What does it matter if you blow off Mrs. Blackwell?

Your job will still be waiting for you on Monday.

It's not like your uncle will fire you.

"Nate," she'd breathed against my mouth. "Come on, baby, it will be a good time."

A good time for Rachel was code for getting wasted and having sex, which were two things I wasn't all that interested in anymore. At least not with her. Not since that night.

"Nathan?" My uncle's voice cracked through the cell.

"Nah, I'm taking it easy tonight. I'll work 'til five," I answered and then pocketed my cell. Or later. There was nothing for me to come home to, and without the band or Rachel around, what was there for me to do?

The walk to Oak Run Plantation was brutal. It was hot and muggy, and by the time I got there, my T-shirt was long gone. My feet were just as sweaty as the rest of me, and I was irritated that I'd decided to wear work boots instead of something more sensible like my Chucks or sandals.

The driveway was impressive if you were interested in that sort of thing, lined on each side by huge oak trees that were generations old. Their branches spread over the top, reaching for the other side like a canopy, and I enjoyed the shade as I walked toward the main house.

Several cars were parked beside a small outbuilding to the right, and at the last minute, I paused, because I was pretty sure Mrs. Blackwell didn't live in the main house anymore. I spied a smaller place on the other side, set back a good twenty feet. There were flowers planted in the front, beneath the veranda. Purple and white petunias just like at my grandparents. Old lady flowers.

I decided to start there first.

I dropped my bag on the bottom step, took the stairs two at a time, and rang the doorbell. A few minutes passed and I rang it again, this time pressing hard for several seconds. I could hear it echoing inside and took a step back.

"Shit," I muttered, glaring at the door—like that was going

to make it open. I was hot, sweaty, and didn't exactly feel like searching a freaking plantation for some creepy burial site.

One more minute ticked by before I decided that's just what I was going to have to do, when I heard a scuffling noise and the door swung open.

I'd just tied a bandana around my head to keep my hair out of my eyes, and with a smile plastered to my face, I turned back to greet Mrs. Blackwell.

Only it wasn't Mrs. Blackwell who stepped out onto the porch.

It was a girl. I knew that much. How old was she? I couldn't say exactly, because in that moment, I couldn't even tell you if she was pretty or not.

I was way too focused on a pair of eyes that hit me in the chest like a hammer against stone. The color was unusual—a light gray/green—and sure, they were pretty damn striking, exotic even, but it wasn't the color or shape that got to me.

It was what I saw inside them. Something indefinable and yet so familiar because it was like looking in the mirror, and my first thought as I stared back at her, my smile slowly fading away?

Man, that sucks.

Chapter Three
Monroe

The boy who stood on the porch was sweaty and half naked and not the old guy I was expecting. At all.

I suppose he was going for some kind of badass look with a red bandana wrapped around his head and his jean shorts hanging so low off his hips I could see the top of his boxers, but seriously?

Did all guys think us girls really gave a crap what brand of boxers they wore? Personally, I thought the whole look was ridiculous and couldn't imagine what it felt like to walk around with your pants falling off. Uncomfortable maybe. Ridiculous for sure.

He wasn't wearing a shirt either, and I'm sure that's why my eyes automatically focused on his tattoo. It was interesting to look at—exotic symbols in black ink—starting from the top of his shoulder and traveling down to just above his bicep.

I had never wanted a tattoo, but the summer before my world went into the toilet, I'd wanted a belly ring. Badly. All the girls at school were getting them, and I didn't think they came close to tattoos on the trashy scale, maybe a seven out of ten, but my mother was horrified at the idea. Her comeback had been, "that's something you can think about when you're old enough to vote."

End of story, because my dad is a wuss and always sided with her.

"Hey," he said.

I didn't answer at first and moved so I could peek around him, but there was no old guy, and he seemed to be alone.

"Are you here for the fence?"

His eyes narrowed slightly, most likely because I came off sounding rude. But in my defense, he was late and had interrupted my nap. And these days, napping was a pretty important part of my day. Too important, according to my parents, which was one of the reasons they'd sent me to Gram's for the summer. In the city, they were at work and I was alone—free to sleep as long as I wanted to and free to spend my days in pajamas.

Gram didn't let me hang in my pajamas. She might not have figured out how to make me brush my hair every day, but she sure knew how to guilt me out of my pajamas.

"Who are you?" he asked instead of answering my question.

"Who are you?" I shot back.

"I asked first."

Okay, what are we, like, five?

He scrubbed at his chin and sort of sighed. I got the impression that he wasn't exactly in a great mood, but then I wasn't either, so I guess we were even on that count.

I'm not sure how long we stood there, staring at each other with only the buzzing of the bees in the honeysuckle to fill the space between us. I shifted my weight, suddenly aware that my hair hung down the back of my neck like a limp rag. A limp, tangled rag that hadn't been brushed in days.

"Monroe," I finally answered.

"Monroe," he repeated, as if he didn't believe me.

I tugged my cami strap back into place.

"You have a problem with my name?"

He shook his head, "nope," and ran his hand across the back of his neck. I'm sure he did it because it pushed his chest out.

Pushed his chest out and emphasized his abs. Not that I was looking or anything, but it was kinda hard not to notice when he was so...naked.

"I'm just here to do a job." He stood back. "Do you know where the family bones are buried or not?"

I considered lying, but what was the point? Gram wouldn't be impressed, besides, it's not like I had to stay out there and keep him company. The sooner I showed him where the crypt was, the sooner I could get back to the important business of having a nap.

"Follow me."

I pushed past him and waited for the door to slam shut behind me before heading down the front steps and out to the